TARA BRAZEE

New Fighter Unlocked

The Second Outrider Adventure

For Tori and Tesa
seeeeeeeesterrrrrrssss

Contents

Acknowledgement   iii

 1 Where'd We Leave Off?   1

 2 Takes Three to Conquer   9

 3 The Gang's All Here   15

 4 They're Called Pawns for a Reason   19

 5 Super Chill Night In (Space)   23

 6 And the Drones go Boom   33

 7 The Lucky Winner Is…   39

 8 *Whistles Casually*   42

 9 Fighting Evil by Daylight   49

10 Team Building 201   53

11 Had the Weirdest Dream   62

12 Very Serious Conversations   67

13 Bright Shiny New Toy   71

14 Warm Up   75

15 Bad Vibes   80

16 Little Alien on My Shoulder   86

17 My Brain Feels Ick   89

18 You Ask How High   100

19 Attack the Darkness   110

20 So Your (Kinda) Girlfriend Might Be (Kinda) Evil   119

21 Sometimes They Can Hear You Scream in Space   125

22 Talk Things Out   132

23 Can't Wake Up   142

24 The Plan Is Changing   147

25 Praise is a Hell of a Drug   151

26 That One's On Me   158

27 This Would be a Good Spot For a Villain Song   169

28 Must Be Proficient in Multitasking   175

29 We Did Get Better, Right?   188

30 Three Good Bois   197

31 We Should Get Matching T-shirts   205

32 Not in my Job Description   215

33 Freeze Frame   218

About the Author   223

Acknowledgement

Raise your hand if you're surprised I managed to do this a second time.
  (It's okay, my hand is up too.)

As before, and as always, thank you to my family. You guys are alright. Thanks for cheering me on.

To the best of the besties, Stephanie. Simply put, you keep me sane. But I'm always scared you'll hate your namesake, so just never tell me if that happens. Okay?

I somehow found the best writer friends around. To my beloved crows in Chaos Chat and patrons at The Tavern, I don't know how I got by without all of you before this. I hope we do fictional crimes together for the rest of our lives.

I don't tell any of you how much you mean to me enough. I spend a lot of time in fictional worlds, but you all make reality pretty spectacular too.

1

Where'd We Leave Off?

Mina was getting an air horn in the Comps. She'd let the confetti cannon go, after Steph reminded her of how environmentally damaging confetti was. The horn she would have. Comps were incredibly dense because of how much was compressed inside them, making their ability to fly all the more impressive. Everyone, including Nek, suggested at some point over the last two weeks how putting in a soundbite of a horn would be a simple and quick solution. That wasn't good enough. She wanted to see the little horn pop and toot their victory. A physical, practical, tangible thing. No easy routes with soundbites.

She spent two days fabricating a collapsible version that made a satisfying enough sound, a process streamlined with the help of her new personal workshop on Outrider. Complete with a mini-fabricator right in the room. She'd moved every tool and work surface from her bedroom up there the day Nek mentioned the extra spaces available to them. The switch left her room looking rather bare, but that was a boring problem. There were far more pressing matters on her to-do list.

Not that a Comp horn was far up on her list either, but this was her compromise with Zane. Working on a not so serious task as the group hung out at Restoration Cafe while Steph and Sean closed up. She'd also promised that she wouldn't spend the entire time obsessing over how they needed to locate Capri and the Lenians before they tried destroying the city again. Or how they needed to figure out what Capri's actual deal was. Or harping about training in the suits and Guardians. All while avoiding being detained by one of the several government or private organizations lurking around Hurst. Mina gave her head one quick shake, breaking up the churning to-do list in her head. She rubbed the base of her neck to loosen the tension that lived there now.

Mina would not allow the unending questions to distract her after she'd finally focused on the Comp schematics. Her current tactic was reorganizing components on the Comp decks, trying to configure pieces in whatever perfect way that would reveal a hidden half of an inch for her horn. There was a jab to her side, come back to Earth. Opps. Mina tuned back in to the group around her.

"We can settle this wild west style," Sean was saying as he wiped down the pastry display case.

"You sound mighty confident there partner," Zane drawled from next to her. He flicked the edge of an imaginary cowboy hat and gave her a wink when he noticed she'd started paying attention.

"I got five whole dollars that say I'm right," Sean countered with his own southern accent.

"The money is lying to you," Emma said from the table nearest Zane and Mina, not joining the game of voices.

"Now you listen here," Steph chimed in behind them, with what Mina thought was the best accent out of the three, "These here tips are split between us and I don't take mighty kind to the idea of you losing my hard earned money over your foolishness."

Sean threw his rag to the floor. "Foolishness! Them's fightin' words. Nevermind this fella, you get out here and draw."

Emma tipped toward Mina, clearly picking up on her confusion. "Sean thinks he can beat Zane in a quick draw."

"Thinks?" Sean shouted. "Betrayal and distrust. From my own family! My blood. Now you draw."

Emma finished the last of her tea, a new drink habit that no one mentioned (to her face) allowed her to chat with Henrie more often. "You can't shoot out everyone."

"Watch me." Sean backed up to the end of a row of tables. Hands held out far from his hips.

Zane pushed off the counter and sauntered over to the other end of the row. "Now what kind of man would I be to let these ladies fight my fight?" He cringed at the groans all three girls gave him. "I know, I hated it as I said it. Sorry. But nonetheless!"

Mina watched him swing around to face Sean, hands out. She caught a faint green light from his pants pocket, a signifier that he intended to activate his Pak in some way. There was a similar orange hue behind Sean's apron.

"No!" Mina dropped the tablet on the counter and jumped to the row the boys stood on either end of. "No. No. No. Hands down."

Zane dropped his immediately, losing his entire cowboy persona. "No, yeah, sorry."

"I can do it! Come on, Mina," Sean begged from his end, but his hands dropped and the orange light faded.

Waves of bright colors filled the fake smartwatch that covered her suit's armband. Nek projecting directly out from their wrists was a little too obvious for the day-to-day. They swirled on each of the team's small screens now. "If I can assist. Based on our training sessions, Warden Zane has Warden Sean beat by nearly half a second on reaction time."

"All the more need for practice," Sean insisted, hands back up at his sides. "We're alone anyway. Mitch is too trusting to have cameras. And the suits will take the hit. We're golden."

"And if you miss and break something?" Emma countered.

"Fabrication. Have a new whatever by morning."

"Dude." Zane walked back to the counter. "She's right, not here."

Sean slumped, fully defeated. "Standoff this weekend on Outrider?"

Zane laughed, "Yeah man, you're on."

Mina kept her stance in the row as Sean moved back to the display case because she was wondering where in their training schedule a duel was supposed to fit. "I'm sorry. Did you guys catch Capri without me?"

They all looked at her, clearly confused at her sudden questioning. Especially since they all knew their only lead was Nek monitoring for Capri's Pak's altered signal, they'd managed to lock in on it while the team fought her downtown. Next time she showed up in Hurst, with her suit activated, they'd know. The downside, that required her coming to them since they couldn't determine where in the entire solar system she was hiding. Thank you, Lenian cloaking.

"Did you stop the Lenian problem too while I was rebuilding Comps?"

Steph leaned over the counter. "We're just goofing, Mina. Nothing serious."

Nek bobbed on her wrist. "Warden Mina, your heart rate is-"

"Backs all done!" Henrie announced as she came through the archway, pulling one earbud out as she got closer. Music blasting from her hand.

Mina slapped a hand over her watch. Nek was gone, but she wanted the extra cover.

Henrie dropped a set of keys into Steph's waiting hand. "Good if I head out?"

"Totally!" Steph answered brightly. Mina was glad there was an actress in the group.

Henrie pointed to the empty mug Emma held tightly in her hands. "Did the lavender tea treat you alright?"

"Yeah!" Emma angled herself away from everyone else. "You'll have to give me another recommendation."

"I'll update the spreadsheet." She laughed at that more to herself. "I'll think of something good for you."

Mina caught the edge of Sean's face, he started smirking as he continued to clean.

They all, directly or not, watched her leave. Emma stood from her table as the last of Henrie's taillights disappeared.

"Is the damsel go-?" Sean asked.

"I'm being courteous," Emma answered before he finished.

"All alone!?" Zane and Steph shouted directly at Sean.

Mina rubbed her neck, that knot wasn't budging. She'd dropped her guard, allowed her team to act too boldly in public. Even participated herself, talking about Comps and Capri and Lenians. Who knows what they'd said while she was zoned out. What could've happened if Henrie pulled out that earbud sooner? How would they have fixed that? Swear her to secrecy? Lock her away on Outrider? What were the odds that one of them rattled off something they shouldn't have in the last two weeks? They spent a good amount of time together, but not every single second. How was she supposed to keep them all in line?

New questions added to her list as the group shifted back to their previous stations around the cafe. Too many variables she didn't hand answers for. Buzzing thoughts turned to static in her ears. A black spot, one she could almost feel, appeared in her head. The darkness expanded, a void spreading through her mind, taking her rising panic first. Taking the concern for her friends. Taking the ever constant dread of her parents returning. Taking everything. She went from too many thoughts to none within seconds. No emotions left, the fuses were all blown. Mina felt in no rush to flip the breaker, opting instead for the straightforward work of her Comp schematics. A simple task with an answer to be found, she had work to do.

She kept rubbing her neck, vaguely aware she was pulling more now. Nek, with the armband so close to Mina's ear, spoke only to her, "Warden Mina, are you okay?"

"Mmhmm." Mina forced her feet toward her stool and pried the hand from her neck to pick up the tablet. She tapped the screen awake and scrolled through her schematic.

Zane crept into her peripheral vision. "Mina."

"Mmm?"

"You shut down."

Mina decided to strip all the components off the decks, clearing them off with her stylus. Giving herself a fresh Comp to build from the ground up. She dragged her horn piece on first.

Zane set a hand on the screen. "Look at me."

She tightened her grip, knowing he'd try taking the tablet next. She almost asked Nek to create a new teleport waypoint right there, but that was definitely on the 'Don't Do In Public' list. Even if they were truly alone now. Her social awareness wasn't always great, but she assumed people would get offended if she started teleporting out of conversations. As lovely as that sounded.

"Where'd you go?" Steph lightly covered one of Mina's hands with her own. "Please come back."

Mina gave a weak tug on the tablet. Her jaw felt wired shut, opening her mouth and forming words took effort. "There's a lot to do."

Zane wrapped his other arm around her shoulders, pulling her to him. "You're not doing this alone."

Steph kept holding her hand. "Sorry. We got carried away. That was honestly too close. I don't know how I forgot Henrie was back there."

"I'm supposed…to be…in charge," Mina stumbled through. "I should have…I should have…"

"Please breathe for me." Zane gave her a squeeze. "Think later, breathe for right now."

That must be why her chest felt tight. She manually took a breath in and some of the static fell away. Mina dropped more of her weight on Zane, knowing perfectly well he could take it. The three of them stayed there for a long moment, Mina taking several deep breaths before she finally pulled away. "Well that was embarrassing."

"Don't mention it," Emma said from her table. "You're right, there's a lot for us to do."

Mina turned around to her. "Me freaking out doesn't help anything."

Sean moved in from the case. "Honestly? Makes me feel better. Means I'm not the only one. Lots of staring into the void. Bad insomnia."

"Really? You didn't mention anything."

He shrugged. "Like I said, I thought it was only me. Figured I'd shake the nerves and catch up to the rest of you being chill about this."

Steph gave Mina's hand a squeeze. "My screen time has skyrocketed. Lots of doom scrolling as distraction. And my appetite hasn't been the best."

Zane nodded over Mina's head. "Ditto on the appetite. For obvious reasons," he looked to Sean, "and insomnia too."

All eyes shifted to Emma, waiting for a potential confession. She stood, cleared off her table, and dropped her mug in the sink before admitting, "I'm on thin ice at the gym. Couple different trainers have caught me going too hard. Nearly passed out on a treadmill two days ago."

Mina wasn't sure if all this new information made her feel better or worse. Her team was overly stressed, but it did feel nice knowing her friends understood. All of them together on their struggle spaceship. She saw Nek quietly waiting on the smartwatch. "Some mess of a team you've got here."

"Warden training, traditionally, is years of work and conditioning. While you were eager to take on this mantle, it'd be unrealistic of me to expect a completely smooth transition." Nek pushed themselves out as a hologram from her watch, letting all of the team see them. "I should have checked in on your mental well-being sooner. I apologize for that."

Mina knocked on the countertop. "New team rule. Mental check-ins, as often as anyone needs them."

"Aye, aye captain." Zane gave her a light shake.

Sean and Steph got to flipping chairs onto the tables, Zane and Emma helped. Mina grabbed the broom and dustpan to follow behind them. With their group effort the final closing tasks were done in no time. Steph locked the doors on their way out. They all waved from their different cars around the otherwise empty lot, Mina did so from the passenger side of Zane's car.

Finding a new car was on her list. There were dealerships offering "deals" for people who lost vehicles in the insane two days Hurst experienced, but they required proof. Her car was completely vaporized. There was a chance that if she told her parents the car had been destroyed they'd arrange for a new one without any fuss, but expected revealing that she was anywhere near the goings-on would lead to them questioning her down the line. From what she knew they had yet to check in with Hephaestus Labs, but with the amount of buzz happening around town their return was only a matter of time. Not to mention The Expo coming in a little over two weeks, they wouldn't miss their time to show off.

Grabbing rides from her friends was easy enough, not to mention the teleporting option. A car was definitely an issue she could leave low on her to-do list. Anything concerning her parents was easier to ignore, out of habit.

Back at Zane's house, he walked her through the side yard and out to their shared gate. He matched pace with her toward his own backdoor, where they waved before heading inside. Acting as if their group chat wasn't going to be active for another hour or so.

Her near empty room greeted her. Steph's thrifted beanbag chair sat in one corner, claiming the spot as her own permanent seat for when they hung out. This one matched the one Mina used at Zane's. Having a group of friends wanting to hang out with her, at her house, was a new concept. Though there wasn't much time for sitting around, which was fine by her too.

Mina tapped her miniature Thunderbird, a cry that now matched her Guardian roared out. The group chat was filling up her armband's feed. Without changing her clothes, barely remembering to kick off her shoes, Mina burrowed under her comforter as she responded to Sean's inquiry on which tail of his Kitsune would work better for a jump. She felt safer having these conversations via text; no one was breaking into their Pak systems.

Nek appeared in the chat to provide a series of short simulations featuring Sean doing a dive and twist from different tails. Everyone held fast to their favorites, defending them like this might truly be a move he needed for an upcoming battle. Responses came slower as the night carried on, everyone drifting off to sleep.

A final text from Zane popped up directly to her. **Change your clothes. Wash your face. Goodnight.**

She rolled her eyes at her window, hoping he'd sense the gesture. Then got out of bed to follow his orders.

2

Takes Three to Conquer

One day, in the very near future, Capri would learn how to make these damned Lenian monsters on her own. With the amount of blueprints saved to their tables, she could get by for a while. All she needed to do was tell the Pawns which design to follow, right? Capri wondered if one could build a single reliable Lenian engineer from the parts of two others. Cut out the bothersome personalities. She'd dig through their database, do some research. Because spending most of the last two weeks laid up, enduring their company, had been maddening.

"That was embarrassing," from Gregory as he'd checked a bandage. She'd tried to shove him off and nearly fell off the couch they'd dropped her on.

"Sure showed those children," Maxwell added, while adjusting cushions to keep her in place. He dodged the pillow she'd weakly thrown at his head.

"How many hits did she foolishly charge into?"

"I stopped counting at twenty. Did any of our Pawns come back in one piece?"

"Not a single complete one. The bounce-back protocol pulled most, but we lost a notable amount of materials to grabby humans."

"We should put that protocol on her if she's going to get knocked around like that. Hell of a time locking on to her."

She'd passed out somewhere after that, but various versions of that conversation occurred whenever they ventured up to the suite. She'd eventually mustered the energy to boobytrap the elevator, sending them crashing back down once the car topped out. Capri laughed herself into exhaustion watching the replay via a Comp's feed. They'd come back that night via a hidden staircase she'd been unaware of, spoiling her fun. Until they reset the elevator and pulled the same drop on the Maintenance Crew.

Once she could stand for longer than ten minutes at a time, Capri moved herself to a workroom on the floor above the engineers. Taking one of the actual living quarters felt too familiar, she also liked knowing she was above them. The cot from her escape pod was easy enough to detach and drop in the corner farthest from the entryway. Capri also made the Maintenance Crew install a set of sliding doors for extra privacy. The built-in cabinets stored her slim goods; during their attack a pair of Pawns had grabbed food and clothes. Unfortunately, given what Lenians considered nutrition, the hunt resulted in meager returns and she was close to needing more. Not to mention the drab options they'd found for clothing. Several pieces were pulled off dead people. Blood splatter, scuffs, and holes made them less than desirable to wear. Nothing fit as nicely as her training attire from Outrider, but those were also severely bloodstained. While stuck prone she'd researched more Earth options, as basic as they were, to provide better direction for the next venture.

With her energy levels on the rise, she focused on preparing herself for another trip to Earth. Capri attempted to recreate a training routine like they'd run on Outrider. She'd dug through her personal drive and found a set of exercises to follow along with, a tweak to the hologram gave her a silent Rin to work beside. Her time with this imaginary Rin doubled as a sort of meditation period, bringing a little peace to her day.

That was until a tiff between the engineers cut through, making Capri regret leaving her doors open that day. As they grew louder, she popped out and called over the railing, "Cut it out or I will shove you both off the roof."

"More damage than you did-" Maxwell didn't finish the insult once the blaster bolt clipped the doorframe next to him.

She was rather satisfied with her reaction time on the draw, using Pawns for target practice kept her sharp. Capri took the stairs down to their floor, expecting to put a bolt or two in whatever new pet project Gregory was working on if he had another insult for her too.

As if knowing he'd need to protect his work, Gregory met her at the landing and took the risk of holding out a hand to her, an easy target for a bolt. "Alright, we've been a little curt. Our...apologies for that. Though I do think it's fair to say that a smidge more preparation might have helped with that plan."

Maxwell peeked out from his workshop, now on the opposite side from where she'd shot. "But we recognize that you felt the situation was rather dire."

This was rather annoying, them being so...civil? Observant? Thoughtful? Their behavior was so aggravatingly hard to pin down. She reluctantly admitted to herself that while the bickering stood out, they'd left her alone to recover in that garish Councilor's Suite most of the time.

Capri thought of her room on Outrider. Simple, but comforting. She'd never over decorated like Caro or let the space become chaos like Jarden. She didn't have that many possessions. Capri was content with basic comforts, only wanting enough space in bed for—one of those ungrateful children to now take up. She could only imagine the mess they'd made of Outrider as a whole.

Her hand tightened on the blaster, but in light of the Lenian's small apology she conceded that they were not the ones truly agitating her. Capri let the blaster recall back to her Pak. "This is all wrong."

"Change is never easy." Maxwell stepped farther out of the workshop, but stopped well out of arm's reach. "Natural to resist."

"You don't know me."

"True." Gregory tipped closer. "But I know you're very angry. And you're very alone. We know we're not good company, but at least we had each other to yell at this whole time. I can't imagine being *that* angry and all alone. It's unproductive. Not to mention dangerous."

This attempt at familiarity bothered her, as it woke something she'd been forcing herself to pretend she didn't miss, the comfort of having a team. This wasn't her team. This would not be her team. These were Lenians, there was a catch somewhere. "What do you want?"

"To survive," Maxwell answered.

Gregory glared at him. "To help."

She refused to believe that was all. They'd only made the first creature out of boredom. They wouldn't be thinking of her well-being now. "You don't care about what I'm after."

Gregory made another risky move, leaning on the railing next to her. "That may be true. But perhaps if we go at the next attempt in a more collaborative manner, we can find common ground."

She pulled away enough to put the previous amount of distance between them. "Why would you help me, again?"

"Felt good seeing a creation in action. Didn't realize how much we missed it."

"Letting us have more say in the next plan would produce better results," Maxwell said. "Rather than simply threatening us to do your bidding."

"But I'm so very good at that." Capri went to casually flick a lock of her short hair, but her bad shoulder pulsed with pain. She tried not to think about that brat Blue laying her out with bolts. A reckless move on their part; one that Capri found herself constantly working to not find impressive. "Couldn't you see I had them shaking in their suits?"

Gregory tweaked his mouth, holding back a smile at her small self-deprecation. "Give us some time to look over the data. Maybe we can find a new angle."

"They've got the advantage of numbers. And the Guardians. And the ship. We'd up our chances if we found some way to catch them not wearing the suits," Maxwell offered up slowly.

They must have started discussing options already. Capri did think that was a smart play, but required knowing who they were. She'd been the only one daft enough to take her helmet down during their fight. Nek's impostor Wardens were nothing more than suits and banter to her. What she needed was time on the ground investigating. There was no way they weren't leaving a trail given their inexperience, but she couldn't casually move about this population. While she looked relatively similar to humans, they were boringly hued; giving her no easy way to pass. She watched her Comp float by on its standard patrol around the tower. Once, she could simply ask any Comp to tell her the status of other Wardens and they'd report back instantly, no matter the distance. This was not an option since she, and them by extension of her programming, were blocked from the Outrider framework. She'd need one in good standing to give up the intel.

She pointed at Gregory. "You mentioned humans grabbed Pawns parts, yes?"

"A handful."

"Did they take Comps?"

"Certainly. I'd have to check the footage to estimate how many."

"Do that," after a beat she added, "Please. And see if you can catch any leads on where the parts were taken. Those Comps would have everything we need to find the Wardens."

Gregory backed away toward his workshop, cautious after receiving the kinder request. "I will get right on that."

"Thank you." The words stuck together coming out of her mouth, she could only stomach this comradery for so much longer. Capri turned to Maxwell. "We'll need someone to check on any possible intel we find. The human agencies and Wardens will be on the lookout for me and the Pawns. But I don't trust a random person to follow orders like I want them too. Do we have a way to, I don't know, enforce commands?"

"They're run by electrical pulses, I don't believe their organic wiring is much different from what we use in creations. I'll have to dig up my old research on human anatomy to see what kind of adjustments are required on the hardware side, but that should be doable." Maxwell stared off somewhere over her shoulder, clearly working on something in his head.

"Okay," she swallowed hard, trying to keep this civility going, "I will leave you to it and will check in at the end of the day."

Maxwell gave no indication he noticed her struggling, she'd apparently found something that interested him, he only nodded and returned to his workshop. Leaving her alone in the walkway, stunned by how they'd agreed on a plan so quickly. Her Warden team never settled matters this efficiently.

Capri flicked her armband and checked for the most recent location of the Maintenance Crew. They'd made a rather remarkable amount of progress on the base, fixing the majority of structural issues and now focusing on cleaning the rust and grime. None of that mattered to her, she couldn't let everyone get off with niceties today.

3

The Gang's All Here

Megan sprawled out across Sam's living room floor, very much a cat in a sunbeam. "I don't think you two realize how good it feels not hearing construction noise right now."

Sam and Henrie, situated on opposite ends of the couch, shared a look and a quiet laugh.

She shut her eyes and stretched out further. "Nothing but air conditioners and birds." Someone drove down the street with an unbalanced amount of bass kicking out from their speaker system. "And, I think, Doja Cat."

"Do they know when they'll be done yet?" Henrie asked. She couldn't imagine that all the noise was good for Megan's mom; who was not so much walking on eggshells as she was made of them. They'd spent the early days staying with family to get away from the round-the-clock noise. Megan convinced them to let her stay at Henrie's once. With the push the city was under to get back to normal, Henrie figured the street level stuff would be nearing done. Giving them back some peace and quiet.

"They say by the end of the month they should have the majority finished. But someone in the building across from us is paying a crew to work near nonstop. Probably want their precious conference room back."

"Would noise canceling headphones help?" Sam asked. "Black out curtains for their lights?"

"That's the thing! I normally sleep great with downtown noise. Even construction. But they blared some overly twang-y country thing last night and there's no glass in yet because they've been lifting materials through the windows. Absolute torture."

"We could break in and sabotage their speakers?" Henrie offered.

Megan pointed in her direction. "That is extremely tempting."

"We are not breaking and entering. And vandalizing," Sam whispered, though neither of their parents were nearby to hear.

Megan moved her point to Sam. "You're not invited, Do-Gooder. Henrie, speak to me of vengeance."

Henrie laughed and gave a shrug to Sam. What harm could a little daydream of crime do? "They probably have a door propped open for their crew to use. We technically wouldn't need to break in."

"The majority of the businesses in that building are open to the public," Megan added. "So no trespassing."

"And we don't have to break any possessions. We could hide the speakers. Or swap it with an identical one that you control."

"I'll play Call Me Maybe until they go mad."

"Few problems," Sam ticked off on their fingers, "even if it's propped open, going in an entryway not meant for you is breaking in. This would also be happening outside business hours, so that is trespassing. And tampering with someone else's property is the definition of vandalism."

Megan groaned and rolled over to give Henrie a pitiful look. "They took our fun."

"Logic ruins many things." Henrie made a big show of blocking her face from Sam and stage whispering, "We'll go without them and make them be our alibi."

"You will not." Sam threw a pillow at her head.

"You'd let us go to jail?"

"If you did a crime? Yes!"

"What a friend." Megan rolled away, curled into a fetal position, and gave a large sigh. "Letting me suffer like this."

Henrie held on to her newly obtained pillow to keep herself from falling off the couch laughing. She felt rather good. The last two weeks were tough, mostly spent waiting for the other shoe - or robot - to drop. The Warden video said they were here to do good, which also alluded that they were here for good. They all but promised more trouble would come and Henrie didn't feel lucky enough to believe the next time would be anywhere but Hurst. Her mom must have thought the same because she kept crazy hours coordinating what the hospital may need when/if the next hit came. Which left Henrie alone for long stretches of time at home with only stuff, dead dad kind of stuff, she didn't want to think about keeping her company.

Sam was being ignored by Megan, so they turned to Henrie and forced a change of topic. "How was closing last night?"

Henrie was grateful as it pulled her thought away from the tiny spiral she'd nearly dropped into. "Dead. I don't know what I'm gonna do when people start staying out after seven. Won't be used to it."

"At least you had good closers with you." Megan rolled over, this time glaring at Sam. "Someone gave me Carter."

"And Michele. Who he is completely intimidated by. I thought that would balance things out." Helping with scheduling was a new responsibility Sam was still getting the hang of.

"Steph and Sean are great, but then their friends showed up. And, I don't know, I feel like I'm interrupting something when they all hang out." Henrie remembered the stiffness in Emma, who was normally chill when the two of them talked alone. Mina had looked ready to throw up as Henrie went by, for some reason. She'd felt several pairs of eyes on her as she left, like they'd been waiting for her to disappear.

"They are a new little clique." Megan sat up to grab her phone on the coffee table. She scrolled and pulled up a group photo from the 'checked in as safe' hashtag. "But they did go through Robo-Day together. That kinda thing bonds people."

"Can't argue that." Their own little group, if not together, spent every day in some form of contact. They'd even joined up with those five once to volunteer for some cleanup work in a less torn apart section of downtown.

"Do you think them hanging out during closing is an issue?" Sam asked slowly, a clear *do I tell my dad/the boss* hanging in the air afterward.

"No, no." Henrie waved off their worry, regretting bringing the encounter up at all. Emma was the only part that really bugged her, but she hadn't divulged the extent of their talks to these two yet. She was pretty tight lipped about relationship stuff, even something that was only a potential relationship. "They're fine. Really. They help close."

Megan swiped through more posts. "I think someone in there has a crush on someone at the cafe, but I don't have Steph's snooping powers."

Henrie clutched the pillow tighter, thinking she might have to out herself.

"Strange how she can do that for everyone else and never goes on dates herself," Sam said.

Megan nodded. "She's the only theater kid I know who isn't a dirty birdy."

"What?!" came from both Henrie and Sam. Henrie completely abandoned the idea of mentioning her own girl troubles.

"That's a thing! That is SO a thing." Megan was typing in her search bar, trying to defend herself with the internet.

This time the pillow couldn't balance out Henrie's fit of laughter and she fell to the floor next to Megan. Sam shook their head down at them. "And you two think you can do crime."

4

They're Called Pawns for a Reason

Capri was carving a channel in the rug spread across the Councilor's Suite. She'd been a fool to give them until the end of the day. She should have been demanded hourly updates. Because holding herself to this agreement of leaving them alone was nearly insufferable. Scaring the crew only took up so much time, and sadly the act was starting to lose its flair. She'd moved on to her personal project of outfitting the escape pod with the better defenses of the scouting ship. Her thinking was to have something ready in the chance a quick exit was needed and teleporting was no longer an option. The Lenian drone ship was too small to fashion a cockpit out of without ruining the functionality, as far as she could tell. Hardware was not her specialty. While she'd managed to get the two systems talking with each other in a snap, they remained two separate ships. Meshing them together was proving a larger challenge than expected. Given her near constant level of impatience anymore, Capri made herself walk away after only a few hours of work.

Loitering in her own room put her too close to the engineers. Their faint sounds of working would push her over the edge. Which brought her to pacing the suite. There wasn't anything good to snoop through up here, she'd found that out during recovery. The quarters were designed with some specific Councilor's taste and comfort in mind, but no personal effects were about. She'd assumed they were lying before about how no one checked on them, but the only scraps she found were food wrapping, lazy sketches of creature designs, and balled up insults either pair must have chucked at each other. All trash clearly from the four residents below. They'd truly been left with no oversight.

Her armband pinged, a Comp informing her that Maxwell and Gregory were wrapping up. The Comp's feed gave her peeks of what the pair were working on throughout the day, but not enough to fully discern their results on her own. The busywork did keep them from bickering all day. She knew that since they were getting along, they'd take an evening meal together down in the dingy little dining room on the main floor. Capri considered grabbing her own food and joining. There was a chorus of laughter in her head, ghosts she had yet to shake.

You'll freak them out.

You barely ate with us.

That may be moving too fast, came a lot softer from Rin.

She hated them. They were right and she hated them for it. On the elevator ride down she reminded herself that all she was arguing with was her own subconsciousness. Perhaps that made the fight easier, filtering this internal conflict as yet another spat with her team to help make sense of everything. She couldn't even say the false voices acted like their once-real counterparts. If Rin was here-

Well, none of this would be happening. That was on her.

"But I was right." She gripped the handlebar inside the lift too tightly, the metal groaned in protest. The Collective, at large, had gone soft, they needed stronger forces to ever truly defeat their enemies. Not simply fend them off. She'd been entrusted to start a new faction, singled out as the strongest on her team. A proven fact given she was the last standing. She would win this stupid planet and take that victory back to the Collective. Capri would boast how she'd done it alone and demand to know why they left her to rot. They'd regret it, she was certain.

Always so sure.

Maxwell and Gregory were stepping out of their workshops as the elevator car stopped at the landing. Capri snapped the door open and stood between them. She realized after a long, quiet, pause they were waiting for her to speak first. No one wanted to potentially ruin this small truce.

Gregory cracked. "There isn't much on the lost Pawns. I've got scraps of intel on who took them, but nothing certain on their current location. Outside of the few being sold online. None of the human agencies are admitting to having our tech."

That left them nowhere. She needed to find Pawns to then find Comps. If these idiots couldn't do that then what was left?

Gregory held up his tablet to fend off her furrowed brow, displaying a design he'd worked up. "Buuuut, I have a plan. We make a batch of stripped down Pawns. Shove trackers all over them. Design them to fall apart."

Capri followed his line of thinking. "More pieces for humans to steal."

"And increase our chances of getting a working signal inside their facilities." Gregory was clearly pleased with his solution.

She couldn't say she hated the idea either. Let the humans do the leg work. Speaking of which, she turned to Maxwell. "Did you figure out anything?"

"Theoretically." Maxwell gestured for them to step inside his workshop. He swung a hand over the display table, a diagram lifted from the surface. A block that looked like her Pak floated between them, until the schematic unfurled. The device now featured one flat pad, with a long spiked tendril rolling out from the bottom and two shorter ones off the sides. "Based on their anatomy, this design should sink in and give us control of a human's functions. And if they wear standard clothing," he pointed to the shirt and shorts Capri was in, "the piece would go undetected. I can also include a small camera that will attach to their front to provide visual feedback of their surroundings."

"Which could be spotted," Capri said.

"Fair, but the camera is small. Gregory can craft a cover. The internal circuitry of humans is too meaty for me to decipher how to go directly through their eyes. Not without further time for research. And potentially a person on hand for testing."

She didn't want to wait any longer than necessary. "The detached camera will do."

A human figure appeared over the table. The block shrunk to match their scale, the pad stuck between their shoulders, right at the base of their neck. Tendrils stretched out across the arms, stopping short of the elbow, and down their entire back.

She pulled the mock Pak off the human, spinning the diagram before her. The tendrils retracted and rolled out over and over. "And the theoretical part?"

Maxwell looked a tad nervous now. "Our programming for creations is rather basic. Punch this. Smash that. But I imagine you would like more finesse. As well, the creations can't think for themselves. We talk a lot about humans being dim, but they could push back. The program will need enhanced to circumvent that. Which will take some time to build."

Capri straightened up. "I can do that."

Gregory coughed and Maxwell's eyes widened a fraction. Neither Lenian seemed to have expected that answer. Maxwell nudged the human hologram, knocking them over. "That would be helpful."

"Send the current programming up to my room. I'll fix it up."

"Sure. Sure thing. Also, this device is rather delicate and may take a couple days to put together properly."

She watched him brace for her response, but surprised herself to discover she wasn't upset with the delay. Not while she had her own project anyway. She turned to Gregory, "How long do you need?"

He answered slowly, checking his quick exit to the doorway. "Also a couple days. To have a decent amount of Pawns ready."

"Sounds fair. Send me the Pawn programming as well. I'll see if I can shore up the tracker signals and make sure the humans can't also dig out intel we don't want them to have. Enjoy your meal." Capri left them and nearly skipped up the staircase. She didn't need a Comp to show her their faces, she'd caught them clearly enough on her way up. There could be something to that kill them with kindness mentality after all.

$$5$$

Super Chill Night In (Space)

Mina sat in the doorway of what could be her bedroom on Outrider. Sleeping quarters, if she wanted to feel fancy about it. The ship gave her a workshop, she didn't need a second bedroom on top of that. None of them did, much less Steph needing a third. Yet the unused space bothered her.

They'd either been training or hanging out around Outrider every day since they found it. They'd all pitched in to stock up on food, mostly snacks and coffee pods to go with a new machine. Sean took charge of organizing everything, his eagerness made Mina realize he must be the main reason the drink bar at Restoration always looked so tidy. Last she knew, he'd moved on with a set of Comps to rework some of the storage spaces. She'd moved her workshop while Zane and Steph rigged up a projector screen in the common area farther down the hallway. Emma hunted through online marketplaces and garage sales to build out the small gym that already existed onboard. Repairing the long dormant, alien equipment was also on Mina's To-Do list. Sean's handwritten notes were stuck under every bit of signage in the halls, one of their group projects was learning the language so as to not rely on the Pak translating all the time.

Bits and pieces of them could be found all over Outrider, but the most to show for her time in this specific room were the few dirty training clothes scattered about the floor and toiletries in the bathroom beyond. She knew everyone else's rooms looked the same. They'd gone back to the bunkroom showers the first few days, but after an extra long morning of cardio Steph caved and used the private tub. One by one they'd all done the same. But she knew no one had touched the beds yet because they'd all been using the blanket fort. Even the nights she'd been here alone Mina slept there.

While she was impressed the fort stayed up all this time without any adjustments, they couldn't hide inside forever. These rooms were part of the whole deal. Part of them taking ownership of being Wardens. The training made them more confident in the suits, but she couldn't shake that nagging feeling they were temporary replacements. That a set of real Wardens would show up any day and take everything away. They'd tell her thanks, yank the Pak off, and teleport her back to Earth. Never to see Outrider again.

That exact nightmare brought her here tonight. She'd initially gone to her workshop to start printing parts for a micro-Comp idea she wanted to test out. A timer ran on her watch for those pieces finishing up. Soon enough Mina found herself here. Sitting on the floor. Willing herself to enter the room.

"One night of sleeping here and it won't be weird anymore."

She hoped.

Mina scooted herself farther in, enough that she could reach out and touch the blanket tucked tightly under the mattress. Comps must have also tidied up when they cleared away the belongings of the last Wardens. As hard of an edge as the blanket looked to have, the material was soft. The mattress had a fair amount of give as she pressed in.

"Stop being weird about a bed." She remained on the floor, but pulled the blanket, finding she needed to tug harder than expected. "Comps may have a future in housekeeping."

She was surprised no one came around to check on her, especially Comp2876. Her armband hadn't even pinged with an overly exclaimed message in the half hour she'd been here. There were always some number moving about the ship completing their unending upkeep and tasks, but at least one would swing by to greet the Wardens when any of them arrived.

On top of that, Nek hadn't said anything either. The team used the saved points to teleport themselves up to Outrider from their armbands now, but usually Nek was waiting when anyone landed.

She needed to get better at being suspicious.

Mina hopped up and made her way through a winding hallway which eventually connected to her new workshop, the charging stations weren't far beyond that. She found the bays full of Comps who'd been working around the ship all day. Nothing weird there. She'd feel bad pulling one out of their sleep mode to answer questions so she moved along.

She popped the map of Outrider on her armband. There were several active points in one of the storage bays. Maybe they were working on the new layout Sean put together. Mina traced a path for herself. Zane could go on about the spoke system all he wanted, these internal hallways got weird. Her and Emma would swear to it. She also didn't believe the amount of rooms on the map should fit. Though given the complicated compression tech Comps utilized, it wasn't hard to imagine the Collective could squish some extra square footage on the ship.

Mina activated the bay door as she approached and immediately met a pair of Comps holding a shimmering green tunic between them. They scanned, folded, and tucked the garment in a silver bag like their training clothes came from. She stepped around as they sealed the bag, printed something on the front, and set it in a crate. There was a large pile of clothing waiting on top of another box, she watched a different pair of Comps pull a piece and perform the same routine. Her stomach dropped as she realized whose items they were sorting. This wasn't something she should be intruding on, yet she stumbled farther in the room. Behind the row of open crates, she found more Comps wrapping items in what looked like fancy, green bubble wrap. How you made bubble wrap fancy, she couldn't be sure, but it appeared higher end then the normal stuff. Intergalactic, space-grade bubble wrap. Mina watched as a Comp carefully covered a bundle of small figurines that resembled how their Guardians used to appear. She picked out the one that matched Capri's remaining Guardian sitting in the level below.

Comp2876 pushed up to her. *Hello, Warden Mina! Can we help you?*

"No. No, I'm fine." She glanced up and spotted Nek's waves rolling low on the panel. Mina thought the colors looked muted. Her face felt hot. "I'm so sorry."

Nek started to say something as Mina ran out of the room, but she didn't turn back. After several random turns through the halls, she dropped into a corner. They'd been packing away the Warden's belongings and she'd walked right in. Straight up barged in on something extremely private and personal.

Mina knew how hard of a task that was from clearing out her grandmother's house. Well, for her anyway. Her mother was clinical, wanting everything done before the funeral so they could leave, only taking the time to sort through papers before calling a company to empty the place out. Mina shoved whatever small keepsakes she could in her own bag as they impartially filled box after box and carried pieces of her grandma away. That moment was the closest she'd ever come to yelling at her mother, before she'd fully dropped out of reality. Mina often wondered if that outrage would have registered with her parents, had she let it out. She hated the idea of her grandmother's belongings basically being thrown to the wind. Now residing with people who wouldn't appreciate them properly.

The heat in her face rose. Mina hated this stuff, but she couldn't shake it. Those Wardens, their own big and complicated lives, shouldn't be reduced to things stuck in a box. They should be here doing...no, because if they were here, Mina wouldn't be and she needed this. She wasn't happy they were dead. She wasn't.

Conflicting emotions spiraled around her head. She was baffled at how hard this was to puzzle out. Why couldn't she nail down one concrete thought anymore?

"Warden Mina," Nek called softly from the panel above her.

She took a breath that was shakier than expected and looking up. "Oh, hey, Nek."

"I'm sorry if that upset you."

"What? No! I'm the one that's sorry. I had no business there. Should have knocked or something."

"Are you sure you're okay?"

She'd been about to make herself cry, but she shook off her memories of unmarked boxes being tossed into a truck and got herself back to standing. She reminded herself that Nek had, in a way, lost their entire original team a little over two weeks ago. Not hundreds of years. Mina needed to support them, not get lost in her own emotions. "Yes, absolutely. Are you okay?"

Nek didn't answer right away, their waves bounced along the panel. "I waited too long to do this."

"That, um, stuff is never easy." For most anyway. There was another memory, one of her mother looking distraught about papers spread across a table. Mina thought she'd finally caught her mom feeling real human emotions. She crept around to see what memento pulled a heartstring in her mother's cold chest, but found she was only reviewing a current draft of her father's latest article. Brought from home to revise while the workers took care of the house. Mina cleared her throat. "But it's good for closure."

"When we...took care of the Wardens, it was hard. But there was so much going on I wasn't able to dwell too much. This. This feels harder."

"Everything in there has a memory. It can seem wrong deciding what to keep when everything feels important. There's no problem with needing some time."

"I keep expecting Caro to argue about her books being mixed with Camden's." They drifted down the hall back toward the storage bay.

While the comment was small, it was the most Mina had heard Nek talk of the other Wardens' personalities. She wanted to tread lightly, and did so literally as she kept pace with Nek. "Sounds like Zane and his movies. Obsessed with the organization."

"Organizing was Rin's jurisdiction. She would vastly disagree with Sean's current arrangement of the kitchen." Nek sounded a little lighter now.

"Nek, if you need a break from everything, no one would fault you. I can take over the deck for a bit. You do whatever you need to recharge." Mina wasn't sure exactly how empty of a proposition that was, given that Nek was an entity living directly within Outrider. There was likely a limit to how far they could detach themselves.

"Thank you for the offer, but the work is how I recharge. There will be rough days, like this one, but I'm glad to go through them with you and our new team."

She couldn't argue the 'dive in to work' mentality without sounding like a hypocrite, but she also knew what it meant to have someone willing to pull you up for air against your own will. Zane had done that for her plenty in the last three years. Mina gave a quick look to the current workload going on over the framework. Aside from the general Comp buzz, Nek was monitoring a lot of local channels. There were new claims of recovered Comps; these were becoming less and less legitimate, but they wanted to ensure as few as possible ended up in the wrong hands. Not to mention the amount of chatter going on about the Wardens. There were also the new personal weapons for the team underway in Fabrication. "I totally get it, but I must insist. Step back, even if only for a few minutes. Let me handle this."

"That is not-"

"Mental health check-ins, remember? That goes for you too. Please, Nek. Focus on their belongings. Take some actual time with it. And then take a breather. You and 2876. I'll get the stuff from Fab and keep an eye on feeds." Nek might not be able to fully detach, but Mina decided this was more of a The-Thought-That-Counts situation.

Nek balled up tightly before stretching out to low waves. "Yes. Okay. I'll do that. Thank you."

"Don't even think about it." Her armband updated with current estimates for everything in Fab, it'd be a while before they were finished. "I'll be up top. Let me know if you need anything. Do not do it yourself."

They moved together through the halls until they came to the elevator. Nek thanked her again before disappearing off the panel, likely moving directly back to the storage bay. Mina hopped in the elevator and took the quick jump up to the deck. She noticed the main display was far more cluttered than normal. The several feeds usually spread throughout the room were running all on the same screen. Nek must have taken the time to arrange this setup for her, keeping her from spinning in a constant circle. The video feeds were all muted with captions running and written posts automatically highlighted phrases as they were processed. She pulled over her preferred chair, which tipped back a half inch further than the others (no matter how much Emma said that was in her head), in front of the console. She got to work sorting information, years of shuffling through social media prepared her for this.

Most articles were easy to flip through, by now they were repetitions of the same things talked about right after Robo-Day. She didn't care for that name, but it'd stuck. Actual social media posts did hold her attention, it felt fair to care about what people said of you while you were trying to save their lives. People wanted to fill in the gaps between The Hill disappearing and the alien fistfight that happened twenty-four hours later. Topped off with the fact that nobody had seen the Wardens since then, there was a fair bit of speculation going on.

Do you think the colors are what their skin looks like?

Silver could throw me around like that robot thing and I'd say thank you.

Does anyone else think they kinda look bad at fighting?

This clip of Purple goes with literally any song you put over it.

Why didn't the big robots become one huge robot? Lame!!!

Orange def does parkour.

Look at how Green goes for Blue here. I ship it.

She had to stop herself from responding to the last one.

Mina fell into a rhythm with the feeds, pushing anything trivial off and dropping the few notable ones to a folder for Nek to recheck. She made another folder for pieces to share with the group. There were niche publications with some not-so-subtle notices of 'exciting potential products coming soon'. Likely whatever Comp or Pawn they'd scrounged up being stripped and frantically reverse engineered. No doubt there was a quiet race going on in Hurst to see who could make a copy and get to market first. While Mina was surprised to not find Hephaestus Labs included, she wasn't about to write them off.

Recovering lost Comps the day of the fight was a rather simple job, as most fell within the few streets where their fight with Capri took place. The remaining Comps had done a pass before returning to Outrider. They'd snagged more from online sales by random people, always using fake names and dummy cash app accounts. Steph said doing pickups made her feel like a spy; Sean said drug dealer. Nek informed her later that Comps were highly encrypted and contained extra measures that were enabled any time they were away from Outrider. Meaning Mina would have had no chance getting into Comp2876's programming back in her room that night. Their concern was that the tech alone could become an issue if the wrong group managed to duplicate it first. Not to mention if Capri found one and worked her programming magic on them. She didn't need more allies.

Mina wished they'd found wherever Capri was hiding. While the Lenians were some of the Collective's oldest enemies, and were well documented in Outrider's newly recovered database, they now used technology several centuries ahead of the Wardens. Whatever cloaking they utilized had so far kept them off any scans Nek attempted. Forcing them to stay on constant alert for any reports of Pawns being sighted or Capri's new activation signal appearing. Not great.

After an hour of sorting, Mina's armband started flashing. The timers for Fabrication were all run down. She left the deck and beelined for that section, thankful that this was a straightforward path. Waiting at the end of several conveyor belts were the new weapons for her and her team. Within a couple days of training, everyone started requesting tweaks or full on changes to better suit them.

Mina never recovered the lost sais from the fight, writing them off as lost in the chaos. The others encouraged her to try again, even after nicking her own hand within the first minute. After nearly injuring herself a second time, they let her quietly set them aside in the weapons locker tucked in the back of the training room. She'd always have the fond memory of a sai bouncing off Capri's helmet, that was enough for her. Luck would have it, after a little trial and error with some other options, she turned out to be a decent shot. Now she opted for the dual blaster setup Zane originally used, but with an added feature of trackers tagged on anything she shot. Ensuring that if she didn't take the Pawn down personally, it'd be all the easier to send Comps or teammates after them.

Zane made the choice to switch to a mace, saying he wanted to free up a hand since he was their second heavy hitter. While discussing designs, he only offered up the nail bat from Stranger Things.

"You wanna be Steve so bad," she'd laughed.

"Who doesn't?" was his only response, during which she could see him physically restraining himself from flipping back his hair. Mina worked in the extra feature that the head could eject the nails for a larger area of effect if desired.

Emma, who did enjoy the morning star, sidelined the weapon to completely free her hands. Choosing a set of spiked gauntlets instead. With a little extra tooling on Mina's part, they engineered them so that the row over her knuckles contained a small boost of their own. When used, they would extend to hit an enemy before her fist caught up a second later.

Steph pieced the tactic together first when the group was staring at Emma and Mina's crude original drawing of the design. "You punch people twice."

"I punch them twice!" Emma was definitely the most excited for her new weapon.

Sean kept the staff, but made adjustments to better suit his style. He didn't always want one full length staff, so now he'd carry two baton sized pieces that could hook together and extend when he wanted. Each contained retractable sickles on the ends for cutting down their flying enemies.

"Surprised one doesn't do flowers," Emma teased.

Steph kept the saber with the blaster addition. The only real change she made was adding some extra design work on the blade. "I feel so wonderfully dramatic swinging this around."

Mina wouldn't argue that. Especially since Steph's weapon having a ranged attack meant more time together doing target practice.

She grabbed a cart to haul everything across Outrider. Mina planned to lay out the new weapons on their beds. That'd get them inside the rooms for a couple of minutes.

Halfway back to the private quarters, Nek appeared on a panel and moved at pace with her. "Thank you for the help tonight."

"I'm glad I could do something for you. Is everything…good now?"

"I believe the Comps and myself are more at peace, yes. We made the decision to release part of the Warden's ashes to the stars. They were always meant to be explorers."

Do not cry, Mina. Keep yourself together. Though that was a wonderfully aching sentiment. She hadn't known Nek was holding on to their ashes this whole time. "That's lovely, Nek. If you ever want, or need, to talk about them, please do. They were your friends too. I'm sure we can learn a lot from them."

"I'll remember that, thank you. But I believe I've asked enough of you for one night. Please get some rest. I believe Warden Emma has another rigorous plan for you all tomorrow."

"Will do. Night, Nek." She watched Nek disappear from the panel and kept going for the quarters. Mina set out the weapons across their pillows, like this was some extremely dangerous hotel. John Wick in space. In her own room, she made herself go in and shut the door behind her. She tried spinning a blaster around her finger. Which only went slightly smoother than the sais, she was lucky these included safeties. After loading the new blasters to her Pak, Mina sat on the corner of the bed and scrolled through her own socials.

Eventually the late hour caught up to her. Her suddenly sluggish brain insisted she wouldn't survive the trek over to the fort or the ten second teleport back home. Mina freed one corner of the blanket and sunk into her new bed.

6

And the Drones go Boom

Henrie stared down the vendor across from Restoration's booth, trying to figure out how they were selling small plushies of the Wardens. A lot of plushies. A clearly not made by this woman in her spare bedroom amount of plushies. She'd been told this little event was to bring local businesses together to bolster the community. True to Sam's word, Hurst really did love an excuse to get a set of booths together. The lady across the way didn't fit that vibe.

The more upsetting fact was how badly Henrie wanted them.

"Henrie," Sam called over from the mobile drink bar. "Can you grab more ice from the van? Smoothies are going fast today."

"Sure thing!" She wound around their makeshift counter, several folding tables on loan from their various homes, and yanked open the back door of the new van. Mitch surprised them all by buying something brand new, one with a thin bench seat included so she wasn't stuck with the crates. Everyone was taking bets on what kind of art Mitch would have commissioned for the exterior. Given the looming threat of another eventual attack, it felt like tempting fate to become attached. For the time being they were enjoying the van while it was new and shiny. Henrie also didn't mind that this gathering's setup, stretched across the parking lot of a nearby shopping center, allowed them to park right behind their canopy, also new and awaiting Mitch's artistic dreams.

She yanked out two bags from the freezer box secured inside and hefted them back to where Sam was putting together drinks. Henrie appreciated being so quickly allowed to join the event crew. Restoration was great, but she enjoyed getting paid to basically hang out with Sam and Megan. She felt much better about this move with new friends, a job, and superheroes keeping her distracted.

Stop that. Henrie chided herself when a familiar twinge hit her chest. To her surprise, the feeling faded away upon command.

Megan nudged her and tilted her head toward the plushie vendor. "Can you believe she wants fifty dollars for a set?"

"Highway robbery."

"I'd split the cost, but there's no simple way to divide the plushies with the three of us."

"Rotating custody?" Henrie bumped Sam's side to get their attention. "But Do-Gooder here probably doesn't want any ties to us scoundrels."

Sam sighed as they poured out a smoothie. "I will bail you out. One time. After that, your life choices are your own."

"Heartless."

"No plushies for you!" Megan called over as she picked up their tablet register. The man waiting to pay laughed at their exchange. "You'd do a little theft for a friend, right sir?"

"Not with those Wardens around." He tapped his phone to the reader. "Too much trouble."

Sam laughed and pointed down to her. "Take that!"

Megan was about to respond when a row of plushies exploded into stuffing. A blue arm rolled across their front table as the woman behind the booth screamed. People in the walkway looked up at something the canopy blocked Henrie from seeing. The man took off running, smoothie in hand, as the three of them dropped under the tables.

Megan shifted closer to Henrie. "Bad flashback."

Henrie crawled out to see past the canopy, spotting those evil drones circling back toward their row. "Yeah, not sure these tables will hold up as well as the benches."

There was a batch of confused people, who'd missed the first sweep, still standing in the row and oblivious about why people were running. Sam left their spot and yelled for everyone to take cover. The drones shot through the tops of their canopies. A container exploded behind Henrie, spilling iced tea all over her back.

She shook off what she could. "Even for me, this is too much."

Henrie watched Sam direct people away and caught sight of two drones coming back up the row. They'd come in lower, likely aiming for targets like Sam who were looking up for another attack from the sky. Henrie didn't have anything to grab this time, but shot out and rammed the first drone. Sending them both crashing through the plushie tent, which didn't make for as good of a landing as she expected. Mostly because she landed on top of the drone. Henrie scrambled, knocking over more dolls, trying to get away before the thing shot again. In her hurry she kicked a chunk into smaller pieces. She realized the drone was fully out of commission after the one hit.

"Feel like I should take that a little personal."

"Henrie!" Sam was looking for her.

"All good!" She patted herself over as she stood. "Weirdly enough."

Henrie stepped around the table she'd crashed into. There was a lot more chaos going on now. People ducking in and out of booths trying to get back to their cars, or behind something not made of plastic and fake wood. Megan joined Sam in clearing their immediate area. Henrie noticed one of their tables now laid destroyed; she expected the decision to move was made for Megan.

Sam yelled over as they slipped between a gap in the booths. "Get to the van!"

Henrie moved to do just that, but was cut off by another drone dropping in front of her. She somehow knew that this one knew that she'd taken out another drone. A fear backed up by three more closing in. The first spread themselves open, while the others folded in. Henrie watched pieces hook together right before her; ending up with something that looked like an endoskeleton from those jump scare games Carter was constantly trying to have them play. There'd been clips of these from the first attack, they were much worse in person. Henrie wasn't sad she'd missed out on them before. The mech-skeleton-thing reached out to her with a spindly hand. On instinct she batted the hand away, three fingers broke and bounced across the ground.

"You all seemed a lot tougher last time."

The person-shaped collection of drones sounded like it huffed before lunging for her. Henrie tipped back and dodged the grab, hooking one of its legs with her own. The stack of drones slammed to the ground, scattering parts everywhere. She'd watched Silver need several hits to take down a single drown before, right?

"Yeah, you did not do that last time."

Henrie got one full second of feeling smug before a shot hit her shoulder from behind. The hit made her turn, allowing the drone to smash into her chest. Sending her to the ground on top of all the other broken wreckage. Hellish Legos stabbed her back. With this new drone added on top, she hoped there wasn't anything pointy stuck in her right now. Henrie shook herself free of bits, but could hear another drone closing in already. She grabbed the biggest chunk nearby and lined up to throw it, but as the drone dropped low a fist shot out from between two booths and knocked the thing fully out of the air.

Silver stepped out and looked around. "This seems easier."

At least it wasn't only Henrie who thought so.

"What did I say about the 'seems easy' thing?" Blue said as they backed out of the same gap. They fired backward and two shattered drones flew out around them.

"Sorry, Boss." Silver came up to Henrie and held out a hand. Her bewildered face reflected on their helmet as she was pulled to her feet. "You again."

Henrie was stunned by the fact that Silver remembered her. "Um, thanks."

"You okay?"

Her shoulder throbbed, but wasn't visibly bleeding. A burn was better than a bullet, right? Her back contained several points of pain, she expected several bruises were forming there. She pushed every ache aside, not about to look uncool in front of a superhero. "Yeah. I'm good."

"Please leave the area!" Green ordered as they charged by taking a swing on two more drones. The evil robots were out of range, but the darts that shot off the end ripped through their backsides. Littering the ground with more pieces.

Orange appeared at the end of the walkway and batted a drone out of the air, but a second swooped by and headed their way. Silver turned at the last moment and punched that drone straight to the ground. Henrie was hit by more metallic pieces, but she didn't care.

Purple came up from behind Henrie and grabbed Silver's arm. "Need your help moving some cars."

"On it." Silver gave a nod to Henrie before the pair ran off.

One of those not-evil red robot things dropped next to her. A little screen flashed *Please move to safety!* at her.

"Sure thing," she said as the small robot jetted after the Wardens. She'd been right in the middle of them. That would've been the craziest minute of her life had she not watched a mountain disappear two weeks ago. And a giant robot fight the day after that. The fighting moved to follow the Wardens. Henrie shuffled through the pile of plushies, deciding they'd earned a set. Henrie made her way around what was left of the Restoration tent and banged on the van's side door. "It's me."

Megan swung the door open and pulled her inside. "You are crazy. And hurt!"

"Nothing too bad. And I got loot."

"That is poor behavior." Sam nudged her to bend so they could check on her shoulder. "That should probably get looked at."

She checked the damage herself, a sting for sure but nothing truly damaged. "Nah, I've had worse burns from mat falls."

The ping of shots ran along the side of the van. Megan dropped to the footwell of the passenger seat. "The Wardens are getting them, right?"

"Those things are practically falling apart this time. But that's not the craziest thing." Henrie smacked the center console with her free hand. "Silver remembered me."

Megan pulled herself off the floor. "Shut up."

"Totally did! They helped me up and said 'you again.'"

"That's not a good thing," Sam warned as they started the van.

"No, it's a great thing!" Megan said, "Oh! Hey. Up close can you tell if it's a helmet or their head?"

"Helmet, for sure," Henrie answered as Sam pulled them away from the dwindling fight. Sam gestured toward Megan's seatbelt.

She rolled her eyes, but pulled the belt across herself. "See Sam, everyone gets a win today."

"What did you win?" Sam asked. They'd been for helmet, Megan for head.

"These four plushies," Henrie said as she passed them over. "I'm good with keeping Silver."

7

The Lucky Winner Is...

Capri stood over the display table in Gregory's workshop looking down at all the markers spread across the city. They'd watched Wardens strike down Pawns and escort people away. She rolled her eyes at how much they'd enjoyed the easy win. They'd been training in the interim for sure, but the group remained far from passable.

Their overconfidence would be more of an annoyance, if letting them win the day wasn't part of Capri's plan. Not long after their departure, other agencies arrived onsite. Capri didn't bother tracking names, that wasn't important. She only needed them to show up and be greedy. None of them disappointed.

They ignored the handful that ended up in residential locations, civilians loved stealing keepsakes on any planet. Instead they focused on the five buildings that held the majority of broken Pawn parts. Tall red beacons shining off the table.

She looked at Maxwell. "Where is your device hiding?"

He pointed to a small green dot tucked away in a building on the outskirts of the city. "We sent it and a pair of proper Pawns here when the rest went to attack. They'll stay cloaked until needed."

"I'd like to test the programming before we send them on an important task."

"Reasonable decision. We can have them attach it to the first human they find, if you like?"

"No, I don't want to waste time pulling it back off. I have some ideas. Let me go over the footage one more time and I'll let you know who to retrieve." She left the workshop.

"Sounds good," he called.

Capri caught the confusion in his voice, which gave her a little smile. After two days of quietly getting along, they still weren't trusting her even temper. To be fair, she didn't fully either. She returned to her personal workspace; only the meager supplies in the cabinets to greet her. They wouldn't be bare for much longer. The test run for whoever she picked would be restocking her food and grabbing better clothing. Much longer and she'd be forced to wrap up in the fabric hanging around the Councilor's Suite.

She dropped onto a stool and spread out several streams of footage from the attack on her table. Capri knew it was needlessly cruel sending Pawns to that gathering. They could have dropped them in any random spot for the Wardens to find, but why be boring? So much entertainment to be found in watching humans scramble and dive. Maxwell and Gregory were sifting through and clipping bits to share between their systems; she'd been surprised to find herself included in that message chain. Seeing the false Wardens looking foolish in a handful made her happy, but she forced herself to focus on the civilians. There was a set that stood out as possible candidates.

Her first potential human immediately ran into the fray and attempted to clear the area, they also helped injured people get away from further harm. They ducked in and out of cover around the different booths, causing one Pawn to take too hard of a turn and destroy itself. They were smart, but a little too safe for her liking.

Her second candidate joined the first, giving aid clearing out people. This one looked frazzled, less sure of being in the middle of the action. Capri knew she could press on those insecurities to weaken any mental defenses, but how long would that work for? Fear was useful, but depending on that emotion alone could break the human before they'd done her any good. Putting her back at square one.

That brought her to the one that jumped on a Pawn. Gregory commented below the clip that the human was lucky these were duds or they would've been ripped apart. But the human hadn't known that and jumped all the same. Did one call that bold, or reckless? Capri switched to a clip she'd saved herself, the same human staring down the Pawns as they reformed. Every chance to run, but Capri watched the human square up with the MegaPawn as it closed in. They'd be no good to her if they got killed on their first outing due to a lack of regard for their wellbeing. That was certainly a detractor.

Yet, there was the way Silver regarded them; Capri'd made a short clip from two different Pawn angles. On an odd suspicion, she pulled up footage from the first attack, scrubbing forward to the final standoff in the street. She'd watched Silver run and save a person then too. Right there on her screen, the same human taking a swing at a Pawn. Capri ticked through frames of the archived feeds and found her first two candidates also at that fight, but there was something about the third one that kept her attention. While she couldn't say they knew the Wardens personally, they had a proven knack for getting in trouble and not being afraid to take a hit. Two things she needed.

She sent a shot of the third human's face to Maxwell, along with the message, **Do what you can to locate this one. I want the device on them.**

8

Whistles Casually

The Wardens returned to Outrider once Nek confirmed the area was clear. Each swiped Pawn pieces on the way out, hoping to gain some insight on more current Lenian technology. Steph had felt silly, scooping up what to her looked like all the same metal and wires. She watched whatever Mina packed away and tried to find similar; wanting to provide something useful. Back up top, Nek directed them to the workroom next to Mina's, the two tables in here held containment units similar to the Pak pedestals on the deck.

"These are designed to block any outgoing signals. At least I hope they will." Nek paced around the panels as everyone set their findings down. "Comps will check them over for anything of interest."

"I think it's of interest how easily they fell apart," Emma said.

Mina rubbed her forehead, Steph could tell she wanted to get her hands on the alien tech. "Don't say easy."

"I mean it though! You guys noticed that too, right? The other ones took a few hits."

"We're just totally ripped now." Sean flexed to help not prove his point, but dropped his arms when he saw the look Emma was giving him. "But no, yeah. They went down quick."

"Maybe Capri still thinks that little of us," Steph offered.

42

"We'll figure it out." Mina took a seat at one of the stations pulling data. "I'll help dig through all this hardware."

Zane grabbed another chair. "I can't really help with that, but I will provide company."

Steph was about to second that when her and Sean's armbands lit up with messages, Mitch sending out an S.O.S. for anybody free to help with a sudden surge of customers.

Steph scrunched up her nose and looked at Sean. "What do you think?"

"It has already been such a morning."

"But we would on a normal day." She figured it'd give them an assumed alibi too. Sean and her couldn't be two parts of the mysterious Warden team, they'd totally been at work the entire time.

"True." He tapped out a response to Mitch. "Nek, we'll need a drop near the cafe, if you don't mind. Since we are such good little employees."

Steph sent her own message off. **Sure thing! Be in soon.**

"Send me too," Emma said. She shrugged off the surprised looks they gave her. "I do the hitting things part and that's over. I'll be more useful going back down to see what's up."

They waited another fifteen minutes before Nek dropped them, to not instantly appear after he texted. Steph watched Mina work on the broken Pawns, the shielding allowing her hands to pass through easily. Mina pulled a piece and began to inspect it, scribbled something down on the digital notepad her armband provided, and instantly forgot the rest of them were there. Steph was mystified about what she could learn from the hardware alone. She pinned the question to send a little later if they were stuck Earthside for long. Asking about tech always got Mina rambling, Steph liked that. While she struggled to keep up most of the time, Mina never tired of answering those questions. She found that cute.

The now familiar pull of the teleport took her over. They appeared in a secluded alley a block away from Restoration and made the quick jog over.

"This does save on gas," Steph whispered as they walked up the back steps to the balcony entrance.

Emma split off towards the front counter once inside. Sean and Steph headed to the office. As forewarned by Mitch, Restoration was buzzing. This attack apparently had the opposite effect of the first, people poured out of their houses. The balcony was packed with those hoping to see giant robots fight. Sean lamented earlier that they couldn't give more of a show this time around. She'd rolled her eyes, but did secretly hope someone got new shots of the Wardens in action. The hours spent watching sword fighting technique videos on YouTube and practicing on the hard light Capri had to pay off in someone catching her in a good stance. Maybe they could arrange a Comp to take pictures. No one could know it was her for now, but maybe one day. Bragging a little might be nice. Just the tiniest bit.

Before opening the office door they caught Mitch's Disappointed Dad voice coming from inside. "I can't in good conscience let you keep working today."

"I'm fine," Henrie protested. "I swear Mitch, I'm good."

"You took a-" Sam was cut off.

"I'm fine! Please let me stay."

Steph pulled Sean behind the back bar so they were clear from the door. Which was good timing as Mitch exited the office. "Henrie, I have to insist. Go home and relax for the day. Have your mom give me a call. If she gives the okay, we'll see you tomorrow."

Henrie looked defeated as she stepped out of the office. She gave a glance toward the not-so-hidden pair at the bar before walking away without a word, holding one shoulder a little stiffer than the other. Steph wondered if Emma saw her get whatever hit that was. Sam appeared next and moved after her. "I can give you a ride."

"My car is here. I. Am. Fine." Henrie disappeared down the ramp.

Steph fought her own urge to follow. There was a small worry that they might be becoming a thing and figured the intel would be good for Emma's benefit, but Sam was always hard to read. Their general demeanor kept them going so far out of their own way to remain pleasant with everyone, making it awfully hard to tell when they were flirting. She also needed to know if Henrie was in a place for that, given the recently dead parent and life upheaval. None of this was Steph's business, she knew and acknowledged that. But also she needed to know.

Mitch gave a small smile to her and Sean. "Have to admire the commitment. Speaking of! Thanks for coming in, you two. I'll have you out as quick as we can."

They took over the back drink counter to free up the others to handle the front. She picked up from conversations that people were giving up hope on any further fight coming, but most remained packed in at Restoration with their drinks, snacks, and theories. Even when the event site was deemed safe by city officials, they stayed passing around videos, pictures, and memes.

Steph spent most of her time filling cups, wiping tables, and trying to figure out the point of this fight. Capri didn't send any sort of demands, or a threat, along with those Pawns. Maybe the Lenians decided to put on their own attack? Maybe Capri stirred up their interest in Earth and now they wanted the planet for their own. So they tested the waters with sub-par Pawns. Because, sorry Mina, those Pawns did go down easier than before.

No. That didn't make any sense. What kind of story was that? A bad one. Steph didn't want to be involved in a bad story. Maybe she'd look over Comp recordings tonight, see if there was anything in particular that stood out. Some trend in what these Pawns targeted. Or something they missed while clearing the site. She could post up at a table in the workroom with Mina, like when they fixed Comps together.

Steph got back to cleaning as she workshopped her 'thought I might hang out here' lines. She ran on autopilot for so long she didn't notice the crowd thinning until Emma appeared at the back counter.

"That was a dud of a mission." Emma looked calm, meaning she was up to probably three cups of something caffeinated by now. "Didn't hear anything all that interesting."

"Yeah, seems all Capri did was give us new glamour shots," Sean said as he went around to clean off a table.

Steph leaned in to ask about Henrie, but Sam appeared at the top of the ramp with a cart of supplies to restock the bar. She tipped back and changed her target. Because while she couldn't figure out Capri's motives yet, coworkers she could do. "Sooo, Sam. Mind sharing what happened with

Henrie?"

Emma twitched her mug but continued to look at her phone. Sam chucked bags of coffee beans inside the cabinet. "She jumped on an evil robot."

Emma dropped the cup, spilling the remaining latte inside. "What?"

"Sweet!" Sean added as he came back, pulling a new rag out to take care of Emma's mess.

"Not sweet." Sam continued to throw items into the cabinets. "So she does that, yeah? She then faced off one of those Terminator things they make. Then gets shot in the shoulder." Coffee bags thudded against the back of the cupboard. "Then shoved on a whole bunch of their broken parts, probably getting cut up all over. Swears she's fine. Then gets mad at me for asking her to get checked over!"

"She told m-" Emma stopped short after an elbow from Sean.

Steph covered for her. "She did look rather upset."

"She got shot! 'Nothing too bad'," Sam gave big air quotes around the words. "I'm not out of line saying she should get looked at."

"No, you're not." She needed to find an exit to this conversation, this was a hotter than expected topic and she didn't want to push too much. There was an art to gathering intel. Steph now felt confident enough to say that Sam's side of this crush was confirmed. Which complicated things for Emma, who she was biased for. Sorry, Sam.

Sean was trying to tug Emma's phone from her hand before she crushed it. "She's an army brat. Probably knows how to take a hit."

"She does-" Emma cut herself off, likely remembering she was pretending to not outwardly be crushing on Henrie. "-some kind of training. I forget."

Steph now realized why Emma was ranting about karate moves the other day, she'd figured it'd been some new rabbit hole she found to torture them with. She tried not to laugh at the two fuming people on either side of her. Glad that their own moods made them blind to how the other was behaving. Best to be gentle with both of them. "She's smart. She wouldn't do anything too dangerous."

Sam was a lost cause, too caught up in their rant now. "And on top of it, she stole stuff from a booth. Megan says I'm overreacting and to not tell my dad, but looting is irresponsible."

"What did she take?" Sean asked as he finally wrangled Emma's phone away and safely set it on the counter.

"Warden plushies. She took a whole set, but gave four of them to Megan to split with me. But I wouldn't take any. Bet she's mad at me about that too." Sam shoved sleeves of cups in the holsters, ripping the plastic case and crushing cups as they did.

"Which did Henrie keep?" Emma asked quietly, eyes locked on the countertop.

They snapped the cabinet doors shut. "I think Silver. I didn't touch them."

None of them responded. Emma was too busy trying not to beam and the other two were trying not to laugh at her. Sam stood up and must have assumed their behavior was all about them.

"You guys think I'm overreacting too." They shoved the cart away. "No one has morals anymore."

"No, Sam. This isn't what you-" Steph tried to catch them, but they charged down the ramp without looking back. She frowned at Sean. "We are definitely getting Carter shifts after this."

Emma was happily tapping away on her phone, completely ignoring them as they got back to work. Mitch reappeared as they were washing mugs. "Thanks again for coming in, you two. I think we can handle the rest from here."

Steph wondered if maybe their departure was anything to do with Sam's mood. That wasn't typical behavior for either Sam, or Mitch, but these were all around strange times anymore.

"No problem!" Steph made a show of wiping down the counter. "Didn't have much else going on today anyway."

Sean snorted and tried to turn it into a cough. "Yeah, happy to help."

"I'll finish up the wash, you two head on out." Mitch nudged Steph away from the bar and toward the office.

Sean tapped Emma directly on the head to pull her away from her phone. "Trains a-leavin.'"

"Yep, sorry. Let's go." Emma tucked her phone away and dropped her own mug in the sink. "See ya later, Mitch."

He smiled. "I'll keep your spot open for you."

Steph considered patching things up with Sam before leaving, but for once found herself struggling to find the right words. We weren't laughing at you, we were laughing at Emma because she's lovesick over the same girl you are. Why was she so excited? Oh well, you see, that plushie is her. Yeah, we're the Wardens. No biggie. Shhhh.

That would go over well. She let the issue go and hoped a good night's sleep might allow cooler heads tomorrow. And a chance to make sure she didn't end up with Carter. But at least she had more to talk about with Mina now.

9

Fighting Evil by Daylight

Henrie knew her phone was going off. Said phone was upstairs, in her room, shoved under a pillow, and far away from her current location in the basement, but she knew. Sam wasn't afraid to over text, another thing to be mad at them about. She felt fine letting them text away all day, but there was a chance she was also missing another message from Emma. Henrie didn't think Emma clocked her injured shoulder as she left, but also expected Sam or Megan had told everyone about her drone fight by now. Emma wouldn't harp, but Henrie wanted to avoid talking about how she was feeling, physically and emotionally, altogether.

She could find more videos on meteor hammer tricks to divert Emma's attention. That'd buy her a half hour or so of talking before Emma might try and redirect to today's attack. There'd be no distracting Sam. So yeah, let them rant via text for a while.

Besides that fuming rage, she was also mad at the speedball hanging from the ceiling at the exact right height to tweak her singed shoulder. Her mother hung it at the height her dad would've needed, out of habit. No way was she pointing that out or fixing it herself. On other days she'd taken swings at the slightly too high bag in silence, but her shoulder was protesting this particular afternoon.

Which meant both her shoulder and the speedball were siding with Sam, making her angry at both. Completely irrational, she knew that, but Henrie was in the mood to stay angry.

She considered kicking the ball, but that seemed too harsh of a punishment for an inanimate stand-in for Sam. Because she wouldn't kick Sam, she didn't think she would at least. Could if she wanted to though. Easy. Pulled harder stunts messing around with other kids at tournaments. Henrie backed up a few steps, worked out the angle she needed, but pulled back before her foot hit the bag. The speedball belonged to her dad, making the kick extra disrespectful. He'd given her a long lecture about respecting equipment back when she was seven, he'd caught her clutched to his sandbag and trying to spin. Her chores always included taking care of their home gym after that, but she never totally shook the desire to grab on and swing.

The hot spot in her stomach that fueled her entire drive home was fading. Replaced by the more familiar knots that often resided there. She hated being alone in the house, everything was too quiet. Her mom put them in a newer development nearly outside the city, to the point that across the road was a cornfield. The houses were spaced out enough that you never heard anything from the neighbors. This neighborhood was supposed to be nice, something new and spacious. No more townhomes stacked side by side. *Look at all this space Henrie*, her mother said right before going to work for nearly 24 hours a day, leaving Henrie and her overly sad thoughts all alone.

Her breathing hitched up and the edges of her vision shook a little. She punched the ball with her bad arm, wanting the pain to chase everything else away. Her shoulder and several points on her back cried out, but the tightness in her chest persisted. She refused to collapse from this panic attack. Henrie bolted up the stairs and pulled her keys off the hook near the mudroom door. She only paused long enough to make sure the lock was set behind her.

Henrie fought the impulse to run straight for the field. A destructive idea she liked, but knew was wrong. *See, Sam. I do have morals.*

Better to keep the target on herself. She ran along the course shoulder next to the field, letting her legs and feet take the beating and not some random farmer's crop. She soon grew distracted by her own breathing, she sounded ragged. Normally she'd drown everything out with music, but her phone and earbuds were up in her room. Leaving her only the option of going faster. Pound her feet against the ground harder. Get her heart pumping right in her ears and cover up the breathing that way.

Her desperate sprint only lasted twenty seconds before her entire body begged her to stop, as she backed off to a jog she caught the sound of buzzing behind her. She took a glance back, expecting a car, instead she spotted the familiar shape of one of those mean drones drawing closer. "Oh, you are really mad at me for earlier."

Henrie expected dashing through the field would work as a shortcut, but why run when they crumbled so easily? Hadn't she been looking for some destruction? She skidded to a halt and braced with her good shoulder forward, ready to take a quick hit and let that be it. The run home would be easy enough, she could see the top of her house over the field.

The drone hit, hard enough to pull her feet off the ground. Henrie was flung several feet back, landing in the middle of the road. The drone, in perfectly good shape, came around for its next attack.

"So the ones this morning were weird."

She gave herself one tiny point for calling that as she scrambled back to her feet, barely dodging the next sweeping attack from the drone. A move that was for nothing, as a second evil box dropped from above. Henrie didn't want to take another hit, her ribs now felt as bruised as her back. Add that to the list of damage she was ignoring. The two drones pushed in. She held still until they were close, only jumping toward the shoulder at the last second. They smashed into each other, pieces of casing fell away this time but both remained otherwise intact. Their few seconds of disorientation gave her enough time to disappear inside the field.

Her great escape plan worked for all of five steps before she tripped over a mound of dirt and was grabbed around the waist by an exoskeleton-thing. She tried twisting out of the hold, but only succeeded in digging the metal arms into her sides. The green corn stalks bent as she grabbed at them, leaf blades slipping through her fingers and doing little to help her resist. Any ways she knew how to break a hold relied on her opponent having fleshy points to take advantage of. Unbending metal did her training no good. She struggled all the same, nothing was getting an easy fight out of her today. For a brief second one of the arms pulled back, allowing her to slip closer to the edge of the field, back to where someone might see her. But the other arm tightened and yanked her back. Her shirt was pulled away from her neck. Something stabbed between her shoulders and her vision went dark.

— — — — — — — — — — —

Henrie bolted awake on her bed, throwing an elbow back at open air. She spun around looking for the exoskeleton until her brain caught up on events and sorted fact from fiction. Yes, she'd started on a run, but the panic attack continued to creep up. Her shirt started to feel too tight, causing her to pull the collar in a mad attempt to catch her breath. The collar hung loose from her now, she'd ruined the shirt. She'd turned back home after that. Her next decision was crashing on her bed and opting to not deal with reality at all. Sunlight was fading outside, she must have passed out for hours. Maybe she'd pushed a little too hard. Blacking out the panic attack like that felt like a blessing, and an omen. Not good for her brain, but also a small relief.

But the episode hadn't fully left her alone. Simply reshaped itself as a dream of a physical attack. She felt a phantom pain around her middle from that arm grappling her. The only damage she saw in her standing mirror was what she'd gained that morning, outside of some serious pillow lines from the nap.

She heard an echo of Sam telling her to get looked over and mentally shoved them away. Maybe she could see herself kicking them. A good hot shower would be enough to shake her bad mood and the aching muscles along her back.

10

Team Building 201

Mina's plan of putting the weapons on their pillows worked. Her team reacted like it was Christmas morning when they saw the new gear waiting after the first bout of training. They'd bounced between each other's rooms, showing off as they could. Until the Pawn attack kicked off. They'd all been more than happy to have something real to test everything on. The fight went so well too! All the reports Zane read out were positive, some noted their improved fighting skills.

Everything was great this morning. Now she was about to cave to failure. She'd deciphered data while Zane pulled out his laptop and distracted himself. Once the articles started getting repetitive, he switched to pulling all the new videos and images for his files. If someone was going to make an epic music video depicting their triumph, it would be him. Her soundtrack for the last hour was him bouncing through song after song trying to find the perfect fit.

The data from the Pawns ran out fast. While she was content at the start familiarizing herself with Lenian engineering, that wasn't giving them much new information. Apparently a good portion of the general hardware didn't change in five hundred years. A lone point of interest was the amount of trackers they recovered, Mina pulled them off of the Pawn parts like ticks.

These devices all sat in a pile on one of the tables with a trio of Comps surrounding them, dedicated to unlocking their signal. The important bits were hiding in the programming, on the trackers and Pawns as a whole, but Outrider's systems were struggling. The concept that their spaceship was technically considered outdated baffled Mina.

While software wasn't her expertise, she aided the Comps the little she could. 2876 highlighted a string of commands that appeared to downgrade their maneuvering abilities. Like they'd been designed to crash. Which made no sense. Then the code stopped giving them anything. There was encryption at the start, but the Comps broke through after some work. Now they hit another obstacle, one that kept the bulk of Pawn programming blocked from them. All they could tell was that this encryption was a new addition. When her eyes started to cross from the code, she gave up and let the Comps tackle the software alone. Mina was more in their way at that point.

Pulling hardware apart would make her feel better. She picked up one of the bigger Pawn chunks to start on when her stomach growled. A glance at her smartwatch told her it'd been several hours since their light breakfast. If she was hungry, Zane was sure to be starving. His eyes were locked on his laptop, given the twitch in his brow she guessed he was making some edit a normal human wouldn't notice but meant everything to him right now. Mina stood, stretched, and waited for Zane to notice her. No reaction came. She got a step closer and waved, he still didn't look up. This was exciting, he rarely got pulled into a project as deeply as she did. Mina crept in until she was near his face. Ten full seconds went by before he noticed her. Zane jumped out of his chair. Mina snatched the laptop before it went down with him.

"Whhhhhyyyyy!?" He curled up on the floor.

Mina used every bit of strength in her to remain casual, holding back a laugh the entire time. "Comps are working on some encryption, going to be a while. Gonna grab a snack. Want something?"

He returned to his seat, not looking at her as he pulled his laptop out of her hands. "I will take some pretzels, thank you."

She found the kitchen area with little trouble, they all had this path fairly nailed down. Even Emma could zero in on food, helped that her coffee was stashed here. Mina dug through the cabinets and pulled out the little stick pretzels she knew Zane would shove away like a wood chipper. Not far away was her box of microwave popcorn. As she nabbed a bag, Mina remembered there wasn't a microwave on the ship yet.

To their credit, that was on the list of assorted things Outrider needed, but there'd been bigger issues to tackle in the kitchen. The oversized fridge had needed serious cleaning, Nek insisted Comps handle that due to them being able to turn off the sensors used to detect smells. The fridge was now sanitized and stocked, mostly with drinks and condiments. There was an equally large, detached freezer box with ample room for all their frozen delights, also newly scraped and cleaned. Sean had organized the assortment of kitchen gadgets and utensils that he recognized in the drawers. The few mystery items no one could name, or felt safe trying to operate, were all shoved away in a drawer and cabinet on the far end of the room. Also at the end of the counter was the Not Microwave, a paper in Steph's handwriting taped across the front door named the appliance so. Nek told them that the machine was meant for rehydrating food, but those of the far more condensed for space travel variety. That information came after Sean figured out how to turn the thing on, his pizza rolls never stood a chance.

Leaving her with nothing to pop her popcorn with. Unless she wanted to figure out the stove and all its dials. No. Not today. She couldn't handle being defeated by more alien technology. Mina tapped out a message to Zane and Nek, saying she was popping down to her house quick and would be right back.

Mina used the saved waypoint of her room for the drop. Teleporting without the suit was an adjustment, but Mina loved the tingles now. Before going downstairs she did a sweep for anything she might take to put in her other bedroom. There was the small Thunderbird on her nightstand, but that stayed here because she liked having a secret little Warden nod in her room. Instead she grabbed the photo of her grandma stuck to the corner of a corkboard and tucked it away in her Pak. That would do for now.

At the bottom of the stairs, she realized her house was not as quiet as it should be. Mina shoved the Pak in a pocket as she moved through the kitchen to the side laundry room. Where she found two carry-on cases open on the floor as the washer and dryer churned away on loads. Her parents always left their bags there because more often than not the clothes went right back in.

She pulled her phone out. No missed texts, emails, or calls saying they were coming back. Not like it'd be the first time she didn't get a heads-up. Her throat tightened. How long had they been here? Did they look for her when they got in? Had they gone in her room and saw everything missing?

"Mina, there you are." The lukewarm voice of her father came from behind her. "Did you just come in? Didn't hear you."

She turned around to see him looking at her over a tablet, swiping through something as he barely kept half an eye on her. His glasses slid down his nose, her nose. Mina knew those wireframes were in her future. "Uh, yeah."

"Out with Zane?"

"Yep." She remembered the popcorn in her hand and held the package up weakly. "Wanted some kettle corn. Heading back over."

He tipped his head back down the hallway. "Come to the office."

Mina shuffled after him toward the lab, unsure if he'd been listening. This was probably something about The Expo they wanted to run by her. She'd be expected to sit and play good daughter while they bragged to investors about their research. Every year she supplied them a list of her personal achievements to mention in conversation, so they could pretend to be good parents.

She stopped at the doorway, out of habit, as her dad continued over to his computer. This was about the chemicals she'd taken for the explosives. They probably stepped inside the house and knew the levels were off.

Her mother was standing over her worktable, printed images spread out before her because she liked to physically move information around. Her pile of dark hair was bundled up in a tight bun, unlike Mina's messy one. She waved Mina in without looking up.

Mina took one, very small, step in the room.

"Question," her mother said, not realizing Mina hadn't come much closer.

"What does this look like to you?"

Did they put cameras up around the house at some point? Well, other cameras she hadn't already moved to make a blindspot and let her get what she needed in the basement. Did her mother go through the trouble of printing out pictures of her sneaking in? Had they checked her room for the missing supplies and seen her missing belongings? The thought made her stomach turn, her parents being in her room. Felt unnatural. While everyone else worried about how much they left her alone, she stressed about how long they stuck around. They kept the lights on for her, but she didn't like sharing air with them.

Mina crossed over to the desk, getting barely close enough to see what her mother was pointing at. Her Thunderbird was scattered across the tabletop. One of those helicopters from the crater must have been a lot better equipped than they realized. The Pak in her pocket took on an extra hundred pounds. Seeing the intricate detailing spread out like that surprised her. Somehow, in all they had going on, Mina never realized her Guardian featured the same detailing she'd engraved on the small scale Thunderbird floating in her room. Maybe she did need to get that out of the house.

Her mother was waiting for an answer. Mina made herself focus on exactly what she was pointing to, the picture was a blown-up shot of a wing. Specifically where the shifting flats that made her feathers connected to the wing. On a real bird, they'd go to the bone, but hers were attached at swivel joints to achieve the quick turning she needed and give them more movement. Mina loved that they could flutter, but that wasn't the point right now. She saw her watch light up, and Nek's waves appeared. They must have noticed her heart rate spiking.

"Looks like swivel joints," she finally said. That felt safe enough to let out. They knew she'd recognize something like that.

"And they look stationary?" Her father asked from his desk in his *I expect a yes* tone. "Not something to be shot off?" Said in a *wouldn't that be ridiculous* way.

Mina never thought of that as a possibility. Why would she mess with her feathers that way? The talons and energy blast did plenty enough damage.

No need for projectiles. She bent over the picture, pretending to study the metalwork more. "They look to be stationary, yes. The joint fully encases the end of the feather piece."

Her mother pulled the pictures away, clearly not getting the tiebreaker answer she wanted. "Thank you for your time."

Mina watched her mother stack the pictures and tuck them away in a file before turning to her computer. No other questions came her way. Her father hunched over his screens. Having settled their disagreement, they were done with Mina. She backed out of the lab, leaving them to their work. Which for the time being was researching her Thunderbird.

Nek turned brighter as Mina reached the kitchen. "Warden Mina, is this-"

"Not yet, please," she whispered and covered the watch. Mina turned on the faucet, cupped her hands beneath, and slurped up handful after handful of water. Why these nerves always made her so thirsty she'd never know. Her parents would tell her if she asked, they loved to give a lesson.

Knowing full well they weren't keeping an ear out for her leaving, she exited out the back and jogged across the yard toward Zane's house anyway. Hoping the whole way that neither of his parents took the afternoon off and were wondering what she was doing without him. Mina ducked around their shed. A set of hedges on her other side kept her out of anyone's eyeline. She hit the saved point of her house for the teleport, but the armband gave her an error.

Nek turned to pulsing waves. "One moment, Warden Mina. Your home teleport designation doesn't extend this far, nor does Warden Zane's. I'm creating a new one for you now."

"Please, hurry." She knew she sounded desperate. She hated it. When teal light finally washed over her, Mina sighed as the tingles returned and she was pulled away.

When she arrived on the landing pad, Zane was waiting for her. He scanned her over. "Nek thought you'd been hurt."

Mina laughed at that. "My parents are home."

He'd been in the doorway until she blinked and he was wrapped around her, squeezing her tight. "I'm sorry. They suck."

"They do." She figured out years ago, before Zane was around, that they didn't hate her specifically. They simply held no interest in being parents. Mina imagined one of them proposed the experiment of having a child, way back when. Shouldn't anatomists who maintained a rather productive relationship give a go at making a human in the traditional way? For a short time, she was terrified of having been a straight-up lab experiment. After a small breakdown over that possibility, Mina was eight at the time, her well-documented parents showed her the hospital footage. Somewhere between her birthday and the day she could handle a microwave alone, her parents lost interest in the kid experiment. More exciting work to do, especially when Hephaestus Labs came calling and moved them here. Grandma helped as she could, but Mina'd often been the one making the phone call asking her to come over. Which got harder as Grandma got older, and impossible once they moved to Hurst.

All that was junk she'd been dealing with for years, and would be forever. Right now, she sank in and took the hug.

"You wanna watch a movie?" he asked.

"Yes," she said against his shoulder. "Can we figure out how to do this popcorn first?"

They dug around in the cabinets for a pot they believed big enough. They dumped in the kernels, figured out how to turn up the heat, and waited. After a minute the first few popped. Quickly followed by the rest, revealing too late that the pot was not in reality big enough. Sending them scrambling for bowls to dump the excess in as the rest continued to bounce around.

Steph and Sean came in near the end of this juggling act. Making no move to help the flustered duo. Emma came after them, grinning at her phone, and absently eating from one of the half-filled bowls. Zane dumped the final, burnt, kernels in the trash.

Mina tried to play off how out of breath they were from the stunt. "How was the cafe?"

"Hectic," Sean said. "But the time went fast."

"People are going nuts over this fight being so public," Steph added.

"Yeah they are," Zane said around his fistful of popcorn. "I'll show you the new montage later."

Mina tipped her head toward Emma, asking quietly, "And this?"

Sean gave Emma a small shove. "This is the result of Damsel stealing a Silver Warden plushie. Because those are a thing now."

Zane and Mina appropriately oooohh'd. Emma dropped her phone enough to roll her eyes at them. "You guys are so immature."

"Then stop smiling like that."

Steph gave Mina a look over. "Everything go alright up here?"

She must have looked frazzled from the popcorn. "Yeah, Comps are working on some tough code. Didn't figure out a whole lot more, except," she looked to Emma, "You were right. These things were made to fall apart. I just don't know why yet."

Emma gave a little punch to the counter. "Everything's coming up Millhouse!"

"You're like a thirty-five year old bro in there." Sean poked her head.

She grabbed his wrist and twisted. "A bro that will put you down."

Steph slid closer to Mina. "Any other discoveries?"

"Her parents are home," Zane blurted out.

All four looked at him. Then three sets of eyes went back to Mina. Who remained looking at Zane, silently begging him to not make this a thing right now.

He wasn't looking back at her. Zane was trying to lock eyes with the other three, looking more stern than she'd ever seen him before. "I'm gonna need sleepovers and hangouts and whatever we can from everyone until they leave."

"Zane, that is a bit much." Mina wanted to shove more popcorn in his face.

He wasn't having it, not about this. "Since we met, my job has been distracting you. I am more than happy to do it, but we have a team now," he looked at the others, "She'll go full lockdown on a project if she gets left with them. Like at Restoration the other day. It happens that fast."

She really hated him talking like she wasn't there. Moreso hated that he was right. Mina grabbed a bowl and made to leave for the movie room. Steph grabbed her hand before she could get away and smiled at her. "Hey, I get crap parents. I got you."

Not we. I. Mina squeezed back and managed a small, "Um, thanks."

"Movie night is up first." Zane grabbed his bowl, and the bag of pretzels, and led the move toward their rec area turned theater. "Anybody have a request?"

Sean shot a hand up. "Have you guys ever seen Scream?"

"Is horror the way to go right now?" Steph asked, continuing to hold Mina's hand as they took seats on the couch.

"I find it rather comforting."

"I think you'll like the meta aspect," Emma offered as she stretched out along her loveseat.

"If anything gets too much for you, I'll tell you when it's safe to look again." Mina gave Steph's hand another squeeze.

Steph smiled. "Let's do it."

"Oh wait," Emma hopped up and came over to the couch. She dropped next to Mina and held out her phone to fit all three of them in the camera. "Squish in, you two. Mina, if my mom Facetimes and wants to chat, we're spending the night at your place. This is as good a time as any to finally break in those rooms."

She snapped the picture, making sure nothing spaceship living room-ish was in the background before returning to her seat. Mina noticed that Steph didn't pull away from where she'd pressed against her shoulder for the picture. Their intertwined hands squished together between them.

Zane looked pleased with himself as he set up the movie. He scooted across the floor and propped his arms up behind him on the unoccupied spot of the couch. Mina stretched a leg out and nudged his side, he pushed her away but kept smiling.

11

Had the Weirdest Dream

lothes. Food. Now.

That was the series of thoughts, stuck on repeat, that pulled Henrie out of bed at midnight and hounded her until she left the house. There was pressure on the base of her neck, tension she couldn't stretch out. The haze in her head was distracting, a fog she couldn't shake. More like she was being guided than acting of her own accord. Like a Sim with a list of demands dominating her small amount of functioning brainwaves. This must be one of those "this is reality, but weird" kind of dreams.

Henrie never had a lucid dream before. Her inexperience showed when she tried getting herself back out of the car. That pressure on her neck increased and her stomach turned when she put a foot on the driveway. Once she pulled back in and shut the door, both disappeared. Replaced by a cool, pleasing chill that trickled down her back. Not wanting to tempt the dream to make her vomit, she relented to whatever was in store for her. She turned the ignition and pulled out of the drive.

Clothes. Food. Now.

The dream wasn't pushing her towards anywhere specific for clothes or food, but she took *Now* to mean the closest option possible. Autopilot got her to the strip mall centered around a TJ Maxx nearby. Nothing in her head told her this was the wrong place. Though phantom nudges directed her to park on the backside of the building.

A dark shape dropped down next to her door, one of those drone things with an odd sort of glow around it. Henrie should have freaked out, given the morning she'd had. Not to mention the panic attack induced dream earlier, but she was numb. More evidence of this all being a dream. She found herself more surprised that she was somehow certain of their name, Pawn.

Kind of lame, really.

Move.

The pressure on her neck increased until she stepped out of the car. The Pawn shot the security camera above the door, and then the door handle itself.

Follow.

She watched the Pawn perform a series of beeps at the alarm box inside before they both moved farther in. Henrie kept herself close because the pressure disappeared when she did. The Pawn scanned the racks of clothing, highlighting pieces she was meant to grab with a laser. This dream was going from mundane to truly bizarre. Her arms were growing full of mainly athleisure pieces. What did a Pawn need clothes for? Had the exoskeletons–MegaPawns, she now also knew–grown a sense of modesty? No longer wanting to walk around with their literal bits showing?

Henrie tried redirecting the dream, reaching for a different shirt than the Pawn had selected. The pressure on her neck increased.

No, hissed in her ear.

She picked out the correct shirt and took the pile to her car, dropping them in the backseat. Henrie jogged back inside, the pressure dropping as she neared the Pawn, and picked pieces as directed. As she stepped outside with the next load, lights flashed at the end of the alley. Henrie crouched behind the front of her car. Green and yellow lights glowed as a security car crept closer. The car came to a full stop behind hers. Not ideal, but she remained low. They might leave if she stayed put.

Remove the obstacle, commanded the voice in her head.

She felt her small bit of awareness pull away from herself as she dropped the remaining clothes and stood. Henrie was glad that somewhere along this dream she'd clipped her hair back on either side, it always bugged her having hair in her face during a fight.

A flashlight blinded her as the guard neared. "Ma'am, I need you to tell me exactly what you're doing here."

A tightness in her jaw told her she wouldn't be allowed to speak. Her attention went to his belt, which held the empty flashlight holster, a radio, and nothing else. Good. Henrie stepped out to meet the man.

His flashlight swung over to the pile of clothes in her backseat. "I'm gonna need an answer for this."

Henrie grabbed the hand holding the flashlight and smashed the wide top into his nose, a messy crack came from the impact. Blood gushed from both nostrils as he stumbled back. That might be the fastest she'd ever broken a nose before. Anything could happen in a dream, she guessed. With him distracted by the pain, she unclipped the radio and tossed it down the alley. She then yanked the flashlight from him and beat the long handle against his now unprotected torso. Her small bit of awareness realized that this guard wasn't much older than her, some college-aged guy working a night job. Not that it mattered. Or stopped her from sweeping his legs out from under him. Which caused him to smack the side of his head on the hood of his car on the way down.

Henrie spotted a set of zip tie cuffs on the back of his belt. The guy was too punch drunk to stop her from taking them. She locked his hands around part of the car's grill.

Not bad, said the hushed voice. Another cool bloom sprouted at her neck and ran down her back as a shiver, the pressure dissipated for a brief second as it did. Henrie didn't think she'd ever felt such a direct hit of endorphins before. With luck, she'd find a way to make that happen more.

She picked up the dropped clothes and threw them on the backseat. The Pawn floated in the open doorway, she suspected having watched her entire short altercation without any intention of helping. Though now the Pawn flew over to the security car and made the same series of beeps as before.

Several pops from somewhere under the hood answered back as the car died instantly, leaving them all in the dark.

"Wha-what the hell?" the guy sputtered.

Leave.

Pulling away took some time, as she had to slowly edge herself around the security car. Only avoiding driving over the guy's legs by inches. He'd yelled at her the entire time.

Food.

She drove to the end of the strip mall for that command. The Aldi's was just as closed, but not as nearly dark inside. Henrie parked in the back as the Pawn took care of the alarm system.

Near the swinging doors that separated the stocking area from the main store Henrie spotted boxes of reusable bags. She dumped several in a stray cart left there as well. The Pawn pointed out items as they combed the aisles. Henrie dropped them in the bags, trying to keep things sorted like her dad taught her. Why a Pawn needed food was beyond her, but this was the dream. Her strange reality until she woke up. Which she hoped would happen very soon.

Henrie became frozen in place, the pressure so intense she could barely make herself breathe, halfway up the candy aisle as the Pawn decided between types of chocolate bars. A new set of lights flashed across the wall of windows at the front. Red and blue this time. That security guard must have gotten free and found his radio.

Go.

Her feet weren't stuck to the floor anymore. Henrie flew through the back of the store, bags hooked around her arms. Why did she take the time to do that? She threw the bags in the backseat, most spilled to the floor. The Pawn stayed above her car, the pressure gave her a weird sense of it keeping pace as she left the back alley. That odd glimmer dropped down over all of her windows, she didn't know what that was about until two more cop cars drove by her as she reached the side street exit. Neither of them looked at her; she realized they couldn't see her. That Pawn was hiding her somehow. Her body kept driving, pulling out to the street and accelerating away from the strip mall. She wanted to go home, that was plenty enough dream excitement for her, but when she attempted to make the first turn in that direction her hands jerked the wheel back.

A vague waypoint appeared in her mind. Autopilot kicked in, she more so watched herself turn down a street she didn't know. The edges of her vision fuzzed over, Henrie dropped further and further into the black. Her hands clutched the wheel, terrified of what would happen if she completely disappeared while driving.

— — — — — — — — — — — — — — — — —

Henrie blinked her eyes clear. She was home. Dream quick travel would be a nice answer, but she'd been heading the wrong way. Henrie glanced at the time, it was almost two in the morning. She wasn't in either of those stores for that long. There was a gap between the strip mall and here. Where had she gone?

She turned to the backseat, sure there'd be a mess of groceries and thrift clothes to sort, but it was empty. Henrie yawned, somehow tired in her own dream, and didn't think much more of it. With that pressure finally gone from her neck, her head filled with thoughts of bed.

Henrie was fine with that. Fall asleep here and wake up in the real world. She slunk her way back inside, tucking herself in without kicking off her dusty shoes. There was a faint level of grime all over her, but she couldn't be made to care. Her sheets weren't really getting dirty. This was only a dream after all.

12

Very Serious Conversations

They'd ended up watching all four Screams, Sean wanted them ready for when the new movie came out. Steph took advantage of hiding behind Mina's shoulder for a few scenes, but managed to watch most of the movies. Mina lost the hand-holding during a jump scare, but the close proximity was a good consolation.

Zane scooted over to the laptop to scroll through options for their next watch until he noticed the time. "Good thing we all said we were out."

Without much talk, they all got up and headed for the private quarters. Agreeing, more so Emma allowing, to give themselves a later start the next day.

Sean scrolled on his phone as they walked and stopped short of going in his door. "Oh dang, my Aldi's got hit."

"Someone has to be real rock bottom to steal groceries." Emma scanned the post over his shoulder. "And clothes, they hit the TJ Maxx too."

Steph shook her head. "Best of luck to whoever stole clothes from a TJ Maxx."

"That one isn't too bad. I've found some decent pieces there."

"Did they catch who did it?" Zane asked.

Sean skimmed the comments. "Nope. They must have been in and out fast. The security guard was knocked around. Police were at Maxx when they got the Aldi call. Want anyone to call in if they maybe saw something"

"Car full of groceries and clothes. Personally, don't think I'd be calling that in," Steph said. Emma gave her a low fist bump.

Zane leaned on his doorframe. "Should we be running like a police scanner or something?"

Their eyes were on Mina now. She straightened up, trying to look leaderly. "I think…given that we don't know why Capri, or the Lenians, sent those Pawns…we need to stay focused on non-Earth originated issues. If we get them squared away, I'm down to refocus."

"What if it's a big Earth thing?" Emma asked. "Natural disaster, terrorist situation, or whatever."

"Um, yeah, those are bad." She realized there was definitely a PR crisis in the future if they only stepped in for alien problems. "I think, in those instances, we go case-by-case. If authorities can handle things, let them. We'd never have personal lives if we stuck ourselves to a scanner or news feeds and went after everything. If there's a global crisis, we'll assess and see what we can do."

"But space first," Zane affirmed.

"Space comes first." That was the right call. She was pretty sure.

"Do you think," Sean said, moving on from the official talk as he looked at his room, "I could swap the bed for a hammock?"

Emma rubbed her eyes, clearly familiar with the topic. "You're going to mess up your back."

"Not if it's here! I'd only use it off and on."

Steph perked up from her spot on the wall."If he's doing that, can I hang a canopy from the ceiling? My mom says I'm too old and the room at my dad's is too cramped for it."

"But the drama," Zane said.

"The drama!"

Mina was glad to be off the serious discussion, but didn't feel comfortable making calls about changes to Outrider. She glanced at the currently empty panel behind Steph. "Nek, this may be more of a question for you."

They rolled in. "I'm looking at some options, but I need clarification. Can you tell me what you're both thinking of exactly?"

Steph fully jumped toward her door, waving Nek to follow. "Okay, so think big and billowing."

Sean opened what were clearly saved tabs as Comp2876 joined him in his room. Emma hesitated in the doorway. She was trying to look grave, but a smile kept pulling up one corner of her mouth. "When he flips and busts his head open, the rest of you get to explain this to my aunt."

"Could make it like a pod," Mina said, an idea pulling itself together, "some kind of sturdy but breathable top to keep him in."

Zane shot a hand up. "Or cover the floor in pillows."

Emma disappeared inside Sean's room, leaving Mina and Zane alone in the hall. Steph described her vision to Nek while Sean showed Comp2876 his ideas. Mina tipped far enough to see the Comp projecting an image from Sean's phone to the room, adjusting it to fit the space.

Emma walked through the hologram. "2876 does that better than I ever get Amazon to."

Mina popped inside her room, releasing the photo she'd stashed away hours ago. She tucked a corner in the vanity mirror, letting her grandma smile out to her new room. Somehow the picture looked happier here. From the corner of her eye, she caught Zane peeking in. "I'm not having a breakdown or anything, I swear."

"I'm just standing here. No biggie." He pretended to slide off the doorframe to prove his point.

She laughed and gave him a poke in the side. "Thank you, for…you know." She always stumbled over this part. Thank you for caring. Thank you for noticing. Thank you for a million things she could point to, but couldn't say.

"I don't need thanks." That was always his response. He bent closer to her. "But I did want to mention that you are over halfway through your month."

Mina was confused until she caught the wiggle in his eyebrows. She poked him harder. "Shut up. Not now."

"Of course not. No pressure yet. But that hand-holding was cute."

She smacked at him until he retreated to the hallway. Training or not, her hits weren't much to him, but it was the principal. "You are horrible."

"And you're in looo-"

Mina lunged to smack her hand across his mouth, stumbling them both back out to the hallway. Emma popped her head out to give them a look but disappeared back inside Sean's room. Mina heard her saying, "2876, do not drill anything yet. No matter what he says."

Zane mumbled a 'sorry' against her hand.

13

Bright Shiny New Toy

Capri sorted through her new clothing options. Some of them didn't look as good here as they did through the Pawn's feed, but she would make due. They were far better than the scraps from before. She'd never get all the blood out of her training outfit.

The food was far better, merely by the fact there were now options for her to choose from. She extended her food stores to the kitchen on the main level as some items needed kept cold. The base was built to one day hold far more people than it currently did, so they weren't fighting over shelf space. Even so, Maxwell hovered as she stashed her goods away. Likely worried she'd nudge some treat of his a fraction out of place. This was a familiar ritual, she could almost feel Rin over her other shoulder.

Afterward, she'd returned to her workspace with something called supreme pizza and set out to dig through her data from the day.

A note from Gregory appeared on her tablet. **I have a highly compelling list of dances the humans have cobbled together. Your new toy might be able to pull them off. If you get bored.**

She glanced at the options before going back to her readings from the girl, who was currently passed out in her bedroom. Her name was Henrie, per Maxwell's report. The Lenian device was tucked between her shoulders, spindles spreading out toward her arms and down her back. They'd surprised her with not one, but two small cameras dressed up as clips, giving them a visual feed from her vantage point. Both looked like little flowers, certainly Gregory's handiwork. They knew from Henrie's perspective the main device peaked out from the arms of the top she'd been wearing during their ambush, but all that required was a command to wear longer-sleeved clothing going forward. Easy enough to add to the coding keeping the girl from registering the device or her injuries.

Henrie performed wonderfully. More specifically, Capri's programming performed wonderfully. Outside that final attempt to avoid the warehouse dropoff. Capri had wanted to attempt fully controlling the human's body anyway, driving the girl's body as it drove the car right from her workstation. The interface was seamless.

An added bonus was how well Henrie could defend herself. The standoff with the Pawns, while short, demonstrated a higher level of fighting ability than Capri expected. Her quick takedown of the guard was enjoyable to watch on repeat. Capri was fractionally impressed.

Not as much as she was with herself, of course. She'd designed everything to run through her Pak, to ensure she was the one in control. They'd modeled the device after her Pak so that only seemed fair. There was an unexpected side effect while the mock Pak was securing itself. During Henrie's spar with the Pawns, Capri watched her Pak put off a faint rosy glimmer without her commanding an activation. She thought there was a similar glimmer around Henrie's fist as she took a swing at a Pawn, but it'd been a flash if anything. Capri wasn't concerned, there was bound to be a reaction with her filtering the code through the Pak's systems. A little more testing and she could lock down whatever weak point was letting that through.

Seeing the response to their small break-ins, she'd sent the other cloaked Pawn stationed at the warehouse back around, was also educational. The parking lot became a frenzy of authorities, all trying to feel important after their helpless response that morning. Agencies she knew they'd be visiting soon stopped by. The humans didn't feel like a threat, but they were paying attention. Prey developed their own means of survival. Much more pushing and they'd start circling in tighter.

Even with any intel Henrie would gather for them soon, she couldn't hit their holding centers like she wanted - quick and maybe loud. As much as they were asking for more involvement, Capri didn't trust the Lenians to coordinate a city-wide attack. No matter how well they were getting along these days. To avoid sending anyone on the run, they'd have to move quietly. More patience and waiting. Neither were Capri's strong suit, but she needed this to go right. She needed the names of those fake Wardens.

None of that could happen immediately anyway. Exerting that much force on Henrie burnt her out. The girl nearly collapsed as soon as Capri steered her back home. She looked peaceful in that deep sleep physical exhaustion brings. Capri was jealous as she was unsure when she'd last slept that well.

A cruel idea came to mind. From her Pak, Capri released her backup drive that held her archive of fights from over the years. The other Wardens said it was unhealthy keeping those so close at hand, studying them obsessively like Capri did, but she wanted to be prepared. Not simply fight the enemy but fight like them, taking any move she was impressed by for her own. In the end, had that not paid off?

She picked a long ago fight with Lenians, to keep things familiar for the girl. A MegaPawn pinning her to the ground with razor sharp fingers piercing her right shoulder while the other hand became a long blade above her. Capri remained mesmerized by the fluidity of that change. She'd originally earmarked the fight in the hopes they'd figure out how to craft a blade like that for her. The memory ended with her being stabbed with that beautiful weapon, one of her rougher spots. Rin, who could be heard calling her name, arrived five seconds later to dispatch the MegaPawn and mend her. Capri sported a scar on her front and back from the injury. Rin always gave the spot a look when she was worried about some particularly dangerous call Capri was proposing. She normally stopped watching before the stabbing bit, but sent the entire encounter to the girl, cutting right before Rin's rescue. Those five seconds would feel like years, she knew that firsthand. Capri wasn't sure how this would filter through her programming, but it would make for an interesting experiment.

The cloaked Pawn keeping watch peered in the girl's window. The results didn't take long. Henrie twitched in bed, hands balling into fists. Her heart rate rose. Capri tapped on her workstation, making sure nothing woke the human yet. She wanted to ensure Henrie received the full effect. The girl's feed didn't provide much, outside of Henrie softly crying out in her sleep. A hand went to her side, where the cut would be. The memory transferred through well. Another spike hit her vitals, Capri knew Henrie was awake. The Pawn showed the girl shooting up in bed, clutching the spot where Capri's scars resided.

The girl rolled her shoulders, trying to shake the tension she must feel there, but won no relief. She did a lap around her room as she fought to level herself out. Her pacing ended at the window, looking right at the Pawn she wasn't being allowed to see. Henrie may not have noticed anyway, Capri could tell she hadn't escaped the memory yet. Knew that far-off look from having to shake her fellow Warden's out of it plenty. Camden got lost often.

Capri tapped through her program, calming Henrie down by force. The girl's hands were shaking as she climbed back in bed, but eventually she settled and fell back asleep.

The full footage played on a loop in a corner of her workstation. Capri watched Rin coming to rescue her. In her mind, the same Rin threw her inside a stasis pod.

Capri sent the dream again.

14

Warm Up

Mina loved the pillows on her new bed. They were so squishy. She woke up completely curled around one. Whatever planet they came from must be good. Her phone buzzed on the nightstand, she snagged it without ruining the perfectly bundled pillow. There was a text from her mother, **Come by Hephaestus when you are free.**

Mina realized she'd never told her parents that she'd be gone for the night. Steph said to say Mina was staying at her place, but she'd forgotten to send the lie between movies. Not that either of her parents had asked. Or had any amount of worry regarding where their teenage daughter was this morning.

She pushed off the ick that was her parents and rolled out of bed, ready to focus on her plans with better people. They'd talked Sean down from his hammock last night. Mainly due to Mina mentioning that if he converted to a Murphy bed he'd gain a secret compartment kind of situation. Steph was fully committed to the canopy. While those two were working today, the others were doing the footwork of checking local furniture stores. As well as hunt out decor for their own rooms.

Given the time, she knew where to find Zane and pulled on yoga pants, a sports bra, and a tank top. With one tap she made her Pak adhere to her hip, a handy feature for when she was without pockets. She redid her bun, shoving the worst of the flyaways back in, before shuffling toward the kitchen. Emma's door was also cracked open, she'd be in the gym with Zane. Mina was glad they had each other to keep up on workouts with. They were all training, but those two needed a different level to maintain what they'd already built. She was happy to let Emma keep him company for the early-early morning bit.

She blended together the post-workout smoothies they both liked, then a regular strawberry one for herself, and made her way down to the gym. The two lucked out that the previous Wardens were also humanoid-type beings. Gifting them with an almost complete gym from the start, once Mina or the Comps repaired the remaining machines. Or Emma found a suitable replacement online.

Emma was doing some kind of lunge thing with weights and Zane was in the middle of a set of leg presses. Both appeared completely oblivious to her entering the room. Mina set their drinks down nearby before swinging herself onto a spin bike. She lazily pushed on the pedals while swiping through her phone.

"Phone curls don't count," Zane called over from his machine, disproving he'd been unaware of her coming in.

"I can't get too big of guns, these babies have to fit small spaces." She flexed her toned, but small, biceps to make her point. He shook his head at her, but the statement was true. Mina helped Comp2876 as they oversaw the repairs to Steph's Pegasus after their first fight. A novel experience, her being the one handing over tools. She'd learned a lot from 2876 over those few days. While the Guardians were huge, there were a lot of smaller mechanisms working to keep them up. Once more items were cleared off her list, she'd pull apart the Guardian schematics like she wanted.

He kept staring at her. She knew what he was after, Mina dropped the phone in the holder on the side of the bike, turned up the wheel resistance, and grabbed the handlebars while putting more effort in her pedaling. Mina held that increased pace for five whole minutes, until Emma dropped her weights and stretched out on the ground. Emma pulled out her earbuds and took a long drink from the smoothie.

Mina swung a leg over to face her from the bike. "You sleep good in the new room?"

"Yeah, it's comfortable. Kinda feels like sleeping in a hotel, you know? Like technically, that space is mine, but not really."

"Same. I think getting more personal touches in there will help."

Emma stretched in the opposite direction, bending farther than Mina thought possible. "Oh totally! Furniture Mart has some nice options. I think it should be easy to find something for the grand magician and his disappearing act."

"And the Hollywood Star, ready for her close-up."

Emma glanced over toward Zane, who was pushing through his last set.

Mina knew he was listening to them over his music. He'd likely knocked down the volume once she'd arrived, well used to her rambling about something while he worked. Emma didn't appear to know that habit, as she shifted to her next stretch and said, "I didn't mean to sound like I was calling you out about the Pawn thing yesterday."

Mina slid down to the floor and started a half-hearted stretch herself. "Don't worry about it. You were right! I'm overly superstitious about saying stuff is easy."

"I…it's like I said. I do the hitting things part. I'm useless after that. I guess I wanted to feel like I was doing more."

"Are you kidding me?" Mina dropped her Pak between them. She tapped in a code and her main display shot up as a hologram above the device. "I only know how to do that because of you. Not to mention this layout you made. Lifesaver."

The leg press clunked into the base, Zane no longer pretending not to listen. He twisted around to look at them. "Same. I was struggling to read the heads-up until you tweaked the formatting."

"That's nitpick stuff though." Emma looked away from them, swirling her smoothie around in the cup. "It's not, like, a skill."

"You do know someone makes the user interfaces for websites, right?" Mina flinched when Emma cut her a hard look. "Sorry. I mean it's definitely a skill. One I, to be honest, suck at."

"We tried making a website about our robot fights and it nearly ruined us," Zane added.

Not to mention that her current website, the one being neglected, used a basic design pack she'd bought from the domain company to avoid any hassle. Mina pressed up on her knees. "And you've taught us so many moves the last few days! We actually looked somewhat together taking on those Pawns."

"A lot of that was Nek," Emma mumbled. "And the suits."

Mina looked to Zane, quietly pleading for him to think of the right thing to say. She wasn't good at this, but he dove for his smoothie and only gave her a thumbs up that Emma couldn't see. He was leaving her alone to finish this pep talk. She was the leader, a fact still weird to think about, and part of that job was encouraging everyone.

"You do a lot for our team, Emma. Really." That was weak. She knew it, and she knew Emma knew it too by the way the other girl kept staring at the floor. Mina rubbed her suddenly clammy hands on her pants and looked at Zane again. Felt weird for him to leave her hanging like this, he was usually so ready to come along on any project. Like following Mina inside a spaceship because she said it'd be fun. Sean and Steph had been nervous, but pretty much game for whatever they found. No one pushed back more than Emma at the start. "You were the most cautious of us that first day here."

Emma shrugged a 'so what' at her.

"You kept asking questions. Kept poking and prodding. I shoved my nose in a Comp and was ready to go along with anything." She saw Emma scrunch up her brow. "I mean it! I would have fixed robots right up to the apocalypse. But you kept pushing. And because of that, we were better able to stay safe."

"Zane would have-"

Mina could see where that was going and cut her off. "Eventually, yeah. But he's my best friend and goes way easier on me than he probably should. You didn't. Even as my actual friend now, you don't. You say exactly what's on your mind and that makes me pull my head out of the wiring and pay attention. And I need that. I have blind spots. I need you questioning things. I need you to keep us safe. We need your ability to sort out these crazy alien systems. And while it is so, so, very far from all you do here, we need you to look cooler than the rest of us as you punch things."

Emma gave up a smile at that. "The gauntlets did turn out pretty great. Thanks for those, by the way."

"Anytime! I will make you whatever you want, as long as you never question your place on this team."

"Deal." Emma didn't look at either of them. Instead, she pushed off the floor and left the gym altogether. "I'm gonna shower and pop in at home."

"I'll text you later about picking you up," she called after her. Mina fell over on the padded floor. "That was so much."

Zane slow clapped as he rolled off the press machine. "When do I get a pep talk like that?"

"I am a tin man and you are my heart. That's all I have left."

"You have plenty of heart." He pulled her off the floor. "You just don't listen to it."

"Fine, then Jiminy Cricket." She hugged him, despite how sweaty he was; the rare time she initiated one. "And for the record, I absolutely, one hundred percent, always need you around."

He squeezed her back, tight as he always did. "Wouldn't dream of being anywhere else."

"But seriously," she pushed him away, "I know how conflict gets to you. But you're here. A lot of this is terrifying, but you're here. Beyond that, most people would have ditched me long ago. I've never been an easy friend. But you always show up."

He tucked her back in under his arm, sweat and all, "That's what real family does. One of these days you're gonna finally believe me."

15

Bad Vibes

"Oh, look. A child's bed. How original," Sean droned as he looked at the picture Emma pulled up on her phone. "And not at all the joke I've been expecting from you all morning."

Emma scoffed, "I thought you'd like the stars and swirls on the bed set."

They were posted up at the back drink bar going over their findings; which were meager and rather eye-opening about the cost of home furnishings. They were redirecting to thrift stores after this. Mina would've loved to knock personalizing Outrider off her list, but she was stubbornly accepting that decorating would be an ongoing project rather than something they could knock out over a weekend.

"We wanted a peace offering for when you saw the prices of the Murphy beds." Zane turned his phone to show the Furniture Mart site with their available options. When the salesman showed them the online listings, because no versions were on display, they'd all backed away from the computer.

Sean paled as he scrolled. "It's just a bed that goes up."

Steph patted his shoulder. "Gotta turn a few extra magic tricks."

"We can probably build one for way cheaper," Mina offered. She'd done a cursory search on the ride over. There wasn't anything too complicated involved.

"You could get a pullout sofa," Emma turned her phone to him, showing the few she'd found in the discount items showroom. "Some aren't horrible and you still get the disappearing act."

"We'll put a pin in that for now." Sean bumped Steph as she passed with drinks on a tray. "At least yours is only a frame with fancy curtains."

Mina swiped over to the pictures of pricing for fabrics they'd found at a nearby craft store. "Depending on your budget, curtains may also be happening in installations."

Steph came around the counter to look at the selection. "Should be doable."

"Should be doable," Sean mimicked her, flicking water from the wash sink.

"Jealous?" She swished a lock of hair as she headed for the balcony.

Mina was sad to lose the contact.

"Yes!" Sean called out as she went through the doors. "How do people fill entire houses?"

Zane stared at the melting ice in his cup. "There were pillows that cost a hundred dollars."

"One of those always cold, memory gel things, yeah?" When Zane didn't answer, Sean stilled behind the bar. "Right?"

Zane looked him dead in the eyes. "Decorative. Purely decorative."

"Liar." He dropped the mug he was drying in the sink, but Zane didn't flinch. "Madness."

Emma leaned toward Mina. "I think this is the most traumatizing thing that's ever happened to them."

"Aliens and evil robots be damned," Mina said.

Sean moved down to ring up a customer. Zane returned to his scrolling of the Furniture Mart website. Mina wasn't sure what he might be trying to find outside of more wounded feelings, but left him to it. She started scribbling out components needed for the Murphy bed on a napkin; if Nek okayed the idea, they could print everything in Fabrication.

Emma stayed close to her side. "You don't have to keep making us things, you know."

"What?"

"Your offer to build a Murphy bed. You don't need to do that. We're not here because you're making us cool gadgets."

She scrunched up the napkin. "Is this one of those 'speak your mind' instances I complimented you on earlier?"

"Yup." Emma took a drink from her shake. "What you can do is awesome. You are one hundred percent the brains here. But don't feel you have to constantly provide proof of it."

There'd been a guidance counselor last year who commented on how Mina might be a smidge obsessive about obtaining achievements and accolades. She avoided that counselor now. Her parents, when she was younger, only responded to reports, statistics, and results. A drawing never made it on the fridge, but a blue ribbon might earn a glance. When Zane's family first moved in, his dad mentioned the garage door opener being on the fritz. She'd fixed the wiring within the hour, and he'd been incredibly thankful, but was begging her to back away from the riding lawnmower not long after. Something about how casually she was working around the blades. Maybe she did have a small bit of a problem.

"I will work on it." That was the best she could offer, this wasn't a habit she was kicking anytime soon. To prove her point, Mina stepped around the bar and threw the napkin away.

She was pretty sure she caught the movement of Emma and Zane sharing a quiet high-five below the countertop. Before she could call them on it, someone collided with her backside. Mina whipped around to find Henrie holding her middle and looking agitated. Had the other girl hit her that hard? They all knew Henrie took some hits yesterday, probably some decent bruising under that baseball tee. Especially if Steph was right and Henrie was lying about how hurt she was.

Mina bent down to pick up the pad and pen that Henrie dropped. "That was my bad."

Henrie pulled the items back, stepping around her to get behind the bar. "It's fine."

Words that were never said when something was fine. Mina slowly walked to her stool. "I shouldn't have been there. Really, it's my bad."

"Fine, it's your bad." Henrie winced as she dropped down and pulled open a cupboard.

Mina caught eyes with Zane, who was no longer lost in his phone. He raised an eyebrow but stayed quiet. Emma stood from her stool slightly to look Henrie over, probably for signs of injuries. The most Mina could see was her hands showing cuts and bruises, those must have happened from her fall in a pile of Pawn parts. They all watched as Henrie snapped one door shut and yanked the next open, scratching items needing stocked on her pad.

Steph came back in from the balcony and caught herself before also colliding with Henrie. "Oh hey! You got the 'all clear' to come back?"

Henrie slammed the door. "I'm fine."

"Are you?" Zane asked.

Henrie pulled herself back up, looking ready to tell him off, but lost her balance. She tipped backward, catching herself on the short ledge of counter there. They all pretended to not watch as she straightened a few toppled cups, outside of Emma who watched her every move. After a long sigh Henrie turned back to their group. "Sorry. I slept like crap last night. That's not a good excuse, but-"

"Been there," Emma helped her out. "All good."

"You wanna chill in the office for a minute?" Steph asked. "I've done it after a bad customer before."

"No, I'm-I'm good." She smacked the pad on her palm. "But if I take a long time coming back from the stockroom, cover for me?"

"Absolutely."

Sean slid in from the other side. "Those bigger bags of coffee beans make oddly good pillows. Don't ask how I know."

"Thanks." She stepped around Steph and headed for the ramp.

She'd barely stepped out of view when Emma snapped around to all of them. "Did anyone catch how hard she got hit yesterday? A Comp maybe?"

Before anyone could answer Emma twisted her arm, the team saw the faint silver glimmer of the armband's hologram display roll out. Zane and Mina immediately blocked her from being seen by anyone else as Emma skimmed through footage from the fight.

"The long sleeves in this weather are kind of a giveaway for being banged up," Sean muttered.

"And the thicker makeup," Steph added.

Mina covered Emma's smartwatch to block the hologram. "Let's not do this right here. We can go somewhere more private if you want," Mina looked up, trying to silently indicate Outrider, "But if she says she's good, you may have to accept that."

Emma flicked her arm, the glimmer slipping between Mina's fingers disappeared, and she slouched against the bar. Mina was trying to think of the next good thing to say when she heard an echo of her own words coming up the ramp.

"-can't force anything on her. She's her own person," Megan said as she appeared ahead of Sam. The pair stepped inside the office, Mina assumed they were clocking in.

Sam reemerged and stalked back down the ramp without saying a word to any of them. Megan came out and gave a weak smile. "Yesterday is still making them a little tense."

"Seems the same for Henrie," Steph said, casually wiping down the counter.

Megan gave a quick look to the group bunched around the bar, but caved to some internal pressure and stepped in toward Steph. "I don't want Sam to know because they'll use it as leverage, but I'm kinda worried about her too."

Emma straightened up slightly but stayed quiet. Steph turned to better face Megan, putting herself between her coworker and the group, letting Megan have some illusion that they were talking alone. Mina felt like she was getting a peek at how Steph was so good at getting intel.

Megan spoke quietly, but enough that the rest could pick up. "This is only my opinion of course. But she's, kind of, stubborn about help. She has like, panic attacks when she gets emotionally worked up. Won't let anyone near her when they happen."

"Like since Robo-day?"

"That's the thing! She was great on Robo-day, she saved my life. I think they started before that. Her dad died, that's why they moved here, but you know that. I don't think she's handling that very well. She accidentally brought him up once when I spent the night at her place and she disappeared for like half an hour. I told her she could talk to me about it, but she wouldn't."

"She wants to pull herself out."

"Right! And then Sam, you know how they are. Born to be a manager. They mean well enough but can push too hard. Just as stubborn." Megan huffed and tucked a curl behind her ear. "I don't know what to do with either of them."

Steph put a hand on Megan's shoulder. "Hey, none of their problems are on you to fix. They have to do the work. All you are responsible for is yourself. Whatever support you give is a privilege to them. Not a right."

Megan smiled. "Thanks Steph. You're the best for this stuff." She swiped a half apron from under the counter and tied the straps around her waist. "Back into the fray. See you later!"

Zane waited until Megan was gone. "That was some real stuff there, Steph."

Steph gave a little bow. "I'd like to give special thanks to the therapist I saw during the divorce."

"You picked an easy damsel to save there." Sean elbowed his cousin.

Emma looked like she had an insult to return, but let it drop. Choosing instead to bend back over her phone.

Mina glanced at her own screen; the text from her mom, technically unopened, remained waiting for her. She put on the biggest smile she could and turned to Zane. "Ready for the next mentally taxing thing of the day?"

He regained the million-yard stare he'd worn over the pillows. "The lab."

"Yup." She didn't want to go, fearing more questions about her Guardian. Hopefully, they'd lose interest soon enough.

"Like Hephaestus Lab? Your parents?" Emma shoved her phone in her pocket. "Oh, I have to meet these people. I'm in."

16

Little Alien on My Shoulder

Coffee beans did make decent pillows. Henrie laid across a set of folding chairs and squished a bag to prop her head up a little higher. She'd been joking about hiding in here at the time, but after stalling out while pulling packets of tea she decided it best to take a minute. An ache between her shoulders kept her from fully relaxing. When Henrie sat up, her body pulsed with several varying aches.

Henrie, mind clouded from her gloom and pain, looked over her bruised knuckles. She was unsure when she'd done that. One of her several falls yesterday, probably. Something was pinching the back of her right arm, she went to scratch under her sleeve.

Don't touch. Henrie's hand stopped mid-movement.

Her phone went off on the nearby shelf, redirecting her attention there. A text from Emma, **Sorry about Mina. And for everyone bugging you.**

No biggie. She typed back. **I'm a grouch today.**

I bet you're pretty stiff. Do you have a good sized tub at home? When I get back I'll send you a pic of everything I add. Might feel a little over the top, but it works.

I'll try anything right now.

Adorable. Cut through her head. *Stop.* Henrie dropped her phone in her lap.

Another text from Emma loaded in. **Did you see the Aldi thing? Wild. How did they not see anything on the cameras?**

"What the hell?" She scooped the phone back up. Typing 'Aldi robbery' in the search bar was enough to find a local article about a break-in the night before. "Absolutely not."

Problem? There was laughing in her head.

That wasn't her. She felt very far from laughing right now.

A second text popped up. **That security guy was in on it, right? "Can't remember their face", sure buddy.**

Henrie looked at her knuckles. She'd hit him so hard. No. Dreamed she hit him hard.

Someone is catching up.

"Stop it."

Weren't panic attacks enough? Now she was crazy on top of it?

Henrie scrolled through the article, confirming that a TJ Maxx nearby was hit first. The security guard's ID picture was included too. As of this morning, he remained under observation at the hospital for a severe concussion.

He'll look different with that new nose you gave him.

"No. Nonono." This was bad. She'd done this, actually done this. But she hadn't wanted to. That Pawn made her do it.

I believe we're done playing house.

Something pinched between her shoulders. That pressure at the base of her neck returned, pushing her toward the door. Henrie fought as her feet inched forward, making an attempt to reach for whatever was on her back.

Stop.

Her hand dropped, fully dead weight this time. The arm hung useless at her side as pins and needles slowly crept up from her fingers.

"What is happening?" Her throat was closing up. The ever-present coil in her chest twisted tighter.

Go home. Now.

Henrie shuffled her way out of the storeroom. The pressure decreased as she obeyed the order, but she felt pulled away from her own body. Like the night before in her (not) dream robbery and assault. She'd never disassociated this hard before; weaving through people, bumping them and barely feeling a thing. Numb fingers pulled off her apron and dropped it behind the front counter. Sam gave her a confused look, but said nothing. They were still upset. The pressure directed her toward the door, the intensity grew as she lagged at the counter. Her jaw wasn't fused shut this time, she could say something. Ask them for help with this psychotic breakdown.

Help, please help, there is a mean voice inside my head and they made me do something bad.

The plea was there, she was ready to beg, until the left side of her head throbbed with pain. She winced from the sudden migraine, feeling some sort of invisible barrier closing in around her mind. Henrie's vision took on a bizarre filter, as if she was watching Sam on a grainy movie screen. Edges of her vision began dimming to black, she feared she was losing control. Words appeared in her head, she heard herself echoing them, "Not feeling up to snuff. I'm going home."

Up to snuff? Something was definitely wrong with her brain.

Sam smiled, happy to hear what they wanted. "Text me if you need more time off. We'll get by."

Henrie gave a weak smile and walked away, the pressure immediately backed off. As she pushed the door open she sighed out a small, "I might not."

Don't be so dramatic.

17

My Brain Feels Ick

"I've never thought about how pretentious the name was until now," Emma said as they parked in the large lot outside Hephaestus Labs. The three-storied structure of concrete and glass situated on the south side of The Park waited for them at the other end.

"What? Because operating under the assumption that your tinkering is fit for the gods is conceited or something?" Mina asked. She hated that she liked the building, always needed to remind herself that the majority was smoke and mirrors for visitors and investors. Good researchers worked on impressive projects that helped people, but they were few in number and worked nowhere near her parents. Also, sadly, the boba counter in their cafeteria was killer. The food on the whole was exceptional. Mina believed they might have the city's best stir fry, which didn't feel fair on top of them being, very likely, evil.

"Wait till you see the statue in action," Zane added as he unfolded from the driver's seat. After a quick stretch he dropped back in and pulled his Pak out of a pocket, tucking it away in the glove box alongside the other two. "Almost forgot."

"I feel weird leaving it." Emma gave hers one last look before Zane snapped the door shut.

Mina made the call of no Paks entering the building on the drive over. She didn't know if they were scanning people for alien tech specifically, but she could guarantee they were scanning everyone for the hell of it. No need to make this easy for the evil scientists, but she also felt strange leaving them behind. There was a void in her back pocket. She'd only held the thing for two weeks, she could go twenty minutes without it. "We won't be long."

They weaved through rows of cars, Mina hadn't expected the lot to be this full. They must have extra people doing prep for The Expo. The statue grew larger as they neared the entryway; a tall, bronze Hephaestus hammering away at an anvil. Mina hated that they'd neglected to represent his disability, simply reformed his image to be exactly what they wanted.

Another difference from myth was the robotic arm welding his blacksmith hammer. Emma stopped as the arm swung down, smashing hammer to anvil; designed of a copycat material that didn't give off as much noise. She watched the arm raise for another swing. "This is too much."

"There's a scanner with facial recognition in his eyes, goes off when anyone not listed as an employee or regular visitor goes by," Mina rattled off as she kept moving, "To impress the plebeian masses."

"So I could stand here and he'll keep going?"

"They sternly ask you to move after fifteen minutes or so," Zane said. "Found that one out myself."

Emma caught up with them. "Absolutely unnecessary."

Mina held her arms out as the doors slid open. "Welcome to Hephaestus Labs."

The entryway was sleek and tidy, as expected with the sharp exterior. The lobby contained the welcome desk directly across from them, along with sets of circular couches on either side for anyone waiting for an appointment. Behind the desk was the elevator bank. On the other end of that short hall was the reluctantly beloved cafeteria. A pair of older women crossed their path, oblivious to the teens as they chatted between themselves, and continued across as the lobby thinned to a walkway that looped the entire first floor. That's where the showrooms were. No, sorry, "testing labs". Mina fought the urge to roll her eyes.

Hephaestus claimed they held an open-book policy about their research and welcomed the public to come see for themselves. Other towns had mall walkers, Hurst had lab walkers. Part of the draw for The Expo was showcasing all the 'newly completed' technology they'd teased in viewings throughout the previous year. The reality was that anything being tested in those rooms was nearly perfected, gave a good show, and was oh-so heavily patented that no one could dream of stealing anything they saw without being slapped with a lawsuit. Or were designs deemed unimportant enough that higher-ups wouldn't care if they did. Or were interns being made to 'look busy', a part-time job her parents attempted to convince her to do when they first moved here. When not in use, the rooms were filled with boards covered in gibberish that didn't make sense if you knew what you were looking at.

But didn't everything look exciting? Smoke and mirrors, all of it. The real work happened on the two floors above. Mina expected more labs were hidden below, but she couldn't prove that yet. Her last attempt resulted in finding Outrider and she'd been minorly distracted since then.

A smiling security guard, badly playing dress up as a receptionist, approached them with a tablet in hand. "Hello, Mina! And Zane. Good to see you both. Please check in on the screen."

She pressed her thumb to the icon. There was a quick animation of a green circle spinning around her finger as the tablet read her print and updated. A message appeared, saying her parents were notified of her arrival. Zane followed with his quick press. The guard tapped a couple of times and turned the smile to Emma. "Can I get a name, please?"

She answered them slowly, Mina could tell she was considering lying. After Emma scanned her thumbprint, the guard held an arm out to the hallway behind them. "An elevator will be waiting for you. I'm sure you know the way from there."

Mina nodded and moved past them, the other two not far behind. A ding directed them toward a waiting elevator.

As the doors shut, Emma asked, "Does the statue tell them who's coming in?"

"If they're saved in the database," Mina answered.

"Too much," she sighed as the elevator took them to the third floor. The doors pulled open and a screen across the hall flashed an arrow pointing toward her parent's lab. Emma scoffed, "2876 should teach their building how to give directions politely."

Her parents were given a regretfully nice office that looked out on The Park. The building wasn't tall enough to see much of the crater, but she knew they could catch an edge from their windows. Every frosted glass door they passed was labeled with the names of other researchers or whatever communal machines were stored within. No shiny glass walls to show off in front of here, she expected because none of them could trust each other. Her pace slowed as they neared the last corner before her parent's door. While entering this lab wasn't as taboo as the one at home, it never felt right.

Zane squeezed her arm. "In and out."

"If it's like my parents, it'll be something they could have texted," Emma added.

Mina felt good about bringing her friends along.

Up until a clipped British accent, coming from a room behind them, stabbed her brain. "I believe your mother requested you alone to come in."

"Well Mel, we were hanging out." Mina turned to see the absolute worst, brown-nosing, grad student–who should have stayed in her family's 'castle' to shed her next layer of skin–walking toward them. Mina researched Mel's family's estate on Google Earth after one particularly long brag, the place was a manor at best. And not even a cute one. How could it be? Housing a hag like her. "And I don't expect to be long."

"Then your pet could have waited in the car." Mel looked at Zane, her pinched face getting smaller, and shuffled papers arm to arm. "Windows down, of course."

Emma took a step, but Mina caught her wrist. Another good reason to have left the Paks behind. Mina fought the impulsive desire of using a boost to knock Mel through a wall, Emma would certainly have more elaborate plans. While Mel technically worked for several researchers, running reports and the more standard tests they couldn't be bothered with, she was somehow always around when Mina came to see her parents. She was a puffed-up secretary in a lab coat. Except, Mina reminded herself, secretaries are vital to their offices. Mel was trash.

"Best not to leave them waiting." Mina tugged Emma toward the door, but refused to turn her back on Mel. She'd seen enough nature videos to know better.

"Yes. Best." Mel followed in step, all the way to the lab. They bunched up in the doorway before Mel elbowed her way in first and walked over to Mina's mother's desk. "I have those results for you."

Not a word from her mother, only a hand pulling the papers closer. Mel idled at the edge of the desk, hands clasped behind her. "Anything else I can assist with?"

"Trial notes need added to the Cranston file," her father said from his perch at their worktable, not looking away from his project. "If that could be expedited."

"Absolutely," Mel said. Given how Mel's fingers twitched behind her back, Mina was guessing she'd been interrupted from that task to procure these test results for them. "I will get right on that."

Mina would feel bad for a normal person working under her parents. Would feel like a kindred spirit with how dismissive they were. She'd shared several 'I know and I'm sorry' looks with other interns who experienced small interactions with them. Mel was not a normal person. She could rot with her nose shoved up–

"Mina," her mother called, "come here."

She and Mel passed each other. Behind her, she heard Zane hissing a small, "Begone demon," as Mel left. Mina dared to step up right next to the desk this time. "More pictures?"

"Yes, but only in reference." Her mother spread out several shots, they were from different parts of Robo-day. All things she'd seen on the news, if not witnessed firsthand, so none of them caught her off guard. What surprised Mina this time was her mother taking her arm and pulling her closer. Her mom turned her wrist over, looking at the smartwatch Mina had forgotten about until now. "I don't recognize the brand."

Mina wanted to tell her to stop touching it, but what came out was, "I made it. Closed system and limited contacts, so we can talk together," she gestured to her friends, their faces telling her that she was saying too much, "Privately. Was pretty easy."

She flinched the second the word left her mouth.

Her father walked from the workstation to his desk. "Easy means not done."

"Early model," Mina corrected. "Prototype. Still testing."

Her mother dropped her arm, the hand moved to Mina's back. She pointed to the rows of pictures. "I wanted your account of these events. From the morning of The Hill to after the incursion."

Because of course her mom would use the word incursion.

"Um, sure. Well, Zane and I went for a hike that morning. Then we went to Restoration, met up with Emma there." She tried turning toward her friends, but her mother's hand kept her in place.

Mina rambled out the cover story they'd come up with. They hung out at Restoration for a while, went back to The Park for a short time (in the chance anyone noticed her car being there), and then the whole group went to Zane's for a movie night. That was where they were when The Hill disappeared and where they remained as everything went down the next day.

When she'd practiced this story alone at home she'd been concerned about sounding too rehearsed, but the physical contact from her mother was throwing her off enough to muddle things. Her parents followed up on various points. Her mom wanted exact times for when they arrived at any location. Then what movies they watched or considered watching. Mina told them Scream as that was fresh in her mind, though it had taken an unusual amount of effort to get the words out. Her father asked questions about the plot of the fourth movie, oddly enough. She didn't think her dad watched movies at all. Her mom then redirected to questions about the Restoration menu, having her list off options. There was a prickling feeling on the back of her neck, something was going on. She couldn't figure out what their angle was. Each time they asked a question, she felt compelled to answer as fully as she could. The urge always stealing her chances to question them back.

"You didn't go to the festival at all?" her mother asked.

An odd point of the story to circle back to. "No, not my kind of thing. We were on the other side because the trails were empty."

"Unfortunate." She shuffled a paper aside.

Mina thought the sheet looked like a map, something the festival made to direct people around the booths and vendors.

"Back at the cafe," her father said, "What does the south wall have for art?"

"What does that-" Mina looked up to her father, for the first time noticing a small camera perched on top of his monitor and pointed directly at her. She turned around, finding a softball-sized box level with her head. The prickling feeling now made the front of her neck itch. The box was hastily made, plates with messy welds casing whatever mechanism was inside. A half inch opening with a telltale pinpoint of light shining in the center gave the box away as being more than decor. The tingling wasn't simply her growing discomfort. "Are you running a test on me?"

"Witness testimony is often unreliable, prone to errors due to faulty memory and perception." Her mother stopped touching her back, instead she plucked the box off the shelf and set it on an empty corner of her desk. "We believe the right stimuli can generate fully factual memory retrieval."

"Remove opinions and influences," her father continued, now typing away at his computer. "Leave only what is. Or rather, what was."

"So you're trying to replicate a photogenic memory with your little machine pointed at my head?"

"And remove personal influences from affecting them," he added, sounding tired of repeating himself all of one time.

"What kind of stimuli were you sending at me?" She knew the Paks contained radiation protection, but she'd left that handy bit of tech in the car.

"Unimportant," her mother said. "Testing is less effective once you're aware. So that will be all." She settled back in at her desk, pushing the pictures into a tidy pile near their little brain altering device.

A quiet 'oh shit' came from near the door, Emma finally seeing what Mina was dealing with. Mina backed away from the desk and gulped out a quick, "Glad to help."

She wanted to smack the horrible little box to the ground. Stomp on the thing until those weak welds gave out. Run out to grab a blaster and shoot the thing until it was ash for good measure. Mina could make something better. She would. Today. One afternoon in Fabrication and…Zane was giving her a look. Time to go.

Mina swallowed hard and squeezed between her friends to leave, expecting they'd keep up as she continued down the hallway. Unless they wanted to be lab rats next. After a few paces she heard their footsteps behind her. As they reached the elevators, Mel stood smiling at the other end of the hallway. She must have known about the test.

Mina punched the call button and fought the urge to flip Mel off.

Emma stepped around, blocking her from Mel. She called down the hall, "Can we help you?"

Once the elevator came, Zane nudged them both inside. They let her lean on the cool metal siding in silence. None of them acknowledged the guard as they reentered the lobby, but the guy followed them anyway to offer a card to Emma. He smiled and said, "This has a QR code you can use to fill out a survey about your visit to Hephaestus Labs. We'd love to hear from you. And you get entered to win some nifty prizes."

Emma held the card until they were passing the statue, flicking the paper towards its face. "Who says 'nifty' anyway? No one you can trust, that's who."

"Good call," Mina said. "The code probably puts some weird program on your phone. Or I wouldn't be surprised if they stuck a microchip in the card to track if you leave here and go directly to a competitor." As the words left her mouth, Mina stopped in her tracks between two rows of cars.

"Everyone is obsessed with tracking these days," Zane said as he continued forward. "Speaking of, I think my new headphones from Amazon got lost. Says it's been sitting in Idaho for three days."

"Bummer!" Emma turned as she spoke, realizing Mina was no longer with them. "What's up?"

"They want to know where their stuff is going."

"That's why I ditched the card, yeah."

"No!" Mina closed the gap to her friends. "The Lenians. They loaded the Pawns with trackers, which makes no sense because they have their bounce-back system. But they didn't use it because they wanted to know who grabbed them."

"Why do the Lenians care about who's holding broken Pawn parts?" Zane asked. "If we can't do anything with them, everyone else is going to have a hell of a time."

That was a good question. Why send weak Pawns to a fight? Why track their broken parts? To know who was researching them? They likely used similar failsafes to what Comps used to keep anyone from stealing intel. Mina knew there were organizations they suspected to be hiding Comp parts. Those same people likely grabbed Pawns pieces too, like candy from a pinata. Giving Capri a short list of those with proven interest in alien technology. Did she want more evil partners-in-crime? What could any human agency do for her? Maybe offer warm bodies as backup. Mina suspected Capri would prefer her own set of Comps over people. Maybe she was after a deal, Capri could give them information if they handed over–

Oh. Duh.

There was a jab in her side. Zane smiled as she focused back on him. "Share with the class, please."

"Capri is going after Comp parts." Mina glanced down to see Nek swirling on her watch. "She sent those Pawns as bait. To see who would take them. We have strong enough protection to cancel the signal out, but anyone down here–"

"Would be easy pickings," Emma finished.

Nek spun tightly before drifting back to waves. "I'll dedicate more Comps to breaking the encryption on that signal. Hopefully we can crack it before she makes a move on any of them."

Zane nudged her and Emma toward his car. "With that settled, I think that's enough superhero-ing in the middle of this public parking lot."

Mina reached for the glove compartment as she slid into the passenger seat. With her Pak clutched close to her chest, she handed the other two over. She rubbed the touchpad, but didn't trigger anything. The tightness in her chest eased as her Pak glowed a soft teal.

"Circling back to the parent thing," Zane said as he backed out of the spot and caught eyes with Emma in the rearview mirror. "You can see why I said she stays out of the house until they leave, yeah?"

Mina gave her knee-jerk defense. "Other people have it a lot worse."

"Doesn't negate your situation." Emma grabbed the back of Mina's seat and shook it slightly. "You're staying at my place tonight. We're throwing darts at Mel's face."

Zane hit the steering wheel. "I was thinking the same thing! The darts at her face part."

"H-L-F-N!" Emma bounced in the seat, any excuse to use the training program got her excited. Hard Light Fight Nights, their new favorite pastime, was too much to say apparently. "We can punch her!"

Nek bounced on her watch. "I can have a usable model ready within the hour."

Emma hit the headrest. "Let's go!"

Mina tried not to smile, thinking it best, as the leader, to not give in to her meaner desires. "I don't think violence is supposed to be an answer."

"But it can be fun." Emma slipped back in the seat. "She's the worst."

Zane turned onto the road taking them blissfully away from Hephaestus Labs. "Agreed."

Nek bounced across the small screen. "This Mel was rather awful by my understanding of human nature."

"That's because she's a snake," Mina blurted out, slapping a hand over her mouth.

Emma laughed, "Mina hates someone. I love it."

Her smartwatch flashed with a text from Emma to their group chat. **Group decree: We hate Mel.**

Steph and Sean responded immediately with gifs of throwing up and flipping off. An additional long **BOO** came in from Sean. Steph sent, **If you have a pic I can make sure everyone (besides Sam) makes her drinks**

wrong forever. Pass it off to other shops.

Emma looked back toward the parking lot. "Do you know what she drives? I'll step on her car next time we have the Guardians down."

Mina knew that wasn't appropriate, and if the event arose she'd begrudgingly talk Emma down, but this little spur of malevolence on her behalf felt nice. She'd wrangle them in later, for now, she sent a gif of someone getting tossed out a window.

18

You Ask How High

The Lenians were back to bickering. She could hear them from the floor below hollering from their workshops, they rarely bothered to cross the short space to argue in person.

Capri checked her feed on Henrie, the girl sat in her car staring at the home Capri wasn't allowing her to enter. The human was so far useless for planetary intel, most of the questions Capri asked resulted in her reaching for the phone to search for a possible answer. Silly of her to hope for a teen-aged shortcut. While Capri could dig through the Lenian database for most of her inquiries, she didn't want to. She'd redirected her questioning to Henrie's personal experience with the Wardens. Making her circle the block until Capri was satisfied with her answers.

A shout rang out below. They were making it impossible to concentrate on her interrogation. She left Henrie to herself and stepped out far enough to better catch what was being said.

"You are ignoring thousands of years of-"

"No, you are! You're refusing to see that-"

"-evolved to have the best possible-"

"-wouldn't recognize true vision if it bit you on your-"

This was hopeless. She couldn't even tell who was yelling what. Capri banged on the railing. "What is this all about? One of you."

100

Maxwell bent over his side to look up at her. "I tried having a reasonable conversation about what base our next creation should use and he's being resoundingly stubborn."

"I would respond better if he brought decent options to the table," Gregory said from his side, not bothering to walk out of his workshop.

Capri rubbed her forehead. "Do either of you have concepts for your choices?"

"Yes," came from both sides.

"I have more," added Gregory.

"Quality over quantity," snipped Maxwell.

Capri needed a way to end this fast, before they devolved to overlapping ranting once more. "Are you in short supply of materials?"

She knew the answer was no, but wanted to hear them say it. There was a surplus of materials lying in wait. Not to mention that the majority of the previous creature was recycled.

"No," came again from both sides.

"Then make both." Blissful silence came back to her. "Then have them duel or whatnot. Prove for certain which is better."

Maxwell disappeared from the railing. Neither gave another remark, she soon heard them both tinkering away. Capri moved back to her room, shutting the door behind her this time. Her Pak laid sprawled out across the worktable, she'd spent more time this morning meshing the interface directly to the table. Now her feed of Henrie's responses and the sentry Pawn were side by side, allowing her to work them in tandem with greater ease.

The girl had used the small bit of freedom to get inside the house. The cloaked Pawn circled the outside, finding Henrie standing in the kitchen. Her camera feed was quiet, outside of her breathing. The human splashed herself with water, hands going back under the tap for more.

You'll break her, Rin warned.

"They're expendable." Capri opened her line to Henrie. "I've decided to be nice. Easier questions for you this time."

Henrie's heart rate spiked, she jumped back from the sink without turning off the water. "I don't know anything!"

"You've well proven that. I'm only after your opinion now. What do you think of the new little Warden team running around?" Capri pushed Henrie's image of the team to her mind, assuming that would trigger her personal memory of them.

"I don't know who they are. I swear. Me being there was a coincidence."

Capri made the girl turn off the water, no need to be wasteful. She notched down her heart rate. "I assumed as much. Tell me what you think of them."

"They're doing good. They're here to protect us."

"That team can't do anything for you." Capri pulled the footage of her first standoff with them on Outrider. She wanted the visual of being attacked by these Wardens to consume the human's mind. Even if the fighting was sloppy.

Henrie tried to physically escape the images, moving around her house in time with the fight's progression. Capri watched as Henrie attempted blocking the phantom of a punch from Blue, nearly clipping her head on a console table as she dove away. These files apparently came through vividly even when the girl was awake, Capri congratulated herself on that feat. The Pawn pulled up thermals once Henrie moved away from any windows. From her direct feed, Capri heard the girl repeating, "This isn't real!"

"Not to you. Now stand still." Capri sent the command, not giving her a chance to fight. "I spied a little figure in your room last night upon our return. Silver caught your fancy did they?" Capri looped the short assault Silver performed on their own. "Congratulations, you picked the least rotten fruit from the barrel."

"Why are you doing this?" Henrie was on the move. Uselessly trying to outrun the ghosts in her head by heading for the stairs.

Boredom was the first answer that came to mind, how Lenian of her. "You're going to help me."

"You already made me steal-"

"Shhh." She closed Henrie's mouth, heard the girl cough from the effort to keep talking. "That was a test. Now we need actual work done."

There were muffled sounds as the girl attempted to respond. Capri released Henrie's jaw. "I...I can't do anything! I'm just...me."

"Then we'll enlist more than just you." Capri directed Henrie to the top of the stairs, turning her toward the pictures along the wall. A man stood center in nearly every one, wearing a uniform she knew to match those at the military outpost recently established within the city. Henrie showed a strong reaction to the images. "Who is this?"

"My dad."

"Wonderful. Time for a chat with him."

"You can't. He's...he's dead."

Capri slumped in her chair. Dead people were the root of all her problems, but not all was lost this time. Other photos contained more uniformed figures. "Who else do you know that would be useful?"

"Uncle J-" Henrie slapped her own hands over her mouth.

Capri made her pull them back, laughing at her futile resistance. "Now, now. Who?"

Henrie fought anyway. "His friend...James...Griffiths. He came to town... last week."

"If you were to show up, would he let you in?" All she got back was a groan, she took that as a yes. She turned Henrie back to the stairs. "Good. We're leaving."

Henrie's feed showed her grabbing for the railing. "No!"

"Okay, fine. I'll drive." Capri triggered the full block on Henrie's mind, locking her tightly away as she'd done at the end of the break-ins. She was proud of her programming as Henrie moved through the house and back to the car, her coding commanding motor functions without the hassle of a personality in the way. There was no kickback as Capri made her pop the trunk for the Pawn to hide inside, to act as backup if a quick exit was needed.

She didn't want to send the girl inside the base alone, but knew the Pawn couldn't sneak around behind her undetected. They were too bulky for full-on stealth operations. Even with its cloaking on, someone would likely bump it. The angle on the human's clip cameras weren't great, Capri would prefer to keep eyes on the girl, but she'd have to make do.

Once the command locked in, Henrie drove herself to the base. The military were using a section of recently developed land for their operations. Long white tents filled the dirt lot on one side of a newly laid parking lot, but Capri expected these were more for menial tasks. Or possibly purely distraction. As the Pawn trackers all sat in the empty office building on the other end of the lot. Henrie was stopped by two soldiers posted at the lot's entrance. One asked for her ID and reason for being there while the other did a walking pass on her car. The girl gave Griffith's name dryly, Capri kept her emotions muted. There was a long stretch of waiting as they radioed in, but they eventually directed her to a parking spot near the building. By the time Henrie stepped out of the car, a man was waiting for her.

He was stiff and straight in his uniform, but smiled and loosened up as she approached. "Henrie! This is, gotta say, this is a surprise."

"I know. Sorry. Should've had Mom call you. I, um," Henrie was stumbling. The speech function needed more tweaking. Pulling enough of her consciousness to give reasonable answers without releasing control back to the human was a delicate process. "I wanted to see you."

"You can come see me anytime, kiddo." He looked back to the building. "Okay, not any time. But you know how that goes." James put an arm around her shoulders. "Like I said at dinner last week, crazy as this all is, I'm glad I was assigned here. Lets me check in on you and your mom."

Capri could see Henrie relaxing once next to James, she was comforted by his presence. Henrie felt safer, which was beneficial for Capri as that lulled the girl's mind down naturally.

"Moving back to her hometown to get some of the quiet life feels like a joke now," Henrie said as they neared the building.

He fussed her hair, Henrie didn't love that. "You two have been through a lot lately, huh." James pushed the door open, waving off a guard that stepped toward them. He pulled her around a scanning station, some luck finally on Capri's side. "Now, without your mom around to perform for, how are you?"

There was a long pause before Henrie finally slipped out, "Fine."

Capri lamented having no visuals on Henrie's face. The vitals made her think the girl was agitated, but the readings from the mock Pak weren't as in-depth as the real thing. She trusted her programming, but being somewhat blind was irritating.

New physical stimuli registered, his arm getting tighter around her. "That wasn't a very good lie."

Capri pressed in a command. "You feel unsafe."

Henrie sucked in a breath, her pulse quickened. "Things are bad here. I don't…don't want…"

The vitals all changed, spiking and diving in unexpected areas. Henrie's breathing hitched oddly. Something outside of Capri's influence made Henrie act like she was under attack.

"Woah, hey, you're okay." James pulled the girl inside an office, sitting her down in a chair before crouching in front of her. "Man, kiddo, I don't think I've ever seen you scared before."

"Dad was never dead before."

Capri pushed back from her worktable, finding herself uncomfortable with the situation she herself brought about. Emotional manipulation was part of Capri's plan, but the sobbing now coming from the girl was far out of her comfort zone. She sent commands for calming the girl down, but something pushed back. Henrie, or whatever else controlled her at this moment, wouldn't let the commands through.

The girl slid from the chair to the floor, hands pressed flat against the thin carpet. "I don't know what to do."

James scooted back to make room for her. His pristine uniform was fighting the unusual posture. "Your dad was always the one with the answers. We're all a little lost without him."

Capri kept pushing commands through, expecting that overloading the system would short out the other emotions dominating Henrie. Allowing Capri to get back on task. Both she and James sat waiting for Henrie to level out, watching the girl's palms grind into the carpet.

Henrie took a long breath in. "I need-"

"The Comps," Capri cut in. Unsure, and uncaring, of where that sentence was originally going. Her patience for this emotional detour was long gone.

Henrie coughed to cover her being tripped up by the command. "I need to know what's going on. What exactly are we fighting? Do you know?"

James's posture straightened. "We're working with everyone else. What the world knows, we know."

"That wasn't a very good lie."

He smiled, but not as warmly this time. "Henrie, you know how classified information works."

Henrie's readings shifted, now to what Capri knew was anger. To be more exact, rage. "Everything is always fucking classified!"

James held his hands out to her. "Hey, now listen. There's-"

"That's so goddamn unfair." Henrie stood, momentarily towering over him. "My dad is dead and I don't get to ask what happened. My mom doesn't get to know why her husband is gone. Thank you for his service, please be quiet. All because we don't have fancy little badges like you." She flicked at his uniform, Capri was impressed at this girl intimidating a grown man. "There are evil robots. Giant robots. Alien freaking robots, all over the city! You know I've been at every event, right? Watched The Hill disappear. Almost got shot multiple times downtown. Got my ass personally kicked around the other day. What kind of clearance does that earn me?"

He stood slowly, keeping his distance from her. "Henrietta, this is not something-"

"What are you doing to make sure I don't end up another memorial on my mom's wall?"

Capri held off sending any command, Henrie was on a tear of her own. As long as this led to Comps, she'd let her be.

James dropped his hands, Capri knew defeat when she saw it. He sighed, resigned to some decision. "You stay close and you stay quiet."

"Yes, sir."

Capri could tell that 'yes, sir' was as much of an automatic response for Henrie as it was for her. As they left the office, Capri triggered some dopamine to reward Henrie for a job well done. She could be kind when kindness was earned. She heard the girl sigh.

The pair moved farther down the hallway, coming to a guarded elevator.

The soldier here was also stopped from asking about Henrie as they stepped inside. On the next floor up the doors opened to reveal a fully open space, broken up only by sets of short walls forming small work areas. Several were occupied with people. As they entered the first row, Capri spied Pawn pieces.

James stopped them between two unoccupied stations, staring Henrie down. "You say nothing of what you've seen here. Is that clear?"

"Yes, sir." After a push from Capri, Henrie continued, "What exactly am I seeing?"

"Our best and brightest are trying to determine where exactly this all came from."

"Easy. Space."

He pointed behind them. "Elevator."

"Sorry. Sorry. Please go on."

"I honestly don't have a lot of answers for you," he sighed. "But I promise you, we are working on it. We are learning everything we can to protect ourselves from whatever these threats are."

Capri made her look around the nearby stations and spotted a flash of red behind him. She pushed Henrie around James and over to the table. Henrie pointed toward the chunk of Comp with nearly an entire deck attached. "These weren't the bad guys."

"Everything unknown is considered a threat. For now."

"You don't trust the Wardens?"

Enemy of my enemy, as far as Capri was concerned. Perhaps she could turn one or more of these agencies to her side. Or align their desires to her own, for however long that suited her.

"We don't know the Wardens. But we're trying to, this stuff is hard to crack."

"Says you," Capri laughed.

"Excuse me?" James asked.

Her elbow was pressed on the channel to Henrie, who must have repeated her words. Capri tipped Henrie's emotions, trying to replicate how she'd reacted before. Once she heard sniffles, she backed off.

Henrie turned to face him but remained close to the table. "I'm sorry. I'm a mess right now."

"No, you're not. This is only a rough patch."

"If you say so." She took an overly shaky breath and wiped away the tears Capri created. "I feel so...not me anymore."

"Grief is messy." James looked away, nodding at someone in the next row over, apparently now self-conscious about being seen in a secure military location with a crying teenage girl. Which was all fine, because that meant he missed Henrie tucking the deck away in her pocket. "You're dad...we all miss him. You're not alone in that." He shook his head and pulled his attention back to her. "Let's get you out of here."

Capri nodded Henrie's head. The ever-helpful James bypassed the same checkpoints on the way out. He rambled about having another family dinner night soon, but Capri locked Henrie away and wasn't listening. She barely bothered to wave before putting Henrie on autopilot back out to the car. As much as she wanted Henrie to immediately pull out the deck and confirm what components were there, she made the girl drive to the same warehouse used for all their drops so far. This saved her the hassle of having the Lenians create a new waypoint, they got so whiny about it.

Once there, Henrie released the cloaked Pawn from her trunk and handed over the deck. Allowing Capri to use its better camera to look the piece over.

Henrie stood locked in place. "Am I done now? This is what you wanted."

"We'll see. Shush." Capri thought the deck looked rather damaged. Human meddling probably ruined her chances, but she'd have to get the piece on hand to confirm. "Standby."

Capri left her room and shouted over the railing. "I need the teleport to pick up the Pawn at the warehouse. Send a replacement for sentry duty."

"Do you want the up first or the down?" Gregory called back.

"What?"

"You can't send something down the same time you pick something up," he sounded annoyed to be explaining. "Would you like the Pawn up here first or the new one sent down first? Takes about a minute to redirect."

She tried to think of any time she'd teleported from Outrider. Had they ever done both? She supposed that made sense. Capri wanted that deck. She knew the trip took a few minutes given how far from the planet they were. The girl would be fine. "Bring the Pawn up first."

Back in her room, she directed Henrie and the Pawn to the other side of the warehouse, where the actual waypoint was set. Then left for the telepad. She wanted that deck in her hands as soon as it arrived. The replacement Pawn bobbed next to her as she waited. Once the arriving Pawn dropped in, she heard the clicks of the system switch to prepare for the departure. Capri held her hand out for the deck, which looked worse in person. Components cracked and broke off as she turned the piece over.

Always too eager. Someone mocked her. She wasn't going to validate them by identifying voices anymore.

If the humans believed they could eventually crack this, she absolutely could with some time and extra care. She could pull apart one of her Comps and compare what exact deck this may be. Something on here would be useful to her.

A Comp dropped to her eyeline. *Issue!*

She briefly worried that the Comp was reading her mind, but pushed that–and the Comp–aside. "Busy."

This Comp switched to a feed coming from the other Comp, which showed her worktable. The table's display was shorting out, flashing lights distorted the feed's quality. That didn't worry her at all, let the table burn for all she cared. What concerned Capri, what got her running for the tower, was the sight of her Pak glowing.

19

Attack the Darkness

Mina sat in the beanbag chair in her room, idly flicking through socials as a way to pass the time. Knowing her parents were locked in to work at the Labs, she felt comfortable enough to hang at the house for a while. On their way back, Emma was informed that in order to get the okay on Mina spending the night she needed to run errands with her mother first. Mina offered to join, but Emma insisted she would be better off not going along.

As they'd dropped Emma off at home she'd said, "There is so much shop talk and probably confidential client stuff she's not supposed to be saying around me. I value our friendship too much to let her bore you to death."

Zane was due back for a family gathering at his aunt's house. Mina could have gone, but they were visiting the aunt who always asked if she'd 'met the right boy yet' and Zane let her avoid that situation. He also tried to skip, but there were out of state cousins coming in and his parents demanded that he participate. Steph was still at Restoration, but rehearsing a one-act play coming up soon. While the cafe was a public space that anyone could wander into, Mina figured it best not to distract her. Also, Mina couldn't guarantee she wouldn't stare without Zane there to pull her back. Sean was, well, she didn't know what Sean was up to outside of that he had the afternoon off. With a tap, the armband told her Sean was in the training room on Outrider.

With a press of her finger she was lifted off Earth and back in her favorite place.

"Welcome, Warden Mina," Nek greeted her at the landing pad. "I was about to message you."

Mina headed for the training room as Nek moved along with her. "What's up?"

"The Comps have decrypted the Pawn tracking signal. This will allow us to track any Pawns within the city, so long as they aren't cloaked."

Mina could tell Nek was disappointed that the cloaking remained an issue, but also knew they needed a win just as much as the rest of the team. "That's amazing!"

"We're currently sorting through initial readings. There are several caches all around the city."

"Which lines up with the Capri going after Comp parts idea."

"Correct. I'll have those locations noted and under observation soon. Comps are cataloging these initial readings so that we can focus on new signals appearing. In the chance of an attack."

"That's a good id-" Mina lost her sentence as she walked in the training room at the same time a suited-up Sean fell from midair. The cushioned floor and suit would take most of that hit, but the smack made her cringe anyway. She helped pull him up. "You okay?"

Sean dropped his helmet. "Yeah, trying to figure out the angle."

"Angle for what?"

A hologram appeared in the air from one of the projectors set around the room. A shimmering Sean took a jump at the wall, ran three steps to the side, then pushed off to send a kick toward an unseen enemy. The figure landed almost aligned with Sean's real life position, giving him a ghostly twin before clicking off. "You'd be surprised how hard that twist is."

"Oh no, I believe you. What brought this up?"

"I kept thinking about being stuck between all those cars last time. And your run on the wall with the Pawn pulling you. Be good to have a move to get out of those spots, ya know? Or to use more of the environment around us. So me and Nek were workshopping some things."

Nek rolled across the room. "This is one of the more feasible tricks."

Mina was surprised. During their bits of training, Emma always took the lead on fighting moves. Sean never once mentioned he was working on techniques of his own. "Do you do this a lot?"

"I mean...practice is always important."

"Yeah, but alone?" She was edging on pot vs kettle territory.

"I want to get them right before showing everyone."

"You should bring this up tomorrow during training. Let us take some falls for you."

"Yeah, maybe. If I can figure out the landing. Maybe." Sean kicked some invisible rock before rushing out the next bit. "I don't want it treated like a joke."

Another surprise for Mina. She sensed a pep talk in her immediate future. "Why would it be a joke?"

"Because a lot of what I do gets teased about. Not only here. Well, less here than everywhere else, but here too. I know I get overly excited. I just...I..."

She was surprised to hear him becoming upset. In Mina's mind, Sean was classified as a showman. Sort of in the acting vein like Steph, but he was always on. Always ready with a line or to steal a laugh when he could. He operated at this high level of go-get-it energy that she admired, was jealous of at times even. Her social battery took major hits on the daily, but Sean was always ready to entertain. Yes, that level of hype could come off as a little unserious, but Mina knew he cared deeply about this team. She remembered how hard he deliberated about his Guardian. How she'd convinced him to use the Kitsune he desired. That it was the Guardian he needed. Mina knew there was that same level of thought going about everything he did. Further evidence to that point–him being up here alone, taking falls to make the rest of them safer.

"You are absolutely in no way a joke to us. If someone says otherwise, okay so, I can't physically threaten someone outside of the suit, but I will sic Zane on them. I'm sure Emma wouldn't be too kind either."

"No one is outright mean, but all the teases kind of..."

"They add up. Like the bed stuff." He didn't look at her, which was enough of an answer. "I'm sorry, Sean. We shouldn't have rode you so hard about that. I can tell the others-"

"Please don't. Then it'll be weird. I'm fine with it coming from you guys, honest."

If she couldn't tell anybody, how was she supposed to fix this? Quietly, she supposed. Not going for the easy joke at his expense and pulling the others back when they did the same. She could do that. Mina would do that for him, but she wanted something to give him right now. "Okay, fair enough. Not a word. But, you have to do something for me. I want to know all your plans. Everything you are workshopping."

"None of them are ready."

"Don't care. Show me the messy sketches." She gestured to the line of projectors around the room. "Or holograms. Whatever you got. I'm in charge, so it's an order. Or, you know, a strong request. You think of awesome stuff. I'd love to brag that I saw them first."

He smiled, "Yeah?"

"You said you get really excited. Me too! And while I just told your cousin how much I appreciate her skepticism, it was nice having someone here that first day who was as excited as I was. Remember, you were the one that talked Emma into coming. Not Zane or Steph. Definitely not me."

"I can be rather persuasive."

"And persistent. You keep up that energy for everything, I find that astounding. Honestly. I get exhausted watching you go at the cafe some days."

"I like talking to people."

"And you come up with such out-of-the-box ideas! That wall move is smart. So come on," she loaded her suit and aimed for the wall, "tell me what you've worked out so far. Let's try this together."

They took turns chucking themselves at the wall for around twenty minutes. Sean was closer to getting the kick added, given his extra attempts, but she was more consistent on the wall run section. The trick was balancing out their boosts for momentum with the adhesive feature on the boots. Mina called for a time-out after a misstep resulted in her with one foot stuck to the wall as the rest of her hanging toward the floor.

As she massaged her strained muscles, and pride, Sean demonstrated a weapon recall function Nek mentioned during their workshopping.

Their waves bobbed along the wall. "I planned on introducing this in regular training soon. The reaction time needed can be tricky depending on the weapon."

"So I could have gotten the sais I threw at Capri back."

"Mmmm, maybe," Sean said. "There's a max radius that objects will respond in."

"Dang. Ah well, I stand by the toss."

Nek flared white along their panel. "A new Pawn signal registered."

Mina knew the other three were stuck where they were. This was bound to happen eventually, an attack that not everyone could answer. No time to fret over that now. Nek teleported them, along with Comp2876, to the site within ten seconds. With any luck, the others would get themselves free soon. Her worry felt unwarranted as the teleport faded and they looked around their immediate area. No signs of Pawns or Capri. All that waited for them was a boarded-up warehouse that must have been abandoned decades ago when Hurst started moving in the other direction. All Mina saw was rusting metal siding, the once parking lot well on the way to being gravel, and weeds.

2876 scanned anyway. *Figure inside!*

"That's definitely a place people get murdered," Sean said, pointing at a battered metal door with a chain hanging from the handle. A broken lock sat in the dirt nearby. Someone must have passed through recently.

"Pretty sure the suits protect against tetanus." She went inside first, not enjoying the creaking sound the door made in protest. Comp2876 came in right behind her, illuminating the space. The darkness inside the warehouse was thick, 2876's light didn't do much more than show what was directly in front of them. The warehouse wasn't empty as she expected. Given the piles of furniture, sagging boxes, and general trash, she suspected this place became a dumping ground over the years.

She switched her heads-up to a night vision they hadn't trained with yet.

All this did was turn the warehouse to a mass of indistinguishable shapes and confirm the entire space was a mess. They were better working off the low light. Which was fine, the night vision weirded her out a little anyway. Mina unloaded the one Daylight she'd packed as a precaution and tossed it farther inside as Sean came in behind her. The orb stuck itself to a stack of soggy, collapsing boxes. The impact tipped the already compromised tower farther away from them. As the boxes fell, slipping through the edge of the light, a figure moved.

The tumbled boxes partially covered the Daylight, now only giving a faint glow of help. They both ran into the darkness.

"You scared of us now, Capri?" Sean called out, he disappeared behind a row of cobwebbed shelving units filled with junk. Mina assumed he was trying to cut Capri off.

Comp2876 sent a bolt through the dark, but only connected with the opposite wall.

She wouldn't be any better of a shot right now. "2876, can you grab another scan for us?"

On it! 2876 moved closer to the ceiling and scanned the interior.

Their heads-up pinged with a point to her left, a lot closer to Sean than expected. "Hey, Orange watch your-"

The crash told her she was too late with the warning. Another pile of boxes fell and a rack nearly tumbled. She caught the shelves, but not before all the contents spilled out and blocked her entire path. Beyond the avalanche of garbage was Sean and, she assumed, Capri. Mina backtracked to where Sean split off, regretting having only the one Daylight. She unloaded one of her blasters and shot a bolt for a second of extra light. Sean was fighting with the figure, or more so holding them off. Her flash revealed him receiving a knee to the stomach.

2876 popped a message on her display. *Capri. Not Capri.*

"What does that mean?" The message kept flipping between the two as she made for where she'd seen Sean. "Either she's here or she's not."

Sean was thrown over a broken couch not far from her. "Help. She's gone feral."

"What do you-" she didn't get to finish because the figure tackled her and sent them both to the ground.

They were throwing punches before Mina regained her bearings. There was a shimmer to the figure that she barely caught in the dim light, some sort of black and rosy hue rolling over the person. Mina swore she could see a Warden helmet. However, being continuously pummeled made it hard to assess the situation.

Comp2876 came in with three more bolts, making the figure roll away for cover. Sean took a swing with one of his batons before the person pulled back into the darkness. That glimmer becoming obscured by all the stupid junk.

Sean pulled Mina to her feet. "You get a tracker on them?"

"I didn't get a chance. Is that Capri or not?"

"She's fully lost her mind, if it is."

Mina corrected her grip on her blaster and shot bolts ahead as she moved. Nothing stirred. Either because she was way off base or they weren't scared. She honestly preferred the former to be true. Sean held a hand out, the Daylight flew through a gap in some shelving to him. He tossed the orb in their new direction. Comp2876 followed overhead. The Daylight landed nearly at the figure's feet. Standing in a place Mina had most certainly been shooting towards, she could make out a scorch mark only inches away from the figure's head. She'd been right, the helmet was there. The suit was there in places, the entire thing didn't appear solid. Patches along their arms were the same hexagonal pattern, but around their torso and legs the material churned like smoke. Mina expected that if she got hands on the figure, the suit might pull off. Or that her hands would go fully through them.

We are not fighting a ghost, she chided herself.

"Capri," she called out, "You're less chatty this time." She didn't wait for an answer before shooting off a bolt.

The figure dodged to the left, behind another stack of boxes. Mina was sick of the endless hiding spots this trash created. Sean moved to follow her. Comp2876 hovered between them but maintained its glitchy message.

Capri. Not Capri. Capri. Not Capri.

Mina heard movement on the other side of a rack and shoved a section over, hoping to block one potential path and corner them for Sean. "Nek, any word on the others?"

"I'm sorry, not yet. We picked up Capri's new suit activation signal, but it keeps disappearing. Very bizarre."

"Very. Much. An understatement," Sean grunted out.

Mina found him once again up close with the figure. They were fighting him for possession of his baton, sending more knees to his stomach and erratic punches to his head as Sean tried to break free. She didn't waste the chance of landing a tracker on them this time, they wouldn't be hiding in the darkness anymore. The figure recoiled from the hit, losing its grip enough to allow Sean to pull the baton free. The odd shimmer intensified, bits of suit along their legs solidified. The extra glow outlined the smoky material surrounding them, revealing a humanoid profile. One she could now tell, even in this low light, was not tall enough to be Capri. Possibly a Lenian got the Pak? But from the little she'd researched they typically featured a lot more harsh angles than what she could make out here.

"Whoever you are, please listen to me. You don't want to side with Capri." Mina debated taking a shot, but found herself wavering on shooting a target she didn't know.

Sean swung for their legs, a move they dodged before grabbing him around the back of the neck and bringing his head to their thigh. As he stumbled, they pulled the baton from his hand, immediately putting two more hits on his back before he fully fell to the ground. The figure twisted the baton, releasing the scythe blade in the end. As their arm swung back for a serious blow, Mina rushed closer. Putting herself between them and Sean. The swipe ripped across her stomach. The suit resisted most of it, but a cold trickle down her side told her she was bleeding as her heads-up did the same. A kick to her damaged gut knocked her down next to Sean. Comp2876 took shots from over the racks behind them. The figure threw the baton and sank the blade in 2876's screen. Mina heard her best little robot clatter off somewhere in the piles of garbage.

The figure stood there, giving off a glimmer of their own. They didn't close in for another attack. Mina realized they were shaking. The person tensed and she prepared to block the next hit, but instead they took off in a sprint. Back toward the door they'd all come in.

Mina rolled over, her stomach angry at the effort, and pushed off the floor. "Stay on them."

Sean was back on his feet and moving before she was fully up. They attempted to follow the direct path back to the door the figure was taking. She watched the figure's arm clip a piece of broken metal, showing no signs of registering the injury, before they disappeared behind a pile of broken furniture. Mina heard the door's rusted hinges screech and saw a flash of light ahead of them before something passed through it. They were vaulting a broken desk when a Pawn came out of the darkness to meet them, slamming itself into Mina and throwing her back across the desk, breaking the molding wood further.

"Forgot there was one of you around," she groaned.

Her midsection was not having a good day. Sean unloaded his second baton and took a swing as the Pawn shot at him once before flying towards the exit. The Pawn barreled through the door, breaking the hinges out of the already weak frame.

Sean pulled her up. "Are you okay?"

"Yeah. Yeah. Get the bad guys."

There was a scream as the pair exited the warehouse. The figure was collapsed on the ground farther out in the broken parking lot. They held a hand out toward her and Sean, like they needed help. The noise cut off suddenly, the person now grabbed for their neck. The Pawn circled, keeping an eye on the Wardens until the tell-tale wavy lines of the Lenian teleport surrounded them.

In an unfortunate bit of timing, Steph arrived in the same instant the figure and Pawn disappeared. She rushed over, pulled Mina off Sean, and looked around for the fight. "What happened?"

20

So Your (Kinda) Girlfriend Might Be (Kinda) Evil

"Honestly, given what I do with nearly all of my spare time, it's shocking I haven't hurt myself worse before this," Mina said while laid out on a bed in the medbay.

There was a machine hovering over her stomach sealing up the short wound that cut through the suit, a rather clean line running from her left side over to her belly button. The machine was being operated by a Comp, she'd watched a little red robot slip inside the top as they entered the medbay. They'd numbed her stomach before she was even lying down. A Comp doctoring her in what was essentially its own medical mech suit would have been cool to watch if the team wasn't actively distracting her. They'd been a flurry of activity getting her and Sean here. Once Steph got Mina situated, she corralled Zane toward a seat because his breathing turned a bit erratic upon seeing Mina. Sean refused to get checked over. Mina knew he had some level of concussion going on, given all the hits to the head she'd witnessed him take, but once Emma arrived the pair teleported back down to the warehouse with another Comp, she believed it was 5712 that went along. She'd made sure to set the task of retrieving Comp2876 while there. As much as Mina wanted to keep her around, she sent Steph after them, wanting as many onsite as possible if that person came back.

"Not funny," echoed out from the trash bin Zane was hunched over. He hadn't officially thrown up yet, but the hard coughs told her that he remained on the verge.

"Just an observation," she offered up. Mina wanted to reach over and pat him, but couldn't with the machine holding her in place.

Nek paced the wall across from Mina's bed. "Meds are highly effective. Your injury will be well on the way to healed by this time tomorrow."

Meds, she assumed that was the name for the machine the Comp was using. That was simple enough to remember. "See? But a flesh wound."

Zane coughed over the bin. "Stop."

"Gotta get cut for the first time sometime." She was glad for it to be her and didn't regret taking that hit for Sean. That was what she was supposed to do. Given how that mystery person was fighting, Mina felt like they got off rather easy. They were targeted with their attacks, but almost feral at the same time. The erratic movement didn't align with the precision blows they'd landed when up close. Mina tipped her head to look up at Nek. "Have you ever seen something like that suit before?"

"Never, a peculiar sight indeed."

Mina raised her arms over her head to tap on her armband. An image of the figure sprang up from her Pak on her other side, looking just as glitched and obscured in the picture. That heavy fog of material clung to them and shifted as they moved, but never broke enough to see the person underneath. "Their suit wasn't fully there. How does that happen?"

"I'm unsure. Once the others are back, I'll look through any records we have in the database on unusual Pak behavior."

Zane lifted his head. "They haven't given any word of trouble, have they?"

"No. They retrieved Comp2876 and were clearing the other side of the warehouse. They sho-" Nek whirled tight before branching back out in a flash of colors. "They're back. Warden Emma is troubled."

Zane was on his feet heading for the door. "Do they need help moving her?" He disappeared down the hallway, calling out toward the landing pad, "Sound off, guys. What happened?"

There wasn't any answer back that Mina could hear. She impatiently waited as the Med taped the final edge of a bandage. She rolled over, pulling her shirt down as she moved, and jogged for the door. There was enough numbing going on that she didn't feel anything from the sudden movement. She found Zane hanging back in the entrance of the landing pad. Mina prepared for the worst, Emma broken and bloody on the floor. Unresponsive, if not…no, she wasn't going to think that. Nek would have told them if more fighting broke out.

Sean, softer than Mina had ever heard him, was talking as she neared. "Emma, take the helmet down. Please."

"We don't know the whole situation," Steph added. "But we'll figure it out."

Mina rounded the doorway. Finding Emma not battered as she'd feared. Their Silver Warden stood on the landing pad completely still with hands clenched. Her helmet remained up, so while it appeared she was staring at Zane and Mina, none of them could be sure. Steph turned to Mina, looking sorrowful with a broken Comp2876 in her hands. The screen was completely shattered and she could tell several decks needed rebuilt.

"Em, I need to know you're breathing," Sean said.

"Her oxygen levels are good," Nek answered quietly behind them. "She's-"

"Stop," Emma cut them off.

Mina took in Emma's posture, she looked ready to fight. No wonder Sean was keeping his distance. Something put her enough on edge to feel like she was in danger and, given the training they'd been doing, the rest were all equally on alert because of it. Emma was a person of action, she wanted to jump into a plan and get things done. Her behavior made Mina think she was conflicted over something, unsure of which way she wanted to move. Leaving her paralyzed. The mystery was what could throw Emma off so much? Mina couldn't think of anything, outside of a mention of her crush on Henrie.

"We'll figure this out, Em." Sean took half a step toward his cousin, who reacted by moving farther back on the landing pad. Her arms raised, ready to throw a punch.

Emma was about to break and she'd likely hurt one of them in the process.

Mina wanted to remove as many variables as possible. She put a hand on Steph's arm and nodded to their accompanying Comp. "Do me a favor, take 2876 to Fab. Let 5712 scan them for damage, get those parts going."

"But we-"

"Please. Go."

Steph nodded and left with 2876 wrapped in her arms, 5712 bobbed along behind her.

Mina pointed to Sean. "I want you in medbay."

Now he tensed up. "She needs to-"

"You shouldn't have left in the first place. You got hit hard, worse than me. Get looked over." Mina realized she sounded exactly like Sam talking to Henrie the other day. "We don't do 'I'm fine' up here."

Emma threw a punch at the wall, the sheet of metal bent from the impact. When Emma's hand pulled back Mina could make out the distinct outline of her gauntlet spikes. At least that was some energy spent on a wall and not a person.

Sean wasn't moving, so Mina turned enough to catch Zane's eye. "Please take him back to medbay."

No argument from him, Zane grabbed Sean's arm and pulled. Sean protested until Zane pulled harder and gave a quick, "She's got her, man. Come on."

Once they were gone, Mina moved further in the room. She stepped close to Emma, whose helmet remained up as she (presumably) continued to stare down the wall she'd hit. Without giving the action much thought, because she'd chicken out, Mina knocked on the side of Emma's helmet.

Mina's arm was twisted behind her back and she was bent toward the floor within two seconds, the gauntlet pressed in her back. A tweak in her stomach told her the numbing was wearing off. Mina held her other hand out in front of her to show she wasn't going to fight back. "You're good, Emma. Only us here."

Emma's helmet dropped, revealing red-rimmed eyes fighting to hold back tears. She let go of Mina's arm. "I'm-I'm sorry."

Mina straightened and rolled her shoulder. "Not the worst I've had today."

"Henrie," Emma blurted out.

Mina was confused. They'd only been down there for fifteen minutes, tops. Maybe Henrie sent some kind of worrisome text while they were there. "What happened?"

"Her car is at the warehouse." Emma's hands flexed and released. "On the other side from where you went in." One shaking finger tapped her armband, a small image appearing between the two of them. Mina recognized the car, the Texas plates being a dead giveaway. "The trunk was open. But she wasn't there."

Mina wanted to be optimistic, even if it was pointless, for Emma's sake. "Do you know any reason she would be out there on her own?"

Emma shook her head. "There was blood inside the warehouse. Some is from you and Sean, but someone else's too. The Comp confirmed everything was human."

She mentally ran through how much damage they'd inflicted on, potentially, Henrie. Mina saw the person clip an arm on the way out, not to mention when she'd stuck them with a tracker. Sean must have landed a blow or two given how much he'd fought them head-on. The suit hadn't fully been there, their hits likely went straight through that smoke to the person below. The person being, maybe, Henrie.

That scream rang in Mina's ears, had it sounded human? The attack hadn't felt human most of the time, more like they'd been trapped with a wild animal. Was Henrie capable of that? And if she was siding with Capri, why was she so unwilling to be teleported?

Mina repeated Sean's words from the other day, "Hell of a damsel you picked to save."

"Why help Capri? Why attack us?" Emma broke her stance, pacing to the other side of the room. "She did come to town right as all this kicked off."

That didn't feel right to Mina. "No, remember, her interview was the same day Zane and I went up The Hill for the first time. Capri wasn't awake yet. She's only been acting off the last couple days. Since the most recent attack."

"So how did Capri get to her? How did she convince her to…" Emma looked at Mina's stomach. "And she hurt Sean. How could she do that?"

"Like Steph said, we don't have the full story. But we will figure it out. We can't say for certain that was her. Might be a coincidence." She hoped, for Emma's sake. They'd all only Henrie for these last two weeks, but given how Emma's phone was glued to her hands when they weren't training she expected they were talking constantly. Mina suspected their intense training schedule was the only thing keeping Emma from asking Henrie out.

Sounds familiar, her mental Zane shot back at her.

Felt like major back luck to have your crush turn evil.

"Sure." Emma shook off enough of her shock to scowl at Mina.

"I'm keeping all non-zero percent options on the table for now. We'll get to the bottom of it. I promise." She stepped aside to clear the doorway. "Once they've got Sean mended up, we can go right back down and start."

Emma nodded, but didn't move. "We should stick together as much as possible going forward. If she can do that to the two of you-"

"I highly doubt she would have done the same amount of damage had it been you and Zane there."

"But if she can, we need numbers on our side."

"Fair enough, group project. Let's go make sure your cousin isn't concussed and then we'll go find your-" she caught a look from Emma, which meant she was feeling more herself, "We'll go find Henrie. See what's up."

21

Sometimes They Can Hear You Scream in Space

Henrie was in space and everything was bad.

That was the last complete thought she'd formed since being taken to wherever this was. Or more so, the last one she'd been allowed to have. The enraged blue-tinted woman didn't relent once getting hands on Henrie.

The initial grab pulling Henrie from the ground was forceful enough to make her head spin. That dark material left her as Capri (Henrie assumed this was the Capri those Wardens were talking about and not some other alien who hated her) shoved her against a glass wall, which made her feel cold and exposed. Henrie watched the material flicker and pull over the alien woman. The foggy substance solidified to the full black suit she'd seen once before. Henrie now received an extra close-up look as Capri headbutted her and tossed her to the ground. Figurative dots of light layered over the actual ones farther away. The number of stars she was seeing made it no wonder her knee killed from trying to smash that other Warden's helmet in.

She tried defending herself by grabbing Capri's foot when she came in for a kick, wanting to pull the alien down. The move worked on the Warden in the warehouse, but Capri was ready for her and pulled free of the hold.

Redirecting the next kick for right where she'd been shot. Or maybe stung? Henrie wasn't sure, there hadn't been time to check her side. Or the gash on her arm. All she knew was they hurt. So much of her hurt. Ever since leaving Earth new parts of her body erupted in pain, injuries she didn't remember gaining were now making themself known due to the agitation from her frenzied fight through the warehouse.

The pain was so distracting she didn't realize Capri was yelling during these first few hits. Capri threw Henrie at the wall, something on her back thunked against the glass, screaming in a language Henrie didn't understand.

Henrie's legs shook, threatening to drop her to the ground. "I can't-I'm sorry. I can't understand you now."

Capri grunted, knocking Henrie's legs out from under her. As she recovered from hitting the hard ground, she saw Capri tapping away on some faint hologram of a screen over her wrist. Before she could move away the alien grabbed Henrie by the shirt and threw her back at the glass wall.

The helmet melted into the neck of the suit, revealing the flushed blue face of Capri. Her eyes were wild as she pinned Henrie against the wall. This time when Capri spoke, the demand came through to her as an echo in her head, a full second behind Capri's actual speaking voice. "Tell me how you did it!"

"I didn't do-" Henrie stopped as her vision cleared enough to register the vast, empty, red span of planet outside this glass, which was biting cold on her cheek.

"How did you call the Pak?"

"Pak?" Henrie was pulled from the wall, she didn't mind that, and thrown to the ground. She balled up as Capri aimed another kick for her ribs.

"Answer me!" Capri screamed.

"I don't know what you're talking about! I didn't do anything."

"Lies." Capri dropped down on her. Henrie braced for more hits, but was shoved onto her stomach instead. Her ruined shirt was ripped open down the back. "You tampered with this."

"With what?" Her answer came via a massive tug on something between her shoulders. Henrie cried out from the pain, how her body was finding more ways to be in pain astounded her. This hit turned her head to static. "What did you-"

Capri ground her face into the cemented floor. "Stay. Silent."

One of Henrie's arms was pinned to her side by Capri's leg. A patch of the suit there flickered, she could feel the wispy material brush her fingers before pulling back to Capri.

"Is your toy broken?" someone called from behind them, the voice sounded amused.

"You can't play with them so roughly," a second voice called out.

Capri held a hand over the small box on her hip, tendrils of material formed the same sort of energy-gun-thing the other Warden used. Once solid in her hand, Capri twisted to fire at whoever was there. "Not the time."

No other responses came from the voices. Capri dropped the weapon to the ground, returning her attention to whatever was attached to Henrie's back. She stopped resisting Capri's weight and sank to the ground as much as she could. When Capri adjusted her balance, Henrie threw her entire body over to the side. The sudden movement tossed Capri off and freed her to grab the weapon. Henrie cracked Capri across the head with the side of the gun. She scrambled away on all fours, putting some kind of console closer to the building between her and the angry alien. Her entire body screamed, now too aware of all the damage she'd been forced to ignore the past two days, but she pushed back to her feet and took aim for Capri. Her dad taught her to shoot, all the while saying the skill was something he never wanted her to need. She'd apologize to his picture if she ever got home. Henrie pulled the trigger.

All the gun did was click.

"Handy trick, huh?" Capri walked toward her, not in any sort of rush. "See what happens when you touch things that aren't yours?"

"I didn't do anything, it just happened. I swear." Henrie pulled the trigger again, another empty click.

"The word of a ch-"

"You're the one in my head! You're the one watching me! You had to see. I'm not lying." Henrie debated sprinting for the building, hoping to find a better weapon inside. She could use the useless gun as a blunt object, but didn't want to risk Capri getting close enough for that unless she was forced to.

Capri bent over the other end of the console. Cold, dark eyes looking over Henrie. Her short hair was oddly tidy for how unhinged she looked. "I'm not in the mood to run in circles here. Speak."

"What do you want?"

"You swear you did nothing. Convince me."

Henrie fought a wave of exhaustion, not wanting to look as beaten down as she felt. She tried recalling that blur of a fight. "You left me there, waiting. The Pawn appeared. There was a shimmer in the air before the Wardens arrived, the Pawn freaked out and cloaked itself. Your device," she gave a weak wave towards her back, "let me move enough to hide inside the warehouse, but they followed me. I tried to get away, but there wasn't another quick exit. The one Warden was getting closer. They thought I was you. That little robot shot at me. I wanted to protect myself and that's when the weird stuff happened."

Capri leaned in farther. "What exactly?"

"I don't know!" Henrie pointed at the box on Capri's hip. "Stuff like what came out of there was all over me. Covered me. Was on my face, making it hard to breathe. Then the Warden found me and your, um…"

"Programming," Capri offered.

"Yeah. That said I had to fight. So I fought. Until you pulled me out."

Capri drummed her fingers on the paneling, the sound echoed around them. "All you did was follow orders from programming?"

"I swear. I didn't ask for anything. Your programming made me take it." Henrie saw Capri stiffen, pointing the blame back at her might have been an overstep.

Capri sighed, "I may have done too good of a job."

Henrie was thrilled to learn that the alien ruining her life was an egomaniac on top of everything else. Fine, if compliments kept any more of her ribs from being broken, she'd gas Capri up all day. "I did sort of go all Terminator on them because of it."

"Terminator?"

"We have it downloaded," shouted one of the voices from somewhere further inside the building.

"Yes, a rare example of quality human entertainment!" the other added.

Capri pushed off the console and looked Henrie over. "You haven't been able to call the suit while here?"

"No." Henrie now knew Capri hadn't noticed the flicker earlier, and she wasn't about to tell her. She also suspected Capri couldn't fully read her mind, something she'd been fearing earlier. "I think it's pretty clear who's had a worse time here."

Capri tapped at the band on her arm, a display appeared a few inches up in the air. The alien was reading something there that Henrie couldn't make out. Henrie pulled a fallen shoulder of her ruined shirt up. A rather pointless move, but she was too tired to care. The adrenaline was wearing off. Her entire body ranged from aching to fully screaming. She felt a sharp jab on her side and her hand went to the spot instinctually, her arm spasmed in pain from the actively bleeding cut. There was something stuck in her side, but she was too nervous to look. Henrie gave a weak pull, but the thing tugged her skin. Her fingers were slick with her own blood.

Capri looked at her through the translucent display screen. "I believe Blue got a tracker on you. Useless this far away, and under the Lenian cloak, but they're annoying little barbed things."

Barbs. That was the resistance she felt. Henrie quietly tried pulling the tracker out a second time anyway. "Yes, annoying."

Capri closed her screen. "I can help."

"I think the fu-" Henrie caught herself. What really were her options here? Essentially only various forms of death in space. Her side pulsed with pain, her head pounded, and something on her back twitched all at the same time. Henrie gave up. "Please."

The gun in her hand disintegrated into particles, forming a trail back to the box on Capri's side. The Pak. Meaning Capri could have recalled the weapon at any moment. Henrie expected she'd only been allowed to hold it for Capri's own entertainment. Look at the dumb human, thinking she had some kind of protection.

Capri pulled a small blade from the Pak. Henrie held out her hand, ready to do the cutting herself. All she got back was a smirk and, "Now I think the fuck not."

Henrie must have looked stunned. Or something on her face was humorous enough to make Capri laugh. In space with a lunatic alien, Henrie was a lucky girl.

Capri stepped in closer, the non-blade welding hand held up. "One small nick, that's all I need to do."

So this was how she died then. Okay. Henrie pulled up the edge of her shirt and looked toward the stars. She didn't want to see the betrayal about to happen. Didn't want to give Capri the satisfaction of looking Henrie in the eye as she stabbed her. She picked a direction, hoping home was that way, and waited for the alien to end everything. A short poke, a small pull, and the tracker fell to the ground. From the corner of her eye, she caught Capri stepping on it for good measure.

Capri backed away. "You'll need a bandage."

"Where-" she cleared her throat, "Where would those be?"

Capri pointed toward the building. "Follow me."

Henrie pressed a hand to her bleeding side, giving the alien a nod as an answer. Capri led the way through an open doorway. Inside stood two robots, as best that Henrie could surmise. They were darkly colored, yellow and green, and rather angular. The Tin Man's rich cousins. They looked as perplexed as Henrie and backed away as Capri neared.

"If your human pees on the rug, you have to clean it," one said.

"Maintenance will clean it," Capri shot back. "Watch your step, she's about to pass out."

Henrie did a self-assessment. Horrendously damaged, yes. But unfortunately conscious. "No, I think I'm good."

Capri touched something on her wrist. "No. You're not."

She could feel the shock that whatever was on her back sent through her nerves this time. Her knees gave out first, dropping her to the floor. Bits and pieces of her went numb in random order; a hand, a foot, her right eye clouded, and then her left ear became muffled. Her body shut down around her. Capri, looking rather pleased, must have done so on purpose. Henrie tried to say that this wasn't fair, she was behaving, but her jaw fused shut. In short order, she was trapped within her body. Her final shred of consciousness left to float in the darkness. A form stepped out of the wall of black, she recognized the MegaPawn from her dream. Somehow, she sensed other forms lurking beyond her range of vision. All waiting for their turn. Henrie knew this was more of the program's doing, Capri leaving her with nothing but monsters. As they closed in, even knowing the effort was useless, Henrie tried to scream.

22

Talk Things Out

Mina checked her phone approximately two hundred times while getting ready the next morning. They'd done a third sweep of the warehouse the night before. She'd tagged the car to know the second it moved. Along with the team taking turns staking out Henrie's house overnight, but she never came home.

Emma went for a run by the house this morning, but saw nothing other than Henrie's concerned mother looking out a window. There were no Pawns around the area that Nek could track, which felt like a good sign. Mina hoped this was a case of bad timing, Henrie merely having a rough few days at the same time a mysterious figure decided to start kicking their asses on Capri's behalf. But the evidence was not looking great.

Her stomach tweaked from more than physical discomfort as she pulled on her shirt. Mina didn't like that their new foe was someone from their personal lives. She didn't know Henrie well, but others on her team were becoming close to her. The person they'd joked about being a damsel made rather short work of her and Sean. If she was Capri's new minion, they had to stop her from hurting anyone else.

That's where her conflict came in, the guilt from the one tracker shot sat heavily on her. Fighting Pawns was nothing, bits of metal and wiring she could tear apart all day. Facing Capri was doable because the ex-Warden was usually shooting first, not to mention the horrible deeds she needed to answer for. This potential Henrie scenario felt complicated. Could she make the team take down someone they knew personally? She hoped something more was going on. Hoped they'd get a chance to talk with her before anyone else got their middles cut open, or worse.

The team's next move was staking out the cafe. Per Sean, Henrie was due for a shift later this morning. They knew she'd bailed not long after they'd seen her yesterday, a tidbit Steph learned from Megan, but were hoping she'd keep up appearances today.

"If she is the bad guy," Mina said out loud. Forcing herself to hold on to a speck of doubt for Emma's benefit.

What they did after that depended on Henrie's reaction. Best-case scenario, she was completely clueless as to what they were talking about and everything was a weird misunderstanding. Next best would be talking out whatever lies Capri told her about the Wardens. Above all else, Mina wanted to avoid a repeat of what happened in the warehouse. She hadn't told the others, but Mina and Nek put a set of Comps on standby if things went bad. They weren't about to risk more of the team, or innocent people at the cafe.

"Today might be the day you get outed as a superhero," she said, giving a final tug to her bun on the way out the door.

She heard machines whirring away in her parents' home lab. Who knew what horrible project they were working on this morning. Probably their stupid little brain wave box that didn't work. If she did come out of the secret identity closet today, they'd have a lot of the same questions she was tackling. Along with some other more nefarious things she'd never think of. Her response to everything would be "Wouldn't you like to know?", if she bothered answering at all.

Zane was waiting at the gate, they headed towards the front of his house. "How're you feeling today?"

"Good."

He clearly didn't believe her.

"I mean it!" Once in the car, she pulled up the end of her shirt to show the red line across her lower stomach. She'd peeled the bandage off this morning. "Nek was right, mostly healed. Ready for whatever happens today."

"Are we?"

"We have to be." She watched his grip on the steering wheel tighten as he got them on the road. "I don't want a fight, but if it is her, we have to stop her. Before she hurts someone else."

"What do you think Capri said to her?"

"Given how little Capri thinks of us, and human life in general, certainly a bunch of lies."

"Is there a way to spin 'I killed my entire team and want to enslave the planet out of spite' as a good thing?"

"She probably left that part out. Bet she told her that Nek is a big evil AI that wants to rule the planet and she's the only one trying to stop it. To her, we're the brainwashed ones."

"Remember when we kind of thought that?"

"That was only for like, a minute."

They pulled in the Restoration lot, which appeared in the middle of its morning crowd. Inside they found Steph and Sean holding down the front counter and Emma at her normal table with a laptop, fake working on something.

Mina stood at the corner next to Steph as she rang up a customer. "What are the odds of her coming in the back way?"

"Not high, but not unheard of."

"I think we'll sit up there anyway. Have the whole place covered."

Steph nodded as she passed change to the customer. Mina pulled Zane away from the pastry display and toward the back seating area. They went up the ramp and grabbed a table along the section that overlooked the stage area below. This gave them a full view of the balcony if Henrie came in that way while maintaining a sliver of eyeline on the front room. She'd be clocking in back here at the office either way she came, but now they'd have someone tailing her immediately no matter what.

Megan appeared next to their table while Mina was scanning faces outside. "Funny seeing you two here."

"We come here all the time," Mina said.

"Oh, no. I meant back here. Especially with the rest of your group out front."

Mina wasn't used to getting noticed. "Oh. Oh, yeah."

"Don't want to distract," Zane added. "Two on the clock and one working on a summer assignment. Gotta let them be. Us unemployed layabouts must entertain ourselves."

Mina almost kicked back that she technically was self-employed, but she couldn't see going back to farming stock footage anytime soon.

Megan laughed, "Well can I get you anything to drink?"

They gave their order and she headed back to the bar. Mina gave Zane a look, "You were pretty quick on the draw there."

He frowned. "Our recent activities have progressed several branches of my skill tree."

"I'm sorry to make you do that."

Zane shrugged. "I'm being whiny because of what we're here for. Honestly, it's done my nerves some good."

Megan dropped off their drinks and took Mina's cash. Henrie was due to arrive in about twenty minutes. She came up blank for small talk to fill the time and Zane didn't offer up anything either. Familiar silence didn't usually bother her, but she wanted to appear as normal as possible today. Mina pulled out the sketchbook and pens she always kept on hand, slapping them on the table. "We're testing new layouts for my room."

"Are we?" He picked up a pen.

"We need to make it look like we're doing something."

Zane drew a box on a fresh page. "Let me teach you about the concept of minimalism."

She grabbed a pen and immediately started a design on the opposite page. "No, absolutely not. I like stuff."

They were distracted enough with their competing designs that they missed Henrie's arrival time coming and going. An additional ten minutes went by before Emma texted their group chat, **Any sign of her?**

Mina craned around to look over the balcony, no signs of Henrie rushing up the stairs because she was late. The office door pulled open, Mitch popped out and asked something to Megan, who shook her head in response. He stepped fully out and headed for the ramp. Mina texted back, **No. We're not the only ones looking.**

She checked the car tracker, no change there either. If Henrie showed up to work, she was getting a ride from Capri. Or a regular Lyft, Mina supposed that could be an option too. When a scowling Sam appeared through the archway below, Mina downed the rest of her drink and made her way to the bar to meet them there. Zane wasn't far behind.

Megan was also there waiting. "Is Henrie with-"

"Nope." Sam stepped inside the office and snapped the door shut.

Megan looked from the door, to them, and back to the door. "Do you mind if I-"

"No worries, go right ahead." Mina sat on the last stool at the bar. "We're good."

Megan gave a tweak of a smile before following Sam, shutting the door behind herself. Ignoring the fact that anyone else back here could see them, Zane and Mina pressed against the door. Not that they needed to be close, Sam wasn't trying to whisper anything.

"No call, no show." They sounded like they dropped into the chair inside.

"Maybe she can't get here for some reason," Megan said. "You did say she could take more time off."

Being in space was a new kind of commute.

"She still needs to call!"

"Okay. Yeah. Maybe something happened to her phone?"

Mina knew where Henrie's phone was, sitting dead on the passenger seat of her car.

The office chair squeaked. "You're making excuses for her."

"I'm saying there could be something we don't know."

Join the club, Mina thought.

"And how would we know? Has she talked to you since Dad sent her home? Because she's barely said two words to me."

Several seconds passed before Megan conceded with, "She hasn't texted me back in a while."

"So she gets mad once and decides she can blow us off. Real mature."

Mina felt her phone buzz. She glanced at her watch in the chance Henrie's car was moving, but the notice was Zane informing the others about the conversation happening.

"We don't know everything." Megan sounded like she was trying to grab at something. "You need to calm down."

"I need to get to work. And so do you." From inside they heard the chair smack against the wall. As Sam yanked open the door, still looking back inside the office, Mina and Zane jumped toward the bar. "Morning rush is going and now we're short-handed."

If Megan noticed they were in a different spot, she didn't show it. With a defeated sigh she stepped behind the bar. "You two after the same or something different?"

"Same," Zane answered. Downing what was approximately half of his first smoothie to sell it.

They waited patiently for her to finish up their second round before snatching up Mina's things and heading to the front. Steph and Sean were locked in with customers at the counter, Sam stepped behind them and said something. From their reaction, they were finding out about Henrie not showing up. Mina sent a quick text, **Talk when you're free.**

Mina could see their watches light up, both checked the screen and nodded at her. Mitch came by with a tray full of beverages and snacks, her and Zane moved out of his way. They worked through the crowd to Emma's table by the window.

There was only one other chair, Zane pointed for Mina to sit. "I'll watch for something to free up."

Mina knew he wanted to be on his feet if Henrie showed up anyway and a fight happened, but she let him have it.

Emma flicked her laptop screen partially down. "So what do we do now?"

"We keep checking the spots we know. Here and her house. We watch for the car to move. Nek is watching for her phone to come online, in the chance she takes it and not the car."

Emma completely shut the laptop. "That feels like so very little."

Mina hated to agree, but she did. "So we're thinking Capri is after Comp parts with all those trackers, right? Henrie might be sent to those locations. We can check those out too, but they're pretty spread across the city. And most are heavily guarded. Be easier to do split up, but–"

"Not safer," Zane said.

"No. Unless we bring a batch of Comps down for backup."

Emma dropped her head and groaned against her arms. "More Comps on the ground would only make things easier for Capri."

"So we go together," Zane said. "But we won't know which they hit until they do it."

"Waiting for them to make a move isn't great," Mina conceded, "But we may have to." She hated the looks the other two wore, defeated and agitated. Mina couldn't blame them because she wasn't giving them much hope for things going forward. "I think we should work out what the plan is once we find her."

Zane finally snagged a chair and dropped down to the table. "Avoiding a fight, preferably."

Emma nodded. "Keep her talking, make her hear us."

"Keep her from activating that weird suit."

"Was that a suit?" Mina asked because she wasn't sure. "Or a full one anyway? It looked so liquid-y. Smokey. I don't know, but it wasn't fully formed."

Zane reached inside Mina's bag and pulled out the sketchpad, flipping to a fresh page and scratching 'weird suit' near the top. "She's got some kind of protection, that much we know."

Mine felt a small wave of concern about them talking so openly, but the overall noise of Restoration kept their conversation to themselves. Zane being the size he was kept anyone from seeing the sketchpad. "We'll need to convince her to give whatever she's using over."

"Or take it off her," Emma added.

That felt like the more likely option, given how their first encounter played out. Zane wrote 'Pak??' on the page and drew an arrow down to it from 'weird suit'. Adding a bold 'must be removed ASAP' underneath.

Emma shifted closer to the pad. "You think it's a Pak?"

"Wouldn't it have to be? Unless Lenians have their own super suits to hand out that look like ours." He added 'Lenian??' to the page, Mina appreciated the thoroughness.

"There's no way Capri would hand that over. Especially when she needs it to unlock her Guardian. Though," Mina leaned in farther on her elbows, dropping her voice to say, "2876 wasn't able to visually confirm if that was Capri or not. Nek said they only sometimes gave off Capri's new activation signal. The one she made to sneak back to Outrider. Maybe it's something duplicating the suit? More illusion than real."

Zane lightly wrote 'Magic??' on the page. Then wrote a small 'ask Sean' next to it. Mina grabbed her own pen and scratched out that bit.

"How much protection do you think it's giving her?" Emma stirred her drink, oblivious to their scribbles. "I watched the footage, she didn't seem to mind much until you shot her."

Mina glanced at Emma, seeing if she looked upset, but her face was the same furrowed brow she'd worn since arriving. "We'll keep that in mind. No one wants to hurt her. Or get hurt by her."

Zane tapped the pen on the pad. "A lot of this depends on where we finally catch her."

"True."

"Which we can't be certain about," Emma said.

"True." Mina felt the three of them hitting a wall.

Nek spun up on each of their watches. "I can work on some of the more likely scenarios."

"That might not be a horrible idea," Zane said.

"I'd like to keep busting their cloaking a priority, if we can." Mina felt awful turning Nek down, but she was worried about them overburdening themselves. She didn't want the team relying on Nek solving every problem for them. They were currently aiding Comps in decrypting more of the Lenian programming, but so far the combo of advanced Lenian technology and Capri's codework was proving to be impenetrable. "But, um, keep those

Comps on standby for us."

Emma arched a brow, but said nothing.

Mina needed the other two here. Sean would have plans of attack in no time and Steph would certainly coach everyone on the best ways to talk Henrie down. As she watched Zane darken his arrow pointing to 'Pak??' something deep in her to-do list stirred. One of the farther-off worries that liked to jab to the forefront at three a.m. "Different hypothetical, since this is a lot right now. Down the line, whenever we do get Capri's Pak from her. Who do you think our sixth person should be?"

"Do we get to choose?" Emma asked. "Or will the Pak choose?"

"I mean, we didn't do the normal process from what Nek knows and they worked for us."

"Yeah, but we also happen to be awesome," Zane countered.

"Sure, yeah. But shouldn't that mean we have some instinct for who a Pak would work for?"

"We could arrange some sort of Cinderella's shoe situation." Emma downed some of her ice. "See who it turns a color for."

"But don't we want to make sure it's someone who also works well with us?" Mina was apprehensive of letting a random person join her newly formed tight circle of friends. What if they didn't mesh? What if they didn't like her as the leader? And worse yet, what if they tried taking that position away from her? "I don't see the harm in having a shortlist of potentials. The first batch to test, secretly."

Zane flipped to a new page. "So who gets a chance? Sam? Michele might be cool."

"If we mess with any more of the staff here, we might shut Restoration down," Emma said. "Can we put an asterisk by Sam? They're generally cool, but I do think they need to learn how to unwind a bit." Their group watched Sam stomp across the room, picking up dirty mugs as they charged through. "And that's coming from me."

"Noted." Zane scribbled on the pad.

Emma brought up people they knew from the gym, Mina vaguely recognized some of the names. Zane and Emma then distracted themselves with the several people who would absolutely not be allowed to try out, there was a person called Mr. Macho McGee who was put down purely so that Zane could forcefully scratch them off the list. Mina remembered a story involving a month-long battle over 'the good power rack' from a year ago, Zane was apparently holding on to that grudge.

They eventually drifted off to other topics, the issue of Henrie too much for them to solve at that immediate time. Sean and Steph individually broke away from the counter, sneaking over to catch up. Each added names for potential team members. Mina planned on doing a little vetting before any real decisions were made. Having a list of people her friends could vouch for was a place to start, being able to scratch anything off her mental list felt good. She'd take the small win on a day that otherwise felt like a flop.

23

Can't Wake Up

Henrie wished Capri had killed her. She would have much preferred that to what did happen. Sending her back a full day later, having to face her mother.

The sliver of herself that remained conscious felt panicked and exhausted when Capri dropped her at the warehouse. She'd forgotten her car was here. Henrie wanted to plug her phone in and see what messages were there, but her commands were *Go Home* and *Wait*. There was no wiggle room, Capri's testing over the last day made sure of that.

Her body started the car and pulled away from the warehouse. Inside she was screaming, begging her hands to listen. To make a different turn. To swerve into the other lane. If only to prove that she could. The mental cage Capri crafted via code was stronger, harder to break than before.

Or maybe she was finally too tired. Capri didn't let her sleep peacefully for any stretch of time. Instead, she'd faced a parade of every horrible creature the twisted alien knew of. Each coming with the promise that these monsters were waiting somewhere far out in the stars. There was a species called Mooneaters who were eight-foot tall, cat-like beings. They were flesh and bone, but the one featured in Capri's memory had half of their head caved in and kept on fighting; she found that one extremely upsetting.

Every once in a while Capri would throw in a lecture about how right she

142

was. How much of a hero she'd be for returning with this planet under her belt. Henrie mostly used that time to snatch as many seconds of sleep as she could, but did catch one of those robot beings–Lenians, Capri often said the name like an insult–looking rather concerned as Capri raved about a Collective. The other robot never looked all that impressed.

Henrie pulled in the driveway. Her furious mother was waiting at the door. As soon as the engine cut off Henrie heard her yelling, "Inside! Now." More orders.

Her body appeared to do as told, but Henrie knew that wasn't because of her mother's influence. She shuffled up the steps and through the front door. Her mother slammed it behind her. She then grabbed hold of Henrie's arm, keeping her from going too far away. The device, the weight of which she now felt, allowed this because Capri's command ended here. She was home and could wait right in this spot if needed.

Her mom turned her around to look over the injuries on her face. "Henrietta Holt. Answers. Now."

Nothing good came from her mom only speaking one word at a time. A mix of intense anger and concern that she'd only ever heard directed at her father before now. Henrie wanted to tell her mom everything about the evil, insane, alien woman who lived on Mars with her robot minions and was ruining her life. Her mouth stayed shut.

"I am speaking to you."

And I wish I could speak back. She tried to push her hand forward and grab the hem of her mom's shirt to roll between her fingers, like she used to when she was little and nervous. Nothing happened.

Her mom pulled away. "Okay. How about I tell you what I know and you fill in the blanks?" She counted items off on her fingers. "You got caught up in an attack. At which you were hurt and did not tell me. You then broke into my phone to text Mitch saying I gave you the okay to return to work, which I did not."

Henrie wished she could blame that on Capri. She'd wanted to go back to work and shake off the weird feeling she now knew was malicious programming in her head. Henrie did feel that saying she broke into her mom's phone was a stretch, her mother's password was Henrie's birthday.

Her mom wasn't done. "You stole property from a government facility. An actual federal crime, mind you. One that James has endangered his own position to cover out of loyalty to your father. Whatever you took will be returned. Immediately."

Rather bold to assume that plan worked, huh? That one she could blame on Capri. Henrie expected her mom wanted her to hand over the tech right then and there, but that was back on Mars. Henrie knew saying 'I can't give it to you' would send her mom off, so this time she was happy to stay quiet. Which turned out to be fine, her mother wasn't done listing her crimes anyway.

"You didn't show up for work yesterday, without any notice. You've now been gone for an entire day without a word to me or anyone. And you show up, beaten to all hell, expecting me to accept the silent treatment?"

Henrie wondered how long it'd taken for her mother to realize she was missing. When her customary 'sorry, will be late, make whatever is in the kitchen' text went unanswered? Or when Mitch called after her no show yesterday morning? Or whenever Uncle James called to inform her of Henrie's crime?

Her mother didn't move any closer. "I do expect answers."

Henrie pushed timidly at the walls of her mental cage, afraid of the attention it'd bring. She knew Capri wasn't capable of reading her direct thoughts, but she was watching her mental status. If she showed stress, Capri would come looking at what was affecting her. The last thing she wanted was being forced to harm her mother as a means of keeping her out of the way. Her best-worst option was leaving, but the commands kept her here.

She took a risk and willed herself to move toward the stairs. Her body listened and got her to the bottom step before her mother loudly objected.

"Henrietta. Back here. Now."

Henrie stopped where she was, not turning around.

"I am your mother. You will answer me."

Even as detached as she was from her own body, she felt her heart speed up. The pressure of Capri's attention crept up on her neck, it felt a hand ready to wrap around her throat. She wasn't alone in her head anymore.

A tiny whisper, like Capri was right next to her ear, *Problem?*

Henrie shook her head.

Her mother caught the movement and assumed it was for her. She moved back to the entryway. "Oh, you don't have to answer me?"

"Let me leave," Henrie whispered. "Nothing has to happen here."

No, from inside her head.

"What was that?" her mother asked.

There was a knock at the door, several fast hits in a row. Someone eager to be answered. Her mother turned to the new sound, allowing Henrie a chance to move up the stairs.

Her mom was talking loud enough to hear as she escaped to her room. "No, Henrie can not come to the door. She will not be leaving this house for a long time. Goodbye."

Her bedroom door shut in sync with the front door. She turned the flimsy lock, knowing full well that if her mom wanted in, she'd be getting in. Henrie cautiously stepped close enough to her window to see outside, expecting to find Sam and Megan below. Instead she saw Emma walking back to her car. A hand twitched toward the glass, like Henrie might knock and draw her attention back to the house. Knowing Emma came to check on her stirred emotions she didn't want Capri to see. Maybe Henrie could survive this without Capri ruining every relationship she had.

Who's the friend? Capri asked. *We think she's cute, given your reaction.*

Henrie backed away from the window. "Leave her be."

Her shoulders spasmed from the shot of pain that ran between them. Capri was louder in her ear, *YOU do not give ME orders.*

"I'm sorry. Sorry. Please. I'm here. I'll stay here."

The doorknob twisted side to side. Her mom's too calm voice came after, "If you want locked in your room, fine by me. This is where you'll stay for the foreseeable future."

Henrie could follow her mother's angry footsteps down to her home office below. The pressure on her neck dissipated, telling her that Capri was no longer entertained by the domestic issue she'd caused. Henrie fell onto the bed, hoping that as she passed out this time Capri would leave her be.

146

24

The Plan Is Changing

Capri wanted to blame the girl for grabbing a deck with components that were fried beyond repair, but Capri knew she'd been too quick to act. Too excited at seeing her end goal right there to take the proper time to assess the piece. Or bother to examine others in that room.

She tried to salvage components as best she could. Unfortunately, the deck consisted mainly of tooling. Capri stripped the functional pieces to keep as replacements for her Comps should they need them down the line. She wanted to avoid asking for Lenian parts as long as possible. One chip did contain fragments of data, but only regarding Outrider. Nothing new to her. With some finessing, she extracted the layout of the main level. Once loaded on her worktable, she spun the blueprint around the elevator shaft and walked herself through the halls of the section that landed in front of her.

An alert came to her tablet. **Update on creations. Come down to the telepad when free**.

Why she needed to be involved was beyond her.

Think of how well this has gone so far for you. Keep the peace.

"Outside of the suit glitch, sure." Capri got up and headed for the door.

Outside Gregory and Maxwell were piecing together their monsters. Both were smaller than the first they'd made for her, due to the need for space during assembly. She'd been informed in a previous update, the compression could make up for the difference. Currently, both were a pair of feet and internal framing being joined together, but she'd seen the blueprints and studied up. Another grudge she carried was how many Earth animals she'd learned to make sense of their designs.

Gregory stood below something that looked like the cursed spawn of a lion and spider. Several arms would end in clawed paws. The billowing mane in his images looked purely cosmetic rather than functional in any way, but she supposed he could waste material however he wanted.

Maxwell's was sleek. A salamander crossed with a pincushion and stood up on two legs. No additional adornments there. She found herself struggling to locate the seams between pieces on the legs, his craftsmanship was that smooth.

Capri walked to the middle of the pad. "What is your update?"

"We are ahead of schedule!" Maxwell answered happily without looking away from his tablet.

"And?"

Gregory came over, ducking below two Pawns with a length of an arm between them. "We are on pace to finish late tomorrow. Being such, we thought it time to discuss where the duel might take place."

Capri was confused as to why she was part of this conversation. The entire planet was theirs to use. She gestured out to the vacant space around them to convey as much.

"But where's the fun in that?"

"Isn't the fun you two fighting each other?"

"We discussed changing the parameters of the challenge."

"Because he knows I'd win the original fight." Maxwell joined them. "But he's too proud to concede the point."

Gregory sighed, "You have a city you want to cause trouble for. We have monsters we want to test."

She felt like she knew where this was heading. "Go on."

"A contest of destruction." Gregory showed a small layout of the city on his tablet, their creations dropping in the crater before storming the city.

"See who does the most damage before being taken down."

"If the Wardens can even handle two," Maxwell added.

She doubted that. Their takedown of the first Lenian creation was as sloppy as the rest of their fighting. Capri doubted they'd practiced much with the Guardians since then. Splitting their attention also made it more likely to catch them off guard. Put them, and the city, in enough danger to force Nek into bargaining. "End of tomorrow?"

Gregory looked back at his creation. "Let's say morning of the day after tomorrow, to be safe."

Maxwell tipped out of Gregory's sight, gestured around his head, and mouthed, "Fancy mane."

Capri caught her laugh, but not by much. "Sounds good. Let me know if anything changes."

She left the pair to their work, all three of them remaining on good terms. Baffling circumstances, but she wanted to get back to the new target for her aggression.

Capri took the stairs two at a time back up to her room. Clearing the useless Comp deck away, she pulled up her feeds on Henrie; who remained sound asleep. Her commands put an end to that.

The girl shot awake. "Please. No."

"Yes. A task for you. A chance to stretch your legs."

"Please."

"Didn't you ask to leave earlier? I've kept you cooped up all morning."

"I can't help you. Didn't you hear my mom? They know I took that thing for you. The only reason I'm not locked up is because Uncle James covered for me."

Another failing Capri wished she could blame on the girl, impatience had been her downfall once again. "Then he should help you now."

"I won't be allowed anywhere near that room."

Optimistic to think she'd get to use such an easy avenue twice, but Capri wasn't too upset as there was time to kill. If the girl got eyes on one of the other buildings, Capri could figure out from there how to get hands on more Comp decks. She cut the girl off from her next protest. "I'm reasonable. A compromise. You'll be going out to do some investigating."

"My mom is here, I can't leave."

"I will give you one chance to find a way around her. Or I will make you go through her." Capri pushed Henrie to stand and watched her panic rise. "Clock is ticking."

25

Praise is a Hell of a Drug

enrie jumped from higher places than her second-story roof in the past, granted those jumps were toward pools or foam pits, so the height didn't scare her. She was thankful the roof featured enough overhang that she could clear the row of bushes next to the house. The landing wouldn't be great, but she'd get by. The escape would be easy. During their standoff, her mom neglected to demand Henrie hand over her car keys. Likely too distracted by her silence. Her mom hadn't left her office all morning, which sat at the back of the house. As long as Henrie didn't break anything hitting the ground, there was a high chance of getting to her car and being gone before her mom caught on. What held her up was not knowing what she was supposed to do after this jump. What crime was she committing today?

Move, hissed in her ear.

The pressure on her neck felt like a shove. Henrie tipped forward from the sensation and launched herself into the air. The fall was the longest of her entire life. She spent that eternity in the air wishing some nosy neighbor was watching out a window to catch her. No shout came as Henrie hit the ground and tucked into a roll. Her banged-up knee jumped to the forefront of all her injured parts, but nothing new added to the list.

She jogged over to her car; wishing for her mom to appear and not appear at the same time. The Pawn that usually followed her remained over the house, the shimmering halo around it told Henrie she was the only one who could see the evil box floating there. Capri probably wanted a threat nearby her mother to keep her in line. Henrie was pulling away from the driveway before the front door even opened.

Henrie avoided looking in her rearview mirror as she drove away, not wanting to see the shrinking figure of her mother yelling after her. "She'll call the cops on me."

You can fight cops.

"I will not!" Her head screamed in pain, blurring her vision for several seconds. She was lucky no one else was on the road. "They will absolutely shoot me. With full-on bullets. Not trackers."

She felt Capri sigh in her head. *Must everything be so complicated?*

Henrie held back her desire to tell the alien to find someone else to do her dirty work. Or to come down and do it herself, but her eyes still held spots from that last mental hit.

The next command took shape in her head, she was being sent downtown. *If time is limited, I suggest you get there quickly.*

What's a few more broken laws between enemies? She kept the thought to herself and hit the gas. Henrie was granted enough control over her direction to stay on residential roads for as long as possible, Capri understanding the tactic of avoiding more heavily traversed streets where authorities might spot her. Capri provided Henrie with a location for ditching the car, a public lot four blocks away from the building she was meant to survey. If Henrie's mom gave the police her license plate and car description, that would buy her a little more time.

As Henrie weaved between the construction materials and scaffolding lining the sidewalks, she realized why the route felt familiar in her head. She was across the street from Megan's apartment building. If Capri wanted in here, Henrie suspected there was more than a construction crew keeping Megan awake at night. Someone must have stashed a load of alien technology on one of these floors during the first attack.

She pretended to tie her shoe on one of the new benches outside the entrance, hoping there weren't a million cameras on her. "Only looking around, right?"

For now. Start with the perimeter.

Henrie hated feeling herself relax with the easy task, but did as she was told. She pretended to look over the building's registry sign, muttering under her breath about the number of reception staff and potential guards she saw through the window. Down the first side alley, she found a door propped open with a chunk of concrete. Just like she'd expected when plotting a fictional criminal days ago. Without needing a command, Henrie stepped inside and found herself at the end of a hallway. She could either go in the building or up a stairwell on her left. No other person, or cameras, were in sight. Take that, Sam.

A cool bloom spread from the base of her neck, briefly erasing the pressure of Capri's invisible hand. The relief rolled down her back, melted into her muscles, and dulled the pain throughout her body. Capri was rewarding her.

Henrie suddenly understood addiction a lot better. All the same, she paused at the bottom of the stairs. "Do you want me to go up?"

Not yet. Determine if there are other exits first.

Henrie was fully aware that her steps were lighter and mind clearer as she came back to the alley. While the other street entrance didn't look as heavily used, there was a bored receptionist and guard near the elevator to deal with. The second side alley was filled with garbage, she assumed the other side must have been cleared to make room for workers. There was a door here too, but this one appeared tightly locked. The Pawn could have snapped the locks easily, but this was her solo mission.

Henrie completed her loop at the bench around front, pulling out her dead phone to act like she was making a call. She hated that she was getting used to this. "Into the lobby or back to the side door?"

Before Capri could answer, a voice called out from across the street. "Did you forget where Megan lives?"

She looked up, Sam stood there with a Sax's pizza box in hand. They set the box on the roof of a random car, looked both ways for traffic, and ran across to her.

Capri was in her ear, *Problem?*

"I can make them go away. I swear." She shoved her phone back in her pocket.

The hand on Henrie's neck remained, but Capri was quiet. There was no command keeping her there, but Henrie froze all the same as Sam stepped onto the sidewalk and stopped on the other end of the bench. Henrie wondered how on some level everyone knew to stay away from her, must be something about her face.

They crossed their arms, trying to appear at their maximum disapproving level. "You've really let my dad down."

"Only your dad?" Henrie needed to be mean, needed to make them leave. "You're not holding any kind of grudge at all?"

"Being a no show is disrespectful of our time. And I've be—we've been worried about you." Their eyes darted around to the more obvious damage she sported. Their arms dropped. "What happened to you?"

She was too warm in this long sleeved shirt, as a petty starter. Henrie longed to pull up the sleeves, but the device stopped her. "Nothing I didn't handle. And maybe I blew off that job because I was tired of you lecturing me all the time."

"We're your friends, Henrie. We were worried about you. Your mom freaked when my dad called her."

The hand tightened on her neck, a command coming through, *Hurry Up*.

"I don't need any of you worrying about me. So how about you back off?" She crossed into their space, making them retreat and hit the cage surrounding a newly planted sapling.

Sam tried to keep standing tall. "So what are you doing here then? Too scared to knock on Megan's door?"

A laugh burst out of her; not from a command, but also not something that felt like Henrie's doing either. The sound was manic and exhausted at the same time. Her life had spun so far out of control, only to settle in a familiar spot. She pointed at the building behind her. "I'm casing the joint."

"Funny joke." Sam put the sapling more between them. "If you come back and apologize, my dad would give you a second chance."

"That would only work if I was sorry."

Oh, Capri whispered, *I like that.* There was a tiny bloom in her head. A little less pain holding her down.

Henrie used the boost to keep herself going and got back in Sam's face before they could respond. "I think I've made it clear that I am done with that place and done with you. If me telling you to back off isn't enough, I will be fine making you."

"What happened, Henrie? Talk to me." Then Sam made the mistake of reaching for her arm.

Henrie grabbed Sam's wrist, twisted them around, and used that momentum to shove them between the cars parked on the side of the street. Sam was only a step or two away from stumbling into traffic. They caught themselves on the trunk of a car and turned back to her, clearly stunned at the move. She could tell they weren't going to give up, but she had to end this now. Henrie stepped up to the curb, forcing Sam to remain on the street.

"Hey!" came another voice.

They both looked to see Megan, standing almost in the street herself. Megan looked concerned, but held the Sax's pizza box like she'd beat down Henrie with it if forced to.

Attagirl, Henrie thought and pulled back. Without a word, she started down the block. Away from her target building. She made another fake call to Capri on her dead phone. "I need to get some distance from them. I'll head back on the other side after a couple blocks."

Very well. Another bloom rolled through her.

Henrie suspected she was genuinely smiling. She didn't want to like following Capri's orders, but it felt good not to completely ache from head to toe. Even if she knew the feeling was a lie. Her peace ended as she came catty corner to the lot where she'd parked. Standing on the corner, waiting for the light to change, were Emma and Mina. Emma spotted her, a hand raising to wave her direction. How was she here too? Henrie did not have the energy to threaten someone else she cared about. Not to mention she was certain Emma wouldn't be so easily intimidated. Capri would end up making her do something worse.

Henrie turned and bolted up the block. She knew how fast she could push herself on a good day. This wasn't a good day, but she pushed all the same. Hoping she could get around the next corner before they crossed both streets.

From behind came a far-off, "Henrie! Wait!"

You're a popular one today, Capri laughed.

Her feet pounded on the pavement, carrying her around the corner and down the next street. The bloom burned up, leaving her limbs feeling heavy. Aching lungs worked harder and harder with each step. Henrie ran inside the cluttered alley and hid herself between a dumpster and a pile of broken boards. She yanked a large scrap of tarp over her head for what little good that might do her.

What are we doing now? Capri asked.

"Hiding. If they find me it's more trouble. Emma knows I'm not supposed to be here. She'll tell my mom and then the cops will be on me," Henrie rushed the words out before Capri could send any signal to cut her off. She didn't mention how her mom would somehow beeline for her once she knew Henrie was downtown.

No good help these days.

For a long, quiet moment Henrie was left alone in her depressing hiding spot. Listening to traffic and her own hitched breathing. She fought the urge to lean on the filthy dumpster and close her eyes.

I have to be honest, I'm rather bored with this.

"I can't let them-" Henrie's mouth snapped shut as her body froze all at once, there was no turning her off piece by piece this time. The alley around her blurred as she felt pulled from her body.

If you are currently useless, I'll have to think of something else to do. The hand on her neck disappeared.

Henrie knew she shouldn't stay here long. If Emma was determined to find her, she'd eventually come through the alley. She screamed in her head, hoping the activity would draw Capri back. The pressure didn't return. She'd been left like the trash she hid between, staring at discarded office chairs that had looked chewed on by every rat in the city.

Muffled sounds from the street filtered through. Henrie kept her ears out, as best she could, for anyone calling her name. All that came back were the sounds of the city around her. As much as she'd longed for peace before, the quiet was maddening.

26

That One's On Me

Mina never cared for downtown. The streets and sidewalks felt too small for the amount of traffic passing through. Add on the various ongoing construction projects and they were dodging people left and right trying to get eyes on Henrie. She'd barely held Emma back from running into traffic on several occasions. Not to mention the amount of apologies Mina made while Emma barreled through crowds without pause.

Not having the time to write out a text, Mina tapped the screen on her smartwatch to send a message back to Zane and Sean, who were stationed on the far end of the parking lot. "Sean, come give us a hand and check out the other side of the street. Zane, stay on the car. She might circle back."

A thumbs up came from both guys.

Mina didn't like having either of them alone, especially if Henrie was indeed the problem, but she didn't have much choice. There was too much ground to cover here and they were short one member with Steph being stuck at Restoration. Sean was supposed to be there too, but called out to give the Wardens another person on the lookout. Given that the cafe was running short with Henrie ditching, this was their best option for keeping up appearances in their normal lives. A compromise she was finding aggravating.

A message from Steph popped up on her watch. **Sam and Megan showed up. Sam is MAD.**

Mina wanted to follow up, but was too busy pulling a glaring Emma away from the window of a car with a woman who was vaguely Henrie looking inside.

Nek's waves filled the watch face. "I think this might be helpful. Linking audio from Warden Steph."

Sam's voice came out of the watch, "-shoved me into a car, Dad! She's dangerous."

Mina pulled Emma to the doorway of a tenant building. The pair huddled over their watches to listen.

Mitch was trying to talk Sam down. "Now hold on. Hold on. You came in real hot there. Start from the top."

"I saw Henrie downtown. I tried talking to her. Told her to come see you. She said she was done with this place."

Their voices were slightly muffled, Mina expected they were having this conversation inside the office. Which meant Steph was playing spy right outside the door. She wasn't worried about Steph getting caught eavesdropping, she was good at this kind of stuff.

"Did you say that in a nice way?" Megan asked.

"What does that have to do with anything?! I-"

"Hey," Mitch cut Sam off. "What she means is that you can get rather passionate at times and that can come across as..."

Bless Mitch for not being able to criticize his kid too harshly. Megan finished the sentence for him, "A bit much."

Sam huffed. "I think there's grounds to be upset with her. AND! Are we forgetting that she almost shoved me into the street?"

"What now?" Mitch asked.

"Yeah," Megan confirmed. "She pushed them between some cars. Looked like she might keep going, but stopped when I got her attention."

"Something's wrong with her, Dad, " said Sam.

"I hear you. Here, sit down. Take a breath for me." Mitch must have shuffled around to give Sam the chair. When he next spoke his voice was quieter, closer to the door where Megan likely stood, "How'd she look?"

"Bad. Like she got in a fight. Two fights. Sam said they tried to ask and she blew it off. And when she saw me, I don't know, she looked kind of wild."

Things grew quiet for long enough that Mina wondered if Nek had stopped transmitting audio, until Mitch spoke up again, "I'll call Henrie's mother and handle this with her."

"She needs to-" Sam started but was cut off.

"I will handle it. I know you three got close rather quickly and her recent behavior is upsetting, but if she's out to harm people you have to stay away. I, as your father, am telling you to stay away. She may very well need help. This is not something you are equipped to handle. Do you understand me?"

They both agreed. There was a faint 'oh crap' from Steph as the door must have started to open. Mina heard Steph stepping back toward the drink counter as Nek cut the audio.

Given that Restoration wasn't too far off from downtown, Sam and Megan could have easily gotten back there while the team was searching. They needed to figure out where exactly the other pair saw Henrie. That might give them a smaller radius to search.

She sent a message to everyone. **Where could they have seen her?**

Sean waved at them from across the street and spoke directly at his watch. "Megan lives somewhere downtown, but I'm not sure where."

Steph's name popped up with three dots, but Nek beat her by a second. "Eldenwood Heights."

Mina opened the navigation app on her phone, the apartment building was a couple blocks down on the street behind them. Was Henrie going to talk to Megan until Sam's confrontation ran her off?

A small exclamation point appeared on the building across from Eldenwood Heights. Mina tapped the marker, a message from Comp2876 scrolled across her screen. **Pawn parts stored inside!**

Mina gave the message a little double tap. "That's what she was going for."

"Still could be." Emma headed toward the building in question.

Mina motioned for Sean to follow after them. A voice message from Zane loaded in, "Update. Henrie's mom is here. I caught something about her getting the car back home. Still some cops around. Gonna head your way now."

Sean crossed at the corner to join Mina and Emma. "Only way she's getting out of downtown is walking. Well, we can hope."

Steph texted, **Please don't get caught by cops.**

Sean answered her first, **That's why we made the white guy watch them.**

Zane responded immediately, **It was a privilege.**

Steph sent a bu-dum-tsss gif.

Mina and Sean held Emma back until Zane caught up. He must have jogged the whole way, as quick as he appeared. She watched a patrol car roll by on the street as the four of them neared the target building. They needed to find Henrie before the police did.

"How do we wanna do this?" Sean asked, looking up the side of the building.

"How many of these floors do you think we can get on without being questioned?" Zane looked over the placard naming every business leasing space inside.

Mina checked the board out too, one in particular caught her attention. "Polymetis, that's another name for Hephaestus. No way that's a coincidence."

Their people must have stashed parts here right after the attack and bought the floor later. Better to keep alien technology away from the main office, plausible deniability of them doing any meddling.

"Do you know that because of a phase when you were twelve thing or a sucky parent thing?" Sean asked.

"Little column A, little column B. Point being, they're going to be the ones holding the Pawn parts." Which skyrocketed this building to near the top of Mina's list of things to take care of. Hephaestus made enough ill-intended tech of their own. They didn't need any help from aliens.

Emma huffed at the sign. "Which means if they have any kind of security set up, three of us are already blown."

"We could look around outside. Check for side entrances," Zane offered. "If she's in there, she'll have to come out."

Mina pointed to the nearest alley. "Stay together. Let's see what we can find."

Emma took the lead without a word, kicking at debris as they went. Once their group was fully inside the alley, Mina risked a grab for her Pak. Her tiny recon Comp might get them more information about this problematic Hephaestus outpost. She'd stripped everything out but the scanning tool and propulsion pack to make the mini-Comp as trim as possible. With a few taps the smallest Comp in the swarm appeared in the air next to her.

"Stick close, Spud," she whispered to the little robot. Mina hadn't told anyone she named the micro-Comp, figuring they might find that a little too much, but Spud did look like a tiny baby red potato with a jetpack. She'd name all the Comps if they let her, but the swarm was rather content with their number designations. "I may have work for you in a minute."

Spud bobbed as an answer, moving to hover over her right shoulder. If anyone spotted them, she could shove Spud in her bun.

Emma stopped short of passing a dumpster halfway through the alley. She dropped to a crouch and pulled a tattered tarp away. "Henrie?"

Zane and Sean stopped farther back, giving her space. Mina tapped her armband to move Spud behind her back but stepped around the guys. She awkwardly pushed over a rotten chair with her foot to stand beside Emma. Henrie sat on the ground, knees pulled to her chest, and arms hanging limp at her sides. Looking at Henrie made Mina remember why she never bothered making robots with human faces; the eyes were always impossible to get right. That uncanny valley was a challenge she chose to avoid. More often than not you ended up with something that felt hollow, which is how Henrie appeared right now. While it looked like she was staring back at Emma, no one was home inside Henrie's head.

Emma picked up on this too, she reached out and put a hand on Henrie's shoulder. "Hey, Henrie, can you hear me?"

"Is she unconscious?" Zane asked from the other side of the dumpster.

Mina gave the smallest shrug she knew he would see.

Emma shook Henrie gently. "Can you talk to me, please?"

Henrie didn't shift, didn't budge. The tarp bundled up next to her moved more than she did. Mina realized she had yet to see the girl blink.

"We want to help you, Henrie. But you need to talk to us." Emma put her other hand on Henrie's arm and shook harder. "Please say something."

Sean finally moved close enough to see Henrie. "Is, um, Em, is she breathing?"

Emma stopped her shaking and held the back of her hand under Henrie's nose. They were all quiet. "It's shallow, but yeah."

Something was going on with her, that was certain. If this was Lenian or Earthly influence, Mina couldn't be sure. She tapped her armband, pushing Spud back over her shoulder. "Emma, let me scan her and see what Nek can make of it."

Emma tilted out of the way, her hands still holding Henrie's. "If it's bad, can we take her to the medbay?"

Mina watched Spud run its little scan, not feeling comfortable about making that call on her own. "Let's see what Nek says first."

Nek's waves filled the small screen. "One moment, everyone."

Henrie blinked, an action Mina only caught because she'd been waiting for it to happen. Moreso, her eyes focused and snapped to attention. Not on Emma, but on Mina. No, she realized, not on her. Over her shoulder. Henrie was looking at Spud. Then she started to laugh.

Emma moved closer. "Henrie, hey, talk to me. What happened?"

Henrie pulled her hands away. "This girl has been better for me than expected."

That didn't sound good.

A flash came from Nek. "There's something unusual on her ba-"

Mina didn't catch the rest of the sentence because she was too busy watching Henrie grab hold of Emma's head and shove her into the dumpster's side. The clang from skull meeting metal rang out through the alley.

Henrie's eyes snapped back toward Mina, this time down at her wrist. "Nek! I found your new baby Wardens."

Capri. Not Capri. Capri inside Henrie's head. That was bad.

Sean immediately moved to grab the stunned Emma as Henrie attempted to bash her head against the dumpster a second time. Zane grabbed the side handle and pulled the entire dumpster away, giving Mina more room to close in. Henrie kicked out at her knee, Mina dodged the hit but tripped on the pile of junk boards piled on Henrie's other side. Before Mina could recover, Henrie stood with that tarp in hand. She wrapped a length around Mina before knocking her feet completely out from under her. Mina fell back on the lumber pile. Something stabbed in her back as she tumbled toward the wall, effectively wrapping herself further in the tarp.

"Henrie, hold on," Emma pleaded. "Let's talk."

"Not Henrie," Mina grunted from her plastic cage. There was more fighting going on between the remaining four. She moved to sit up, a board coming with her before she felt what was definitely a nail pull out of her back. Her injury protested loudly as she fought to find the edge of the tarp. So much for not needing a tetanus shot.

"Calm down," Zane said. "We want to help."

A board was pulled from the pile below her. A grunt told her Henrie was the one swinging. A thud and a groan from Sean followed, he must have caught the hit. He coughed out, "Whatever she said about us, it's a lie."

"I don't need to bother lying about you," Henrie growled.

Mina was sick of being caught in this tarp. When her struggle finally revealed brick and not more blue, she pulled her Pak from a pocket. Hoping that she'd appear intimidating as she stood and the suit formed around her. Maybe Sean would appreciate the showmanship. As her heads-up display rolled out, she noticed the aching spot on her back numbed. That was helpful.

Henrie, twisting Emma's arm at a nasty angle and a length of lumber keeping Sean at bay, looked at the Warden now standing in front of her. "Blue! Mina Willow. Good to know."

"Capri, let her go." Mina gained some extra appreciation for the modulated sound of her voice, she felt it gave her a more authoritative sound.

"Which her?" Henrie raised the wood, ready to take another swing at Emma with it.

Emma, one split eyebrow clouding her vision, shook off enough of her dazed condition to free herself from Henrie's grip. While she didn't appear happy to see Mina suited up, she nodded and unloaded her own. She used a boost to jut forward and throw her shoulder in Henrie's stomach before the silver band settled along her side. Giving her enough kick to pick Henrie up off her feet and put her back in the wall. There was an unexpected metallic scraping sound that accompanied the hit.

Henrie groaned and the wood fell from her hand. "Silver. Emma Upton. Hello to you too."

Nek's circle of ribbons appeared on Mina's display. "There is a device on her back. I believe Capri is controlling her."

Henrie was pounding on any part of Emma she could reach, not caring that little was getting by the suit. Her eyes, Mina wasn't sure why she was bothering to notice, remained vacant all through her attacks. She wasn't doing this.

Emma pulled them away from the wall, throwing Henrie to the ground. She went to pin Henrie, but the other girl rolled away and pushed up to her knees. Sean tried for a grapple, but Henrie broke his hold and almost knocked him down before he managed to break away.

Zane unloaded his suit and hooked his arms under Henrie's. This pulled her the rest of the way up, but their height difference took her feet off the ground. Henrie threw her weight back at him, thrashing in his arms. Her feet trying to kick out his knees. Emma tried grabbing her legs, but Henrie caught her in the chest and shoved her back toward Mina. One arm slipped from Zane's hold and allowed her to turn and pummel his, thankfully, now helmeted head. Zane dropped her as smears from bloody knuckles smudged the surface. Henrie redirected for Sean, who was the last without his suit. He activated his Pak right as Henrie's hands went around his throat.

"Green and Orange. Zane Winger and Sean Kane. Wonderful. So that leaves Purple to be," Henrie paused from bashing Sean against the wall, "Stephanie Diaz. Am I right?"

So that was that, Capri knew all of their names. Mina's stomach dropped into her boots. This was all getting too close to home. She refocused on the fight, which was currently only with the Capri-controlled Henrie. No Pawns popped up to ambush them this time. They needed to stop her here.

Emma pulled Henrie off of Sean and took a full-on swing at her face, but missed as Henrie ducked under and kept right on running for Mina. She used a boost to offset Henrie, shoving the girl back into the dumpster's side. There was another ear piercing sound of metal on metal as Henrie crashed to the ground. Maybe they could break whatever was on her back, preferably without breaking her actual back.

Zane was on her next, twisting one arm until Henrie turned onto her stomach. He pulled her other arm behind her back. "Henrie, you gotta stop. You're hurting yourself."

"She wo-" Henrie struggled underneath him, "won't let me."

That sounded different to Mina, sounded like Henrie. She'd mentally come back to the surface, while her body kept fighting them. Zane heard it too, as he pulled Henrie back to her feet he said, "Listen, we can he-"

His words were cut off by Henrie throwing her head back at his helmet. Her frenzied struggle stopped and her head dropped forward. She'd stunned herself with that last hit.

Zane tipped from the impact, but kept his hold. Mina pulled back the collar of Henrie's shirt while they had a chance. Between her shoulders sat a flat square of green metal. Two tendrils stretched out towards her arms with a third going down her back. The edges were black and crusty, Mina thought it was corrosion until she realized they were outlined in dried blood. This device wasn't simply on her, but latched in.

"Nek, I don't think we can do this here." The angle was awkward, but Mina reached in to test how secure a corner of the block was.

Henrie screamed as she came back to life. Mina and Zane were thrown by some force, knocking them into Emma and Sean. They untangled from each other in time to see that black mist rolling out from Henrie's back. A rosy vine circled her head.

Henrie kept screaming, but not at them anymore. "I'm sorry! Capri, I don't want it. Take it back!"

Emma stepped closer. "Henrie, let us help."

Henrie ripped the dumpster lid off its hinges and swung at Emma. The smoky suit billowed out and back in around her body. "I didn't do it, Capri.

I swear!"

Zane went to tackle her, but Henrie sidestepped and pushed him into the broken chairs. They needed to get out of this alley. Henrie must have agreed because she dropped the lid and ran for her nearest exit.

Emma was the first to sprint after her. "Henrie, come back!"

Mina was as close behind as she could keep herself. They charged onto the sidewalk, finding several people watching the smoke-covered figure that was Henrie. One that stood out was Henrie's mother, who'd been not far off from the alley when they ran out. Hopefully that partial suit was enough to keep her from recognizing her daughter running by. She heard the guys behind her and expected Zane would pass her as soon as he got his stride under him. Mina realized where Henrie was headed as they rounded another corner. They weren't far off from the intersection where the Wardens had their fight with Capri, where she'd been taken away by the Lenians. Assuming their teleport systems worked similarly, getting her back to that point was an easier exit than making a new target while they were all fighting. "We gotta grab her before they pull her away!"

As expected, Zane passed her as Henrie ran straight for the traffic ahead of them. Cars slammed their brakes to avoid her, some only doing so by inches. He and Emma were closing in as Henrie reached the next corner and turned onto the street she needed. Someone behind them was demanding they stop. Mina looked back to see two cops desperately trying to keep up.

Sean turned fully around, running backwards along the street. "Not your jurisdiction!"

They both hit a boost to catch up with the others. Emma snagged one of Henrie's arms and tried pulling her to the sidewalk. Henrie countered her momentum and threw Emma at a car parked across the street. She took off again without missing a step. Her smoke-suit formed the bottoms of the boots and partial cover for her back, the rest remained a swirling mass around her body. Zane hopped on the hood of an oncoming car, ran the length of it, and launched himself at her. Knocking Henrie to the ground and rolling them into the very intersection Mina wanted to avoid.

Emma joined, trying to pin her. Henrie pulled hard against both of them.

Sean and Mina stood back, ready to jump in if Henrie broke loose again. The street cops were nearly two blocks back, but other sirens were coming from several different directions now.

"We need to get her out of here," Mina said.

"There's interference. I can't get a lock on you." Nek became a tight ball of color in the corner of the display. "I fear the Lenians have beat me to it."

A heat signature registered in her system, the Lenians sending their teleport like she feared. Henrie kicked and screamed, reaching for the spot where the Lenian teleport was beginning to appear. Emma let her go, Mina couldn't blame her. That scream sounded like the throat tearing kind you only ever want to hear in a horror movie. She twisted enough to get a foot under Zane and shove him off. Once free, Henrie dove for the teleport. The defective suit pulled tight, forming more solid pieces before Henrie disappeared completely. Leaving the Wardens standing there with what felt like everyone in downtown Hurst closing in on them.

Nek spoke softly from their displays. "I'll have you out in six seconds."

She expected the time would feel longer. Figured there'd be an eternity of people shouting, car horns blaring, and sirens ringing in her ears. Thought the cops might finally catch up and make a new problem for them. But it was six seconds. Her vision blurred and she turned weightless before anyone got near them.

27

This Would be a Good Spot For a Villain Song

Capri tried to load out her suit as the girl landed on the telepad, but for the first time since the day the Pak was handed to her, nothing happened. The pad flashed white before darkening to black. The girl stood before her, covered in the broken suit that belonged to Capri. One full leg was fully formed, a span across her middle took shape as Capri circled her. A dim pink coloring was trying to settle along her back, following the lines of the Lenian device.

Henrie turned to keep Capri in front of her, the vapor taking the shape of a helmet broke apart and reformed as she moved. "You have to listen to me, Capri! I don't want it. You called them out. I was getting hurt, but I didn't call for it. I swear!"

Capri found that hard to believe. To be in this situation for a second time in almost as many days was not favorable. She grabbed Henrie's wrists, thinking to pull her inside the building. While one hand felt the familiar rough texture of the suit, the other passed through to skin. A bizarre experience she would've been intrigued by were the situation happening to anyone else.

Henrie dropped to her knees. "Take it back. Please. Please take the suit back!"

Capri expected the material to return to her Pak like the first time. Pieces were, but much slower than before. Given the level of panic Henrie was showing, she realized whatever glitch in the program was causing this must think the girl needed protection. She dropped Henrie's wrists and stepped back, using her armband to force Henrie to calm down. The girl slumped more to the floor, the material pulled away from her faster. As Henrie became partially visible, Capri activated the Pak. This time the material jumped to the command, a sight that soothed Capri, and pulled across the space to fully form around her.

Henrie kept rambling. "I was waiting. Ri—right where you left me. I heard them, b-but I couldn't move."

With the girl hidden away, Capri assumed they could wait out any search party and simply investigate the building at night. She'd left to make food and came back to find people had stumbled upon Henrie and were attempting to wake her up. Thinking they were nothing more than concerned friends, Capri watched to see how long they'd stay at it. Then Blue - Mina - used that minuscule Comp to perform a scan and Capri's system registered the signal. The recon Comp was impressive, small enough that she'd missed it on the girl's feed until that moment.

Running a quick facial recognition program through Henrie's social media accounts gave Capri exactly what she wanted. The faces, better yet the names, of Nek's new team. Without having to mess around with any more breaking and entering. Aside from the suit glitch, the human proved worth the trouble.

Capri dropped her helmet. "I believe you."

Henrie sat on the floor. "You do?"

No. Not entirely. But Capri possessed the intel she desired, that was the important part. Glitch or no glitch, the Pak and suit were hers. She'd proven so right now. The girl never called the full suit either time, but had now held her own in a fight against four Wardens with only the partial suit as aid. Them being poor excuses for Wardens aside, that was useful to Capri. She was in short supply of useful.

"This," she pointed to the Pak on her side, "means a lot to me. This malfunction between us is…upsetting."

Henrie stayed on the ground, inching back to put more space between them. She looked at the Pak, but Capri sensed she was weary to ask more. One side of her face was scrapped up, from one of the several hits against the brick walls she'd taken during that fight. One of the Lenian clips hung broken and tangled in her hair. While she rested back on one hand, the other laid in her lap. Likely tender from those hits she'd made directly at Green's - Zane's - helmet. The back of her head couldn't be faring well either. Her toy needed more mending.

She held a hand out to the girl. "Let's get you bandaged."

Henrie didn't move. She'd looked past Capri to Maxwell's towering creation behind her. Not fully completed, nor at their full height, but Capri knew the creations were a sight to see up close for the first time. How old had she been? Eight, maybe, when they showed them the dormant Lenian creation, used as a display, at the Collective's facilities. Capri wasn't proud to admit she'd been scared that day, thinking the monster would lunge at her if she looked away. Snatch her up and steal her chance to become a Warden.

Henrie's face reflected that same mix of awe and fear as she looked up to Gregory's creation directly above her. Capri nudged the girl with a foot to pull her attention back, her hand still out. "They won't move anytime soon."

The girl pulled her eyes away from the lion's head being set into place. "Last time you-"

"I did bandage you. Correct?"

"Yes." Henrie didn't take her hand, but rolled to the side and pushed herself up. She waited for Capri to move first.

Capri walked them inside and heard Henrie suck in a breath as they cleared the doorway. She'd keep the girl on her feet this time. The Lenians whined about carrying her when Capri refused to pull her out of lockdown before. A Comp swooped down from above to join them. The girl didn't flinch, simply clocked the new addition and kept along with Capri. The trio moved through the main floor. The base contained no official medbay, Lenians could simply repair themselves in one of the dozen workshops. They passed the dining room where Maxwell and Gregory were having their meal. Two shiny foreheads poked around the doorframe as Capri led the human towards the row of private quarters.

She flicked on the light in a room and pointed back to what passed as a bathroom by Lenian standards. Capri preferred the sparse facilities in her escape pod. "The water pressure is atrocious, but it'll have to do."

Henrie cautiously stepped in the room, taking in all the bolted-down metal furniture. She turned back to Capri. "Are the robots made of the same stuff the building is made of?"

"No. Theirs is an organic material. While metallic in structure, the substance grows naturally in their home system. Their kind are crafted and sent out to be nuisances all over the galaxy." She looked around the place, the hard pad that Lenians wrongly referred to as a bed in this particular room did match Gregory's coloring. Capri could see how one could think the two were the same. "But I can see your confusion. They are overly attached to the color scheme."

Henrie walked in the bathroom and started to push the door closed. Capri sent the Comp to catch it. "You understand I can't leave you completely alone?"

"Yes," came from the other side of the door.

"Be mindful of my device. You know how it dislikes being touched."

Henrie's 'okay' came even quieter this time.

"I'll have a Comp bring you supplies for when you're out."

There was a long wait before a faint, "Thank you."

Capri left the door open behind her and tapped out the order of bringing bandages and the drabbest set of clothing on hand. She knew the displeasure of walking around in blood-stained garments. On her way by the dining room, she poked in long enough to say, "Keep an ear out for the girl, would you?"

She hopped in the elevator and headed to her room. On the way up she dropped the suit and triggered the Pak again. There was a three second delay before loading out. That could be due to the stress she'd put on the system. She'd let the Pak run a diagnostic and clear out the bugs tonight. Capri found she was in an overall good mood as she settled in at her worktable, for five very specific reasons.

Mina. Emma. Zane. Sean. Steph.

The annoying children who ran her off from her home. Capri wondered if it was time to return the favor. Learning where they lived wouldn't take long at all. Perhaps Capri would send Pawns to visit their family members and loved ones. See how truly committed to being Wardens they were. She'd seen such behavior from other teams in the past. All's good when you're out protecting other planets. Once it's your home turf things become muddy. Harder calls were made.

Capri scrubbed through footage from her first day directing Henrie, seeing the group standing right there. All of them looking at the girl. How nicely everything had fallen into place for her.

But how to hit all of them at once? She remained uncertain about the Lenians and their coordination skills. Capri, working stealthily and alone, believed she could take out one or two before Nek alerted the others. The survivors would surely stash their families away on Outrider after that, keeping them far out of her reach. She'd be back to causing destruction in the city to pull them out of hiding.

She reviewed the beginning of the footage from the alley, when they'd only been a set of concerned friends–as far as Capri knew. They'd been looking for Henrie, already concerned about her well being. They'd been trying to reach her, convince her to fight Capri's influence, useless as that was. They wanted to save Henrie.

The frame of them all standing in that canteen sat in a corner of her worktable. Why should Capri go through the extra effort? Let them all come to her. Let them try to save their little friend.

She checked the progress of the creations; they were on track for completion by late the next morning. Capri could pull them in enough directions that Nek would have no choice but to deal with her directly–namely returning her Guardian.

Capri dropped her suit and set the Pak on the worktable. After tapping in her code, she watched the pad flash and begin its diagnostic. She assumed part of the latency issue was from the Pak and Guardian being untethered for so long. The two systems were tightly intertwined, it stood to reason the long separation would have adverse effects on the Pak's functioning. Could explain why the Pak was pairing with the Lenian device in such an unexpected way. Once reconnected to her Guardian, the systems would realign. She'd be an army of one, but that was all she needed before.

The Comp updated that Henrie was done cleaning up and now tending to her wounds. Capri peeked via the Comp feed and saw the girl slowly placing a new pad of gauze on her tracker wound. Henrie's face looked red and angry, but Capri wasn't sure if that was more from injuries, scrubbing, or some overspill of emotions. Capri cut the audio feed, not wanting to listen to sniffling, and prompted the Comp to aid in taping a pad of gauze to Henrie's cut arm.

While the Comp tended to Henrie, Capri pulled up one of the fight scenarios the engineers crafted while insisting their monster was better than the other. They'd placed their standoff inside the crater, but Capri changed the creations to start within the city proper. Immediate destruction occurred upon their landings; the damage and lives lost only went up from there. In their ideal imagining of the fight their creations would brawl without Warden interference. The monsters wrestled their way around Hurst until nearly everything laid in ruin.

A transcript from the Comp feed appeared, Henrie asking it, "Do I wait here?"

Capri pushed Henrie into lockdown, with the small kindness of aiming her for the bed, and sent her the fight as a new dream. No more visions of the past, now a prophecy of the future. Her vitals were immediately responsive.

A message popped up on her worktable from Gregory. **Sounds like she might have hit her head down there.**

28

Must Be Proficient in Multitasking

Secret identities were the worst. Sean and Steph were locked in at Restoration this morning. Nothing they could do without causing more suspicion from Mitch and their own parents. Leaving Mina, Zane, and Emma to sort out the Henrie problem, with whatever help Nek could provide. To her own surprise, Mina had a plan. A very loose plan. A potentially bad plan.

"I know we talk about your parents being evil all the time," Zane said as he parked in the Hephaestus Labs lot, "but do we really think that what they are working on is at the same level as what the Lenians have?"

Mina shook her head, even though the device had slightly worked on her. "No. Absolutely not. I think the brain box they made is bad and broken."

"And we are stealing this box because…?" Emma asked as they all climbed out of the car.

"It's bad and broken to a degree that I believe will interfere with the Lenian tech. Mix signals. Confuse their brainwashing block with its wrongness."

"How certain are you of this?"

"Fairly? They are trying to alter brainwaves. What the Lenians built does alter brainwaves. If we put that signal against theirs, that might overload the system. Or at least jam everything up. Give us a window to get that thing off her."

Emma's face dropped. "Did her back look bad?"

Mina regretted giving them the full details of what she and Zane spied on Henrie's back. "There's a lot of contact points, but nothing going too deep. I think the damage is more from how much she's been fighting."

"And there's no option that involves not going in here?" Zane waved to the hammering statue as they walked by.

"Nek and the Comps get a better read on the Lenians and Capri every time we encounter them, but we still have the same problem of the Lenian tech being more advanced than us." She gave a glance back to Emma. "We could pull the block off, but that'll mean getting in close with her fighting us. That will only hurt her more. You saw her reaction last time. Capri won't let her stop, Henrie said so. And she's kind of been kicking me around a lot." Mina rubbed at the puncture wound on her back. She'd spent another short stint in the medbay as a Med treated that small wound.

Emma touched her split eyebrow. Zane paled slightly. He'd told Mina, once they were alone, how unsettling it'd been having Henrie beat away at his helmet with her bare hand. Didn't matter that she did no physical damage to him, the hits landed all the same.

Mina shifted her Pak around in her pocket as they neared the front. She wasn't thrilled at taking them inside but nothing came from them having the armbands on last time, yet. The Outrider tech might be beyond something Hephaestus could scan for, like their personal issue with the Lenians. That's what Mina was banking on anyway. She wanted their Paks on hand in case this went sideways on them.

She looked down at the smartwatch. "Ready Nek?"

Their waves filled the small screen. "Yes. We're sure this will not harm any planetary relationships if I'm discovered?"

"Nobody here is someone we want to be friends with."

"They totally deserve this," Zane added.

"Wait," Emma stalled, "Odysseus works here too?"

Mina nudged her forward as she pulled open the door. "Guy works crazy hours. Never goes home."

Zane threw an arm over each of their shoulders and squeezed as they entered the lobby. "We have so much going on, but I need you to know I'm sincerely happy you two found the space to make a joke right now."

"My body only handles so much sincerity and serious emotions at once." Emma shook him off. "Had to balance back out before I threw up."

He gave her a finger gun. "Been there."

The guard pretending to be a receptionist met them halfway, tablet held out before them. "Hello! Mina, I don't see your parents having visitors listed for today."

She gave her best smile. "Sorry! This was a last minute thing. They asked me to pop by since I was out and about. They were going to send a message?"

"We can have a courier deliver anything to them directly."

"You know how they are. Particular. Are you sure there isn't a message? They might have gotten distracted and forgot. I could call them…"

The guard tapped on the tablet, giving a small 'hmph' as Nek's fake email rolled in. "Looks like they did."

"Great! We'll be two minutes. Tops." She immediately pushed by the guard and walked toward the elevators.

Their hand grabbed her arm. "I still need you to check-in."

They held the tablet out, the glowing fingerprint icon waiting for her. She gave a quick 'oh, right' kind of laugh and pressed her finger to the screen. Instead of the normal solid green circle, a swirl of several colors surrounded her finger. As the guard turned to Zane and Emma, Mina gave them a quick reassuring nod behind their back. Each pressed a finger to the screen, both looking relieved to see Nek there instead.

The guard's tone changed to bored with only a hint of annoyance. "An elevator will be waiting for you."

The group stepped into the first door that opened. Mina looked at her watch. "Good looking out there, Nek."

They spoke out of the elevator speaker. "Once we're leaving I'll clear any camera footage from the system."

"Professional advice, don't spend more time in this building than you have to."

"We don't want you catching anything," Zane said as the door opened.

The screen across the hall read **Concern Noted** above the arrow pointing toward her parent's lab. Mina was beginning to suspect that interacting with their team was affecting Nek's sense of humor, for better or worse.

They passed the same quiet research offices. She knew her parents weren't here. Firstly, their door wasn't radiating an aura of doom. Secondly, they'd talked about being off-site this morning while eating breakfast. With them not being here or at home, yet in town, Mina was certain they were looking at Pawn, and potentially Comp, parts at the outpost. An annoying fact, but one that worked to her benefit for the time being.

She unlocked their door with the spare key they left at the house and let the other two inside. The dumb, horrible, stupid, little brain box was sitting on the shelf behind her mother's desk. Trying to look no more dangerous than a paperweight, a very industrial and ugly paperweight.

Mina pointed to some papers stacked on the worktable in the middle of the room. "Make copies and shove them in folders, should be some in the bottom of that cabinet."

Emma and Zane got to it. Mina stepped around her mother's desk and checked over the shelving, slightly suspicious that if she grabbed the block an alarm would go off. "Nek, do you think it's safe to do a scan?"

They bobbed on the watch. "Yes. The feeds here are tied to your parent's home network, I put them on a loop before you entered."

Mina unloaded Spud from her Pak and set the little Comp right in front of the box, "Alright buddy, tell me if anything is boobytrapped."

The light flickered over the shelving. Nek spun as they processed the data. "The box is clear of any alarms."

"Wonderful." Mina snatched the brain box and loaded it in her Pak. She gave Spud a little pat before doing the same with it.

Nek relaxed into waves. "Mina. There is a small statue to your left, on the same shelf the box was on."

Mina found the piece they were talking about, a little human figure. A body cut down the middle to display the nervous system. "Creepy little thing, huh?"

"Yes, and also a switch."

"What?"

"I can't see beyond this wall, but that is the switch to opening something."

Mina's mental to-do list got bigger. Of course there was a secret panel in their evil lair of an office. Because of course, this wasn't the real lair. She hated being right. No, she loved being right. The pettiest part of her appreciated her parents being tried and true awful people and not simply annoying parents she complained about. One day she planned to expose them to everyone, besides her friend group who already agreed. They were a problem, but one she didn't have time for today.

She pressed a finger in the face of the statue. "I'm coming back for you."

Emma and Zane were stacking the original papers back on the worktable. Stuffed folders tucked beneath each of their arms. Mina put her Pak away and took the folders, giving the room a quick look-over before they left. She nudged the stack of papers to line up with the corner better, but otherwise they'd done good. The group left, she locked the door, and they were back in the elevator five minutes after they'd stepped out.

Zane gave a half-hearted wave to the guard as they crossed the lobby. Nek turned brighter as they left the building. "I've cleared us from the system."

"They'll see the box is gone," Emma said, "Will they suspect us? They know that we know what it does."

"If they were truly worried about it, they should have locked it up," Mina said, adding a 'in their secret lair' to herself. "And I'm sure they have plenty of enemies within that same building who'd love to dig around their stuff."

"Speaking of enemies." Zane pushed himself in front of the other two.

Coming up from the lot was Mel, who spotted them and came to a full stop by the statue. Mina's skin crawled; there wasn't time to deal with minions today. "Just keep going."

Mel moved to the middle of the path, giving them no chance to get by. "What are you doing here?"

"Laps of the display stretch," Emma answered as Zane sidestepped her and they all kept walking.

Mel spotted the folders before Mina was out of reach, blunt acrylics dug in her arm. "What are those?"

"Calm down. They asked me to pick stuff up since we were here." Mina pulled her arm away.

"If they needed something-"

Mina cut her off, "But they didn't ask you, did they? They asked me. Get over it."

"What projects are they having you bring to them?" She eyed the edge of a folder like she might make a grab for them.

"If you weren't informed," Zane said as he pulled Mina further along, "I don't think she should be telling you. Take it up with your bosses."

"Or die mad about it," Emma added, throwing an arm over Mina's shoulders and walking them away.

Hepheasus' arm swung down, bashing on the anvil louder than Mina ever heard before. Mel let out a surprised exclamation. Mina didn't even try holding in her laugh.

Nek was a bright ball of colors on their watches. "I think that spooked her well enough. She's heading inside now."

"Bless you, Nek," Zane said. "Will she be a problem? She's likely calling your parents right now."

Mina pulled herself back together. "If they bother to answer. Cameras will only show her in the whole building. They could ask the guard, but the log won't show anything thanks to Nek. And I have no issue lying to them."

"Ah man, if she could take the fall for this, that would be so great."

"Calm down, Icarus," Emma chided.

"Another one!" He shoved her gently, jostling both her and Mina. "Look at you go."

Mina felt her phone buzz in her pocket, she glanced at the watch to see a new message from Steph. **Henrie is here.**

Emma's arm disappeared from Mina's shoulder as they all jogged the rest of the way to the car. Zane had them on the road a minute later. Mina texted back, **What is she doing?**

Nothing yet. Came from the balcony. Sitting at the back bar.

"How fast are you comfortable driving, Zane?" Emma asked.

"About right where we are at now." Which was floating around ten above the speed limit. "Getting pulled over isn't going to help us."

Emma reached forward to show her phone to Mina. There was a text from Henrie. **Bring the rest of your team to the cafe.** She fell back and started typing.

Mina texted their group chat. **Keep eyes on her, but from a distance. We don't need her going off inside the cafe.**

So *today* might be the day she gets outed as a superhero. From her Pak, Mina unloaded the box and a set of compact tools. Doing this on the road wasn't ideal, but they didn't have time to be picky. The welds on the sides were shoddy, taking barely a touch from the tiny Comp torch to cut the back and top panels out of her way. With only a slight singe to her pant leg to show for it.

As Mina suspected, they'd designed the signal to be triggered remotely. That was how they could set her up at the desk and turn the device on behind her without moving. She could rip out the receiver and reconnect the wiring, but that would leave the signal on constantly. That didn't feel like a good option given that she didn't know what this beamed out. Mina dug in her bag for whatever spare hardware was inside, buried at the bottom was her mayday fidget cube for when being on her phone was 'inappropriate'.

The torch would melt the plastic too well, ruining the switch she wanted to steal. Without turning, she handed the cube and a screwdriver with the widest handle back to Emma. "Please break this. I need the switch."

"With pleasure." Emma snatched the cube from her and immediately set to work. She soon passed back the broken side panel with the switch.

"Thank you." Mina didn't bother breaking off the final bits of plastic. She snipped out the remote trigger, stripped the wire ends, and connected the switch to the circuit. Her work was as messy as her parent's, but she had a reasonable excuse. Making sure to aim the lens away from herself, she flipped the switch to test her work. The red light bounced around the roof as Zane sped them toward Restoration. Nothing there burned or melted, that was a good sign. She stuck a hand over the beam to be extra sure, no burning or melting, only that vague tingle. Mina turned the box off. Parts of the actual mechanism inside were attached to the remaining panels, so she couldn't strip anything else off easily. The torn open box would be impossible to hide, but she'd make due. "I can't truly test this until we've got her, but I can turn it on."

"You're so cool," Zane said as he turned onto the final stretch before Restoration.

He parked in the public lot behind the cafe, and their group made a beeline for the balcony staircase. At the top of the stairs, Mina dropped the box in her bag. There were far too many people either on the balcony or in the back area to try anything right away. Especially since all of those people were looking right at Henrie and Sam, who was yelling at her. Through the glass they saw Sean and Steph keeping their distance as they watched, gently gesturing for some of the patrons to move elsewhere.

Mina yanked the door open as Sam let out, "You have some nerve coming here."

Henrie was looking at Sam, but not saying anything. She looked uncomfortably warm sitting there in a full tracksuit.

Which only appeared to anger them more. "I could, I could call the cops. And I should! After what you did."

Steph spied them walking in, she nudged Sean and they moved behind the counter. This way they'd have Henrie on both sides, whatever that might do for them.

Sam was getting further enraged by her silence. "You need to leave!"

Sean put himself between the two and pushed Sam toward the office. "Hey, we got customers. You're too hot. Let me walk her out."

"She needs to explain herself."

"Do you want me to leave or do you want me to explain?" Henrie drawled out. "You'll have to pick."

Mina could tell Henrie was speaking, not Capri talking through her. That unnerved her more.

Sam fought against Sean. "I don't know what happened to you, but-"

Sean pushed back harder, getting them nearly to the office. "Not here, Sam."

"Your dad wouldn't like it," Steph added, setting herself directly across the counter from Henrie.

Sam stopped at the mention of Mitch. "No. No, he wouldn't." Their eyes snapped back to Henrie. "How about I give him a call? Let him deal with you."

People began muttering as Sam disappeared inside the office. Some turned away, but several kept eyes on Henrie. Mina, Zane, and Emma closed in from behind. They were now drawing attention, especially since most of them looked some level of beaten and bruised.

Henrie turned her head far enough to side-eye the three of them, her cheek was scabbed and red. "Good of you to join us."

"Capri," Emma growled.

"No, just me." She turned more on the stool to get all five of them in view. "I have a message."

Mina didn't like being right this time.

"We should walk you out," Sean said, loud enough that it'd carry back to the office.

Henrie sighed. "Sure, yeah. I can go as far as the balcony."

Mina touched the box in her bag. "What does that mean?"

Henrie slid off the stool and gestured around to the back seating area. "I was told to be at the cafe with you. That's as far as I can push the command without getting in trouble."

Emma and Mina stayed within close range of Henrie. Steph and Sean brought up the rear, pretending like they were good employees ushering them out. Zane backed up to pull the door open, waiting there as they all filed through. Mina stood by the top of the stairs, blocking that easy exit. The few other customers out there picked up on the tense vibes and moved inside. While the Wardens surrounded Henrie, Mina didn't feel like they had the upper hand here at all.

Mina eyed the several people watching them through the glass. "We're hoping to keep this calm. Lots of eyes here."

"They'll be distracted soon enough. But all I've been told to do for now is give you a message." Henrie stayed closer to the building, as close as Zane blocking the door would allow her. Like she was nervous to step too far out of her apparent safe zone.

"So what did Capri want you to tell us?"

"It's a question, actually." She took a deep, shaky breath in. "Are you ready for round two?"

There was a boom over The Park, a cloud bank was forming. Another Lenian creation was on the way to Hurst. There was maybe a minute or two before the monster landed.

Henrie turned to Emma, rushing out, "She showed me what's going to happen. You have to give her the Guardian."

"Henrie, she'll do worse if we do." Emma reached out to touch her arm but pulled the hand back. "We can't do that."

"You have to! She's sen-" Henrie grunted and doubled over, only managing to get out, "Two."

There was another boom, far off on the other side of the cafe. Mina didn't like that, nobody liked that given the concerned looks she caught through the glass. They weren't going to have this balcony alone for much longer.

Steph was looking at the growing bank over The Park. "We need to go."

Nek spun on their watches. "Guardians dropping shortly."

Henrie straightened and grabbed at Emma's watch. "Drop hers! Please, she's going to kill everyone. I've seen her plan. You have to give her Guardian back."

Emma peeled Henrie's hands off her arm, more gently than Mina imagined possible with their general tension levels. "Listen, you know she's bad. We can't-"

There was a smaller set of rumbles above The Park, their Guardians coming through. Nek could teleport them, but they needed to get away from the crowd first.

Henrie kept looking at Emma's watch. "She won't stop until you give it up. She'll keep sending them until everyone is dead."

"I don't know if Capri is listening, or if you'll have to tell her, but we're busy using her Guardian as a punching bag for practice. So that's never going to happen." Mina turned to her team. "We gotta go. Now."

Zane and Steph immediately broke for the stairs, moving around Mina.

Sean hesitated, eyeing his cousin who was still holding on to Henrie, but followed.

Emma wasn't moving. "Did she give you any orders for after you talked to us?"

Henrie's eyes went to the crowd inside. Her face scrunched up as she fought to get the words out, "She mentioned. If you leave. No one. Is here. To protect. Them."

The idea of Capri putting Henrie back in that feral fighting mode and setting her loose on random people was sick. Especially if that smoke-suit returned and gave her near-Warden level abilities. Mina spotted Sam stepping out of the office as Megan came up the ramp, there was no way those two wouldn't step into the line of fire if Henrie was set off. Capri would ruin Henrie's life, if not end it, for the sake of dividing their attention.

Emma looked at Mina. "We have to get this off. Now."

More things on that stupid to-do list and there were monsters appearing any second. "We don't know what kind of time it'll take. Maybe we can tie her up somewhere—"

"Please." Emma's face held some emotion Mina couldn't name, but it made her heart ache.

A thud shook the building, followed by a smaller one from the opposite direction. Henrie stepped away from the rattling glass. Their Guardians would arrive next, the others would need them, but Mina knew they couldn't leave Henrie alone. Tied up or otherwise.

"We can't stay here. Henrie, are you sure you can't leave the balcony?"

Henrie cautiously approached the staircase and stepped down once. Then took another slow step down. Her shoulders relaxed. "She's not watching me. She hasn't set the next command yet."

"Probably watching the monsters kick off." Mina started taking the stairs two at a time, expecting the pair behind her to keep up. She called down to the others, who'd been waiting below, "You three hold those things best you can. We'll take care of Henrie and be with you as soon as possible."

There were now people leaning over the balcony railing above them. The group ran up the street, finding a cut-through between businesses that was clear of anyone. Mina didn't realize superheroing would entail so much time in alleyways. A set of thuds rolled out from The Park, followed by Zane, Steph, and Sean disappearing.

Mina pulled the brain box out. "Here goes nothing. Emma, maybe you should try holding her?"

"Capri still isn't paying attention," Henrie said.

Mina got herself lined up with her back. "There might be a failsafe."

Emma grabbed Henrie's arms. "When this is done I have a couple moves to ask you about."

"Deal." Henrie tipped her head toward Emma's.

"If this hurts, I'm sorry." Mina flipped the switch and aimed the beam toward the spot she'd seen the block.

"Nothing worse. Than my last. Couple days." Henrie grunted and pulled slightly on Emma's arms. "Doesn't like that."

"Thought as much. Emma, suit up." Mina tapped her own Pak, their suits unloading at the same time.

Henrie gasped and dropped her head to Emma's shoulder. "Really. Doesn't like. Seeing Warden suits."

Updates from the others loaded in; Steph and Zane were in the crater with a very pointy lizard thing while Sean crossed through the city to grapple the several arms of a lion with his tails. Henrie kept her control well enough to not physically fight back. Mina struggled to keep the beam aligned as Henrie twisted from the pain, but she noticed dots of red beginning to appear along the girl's back. "Emma, check the device."

Emma, now holding most of Henrie's weight, slowly pulled back the collar of her shirt. "The tendrils you mentioned aren't there. Just the square."

"Can you pull it off?"

Emma slipped her hand down the back of Henrie's shirt. The moment she pulled on the device was clear as Henrie cried out, causing Emma to immediately stop. "I'm sorry."

"Do it," Henrie begged.

Emma pulled again. Henrie screamed, knees buckling this time. Emma pulled her hand back and looked at Mina. "It's hurting her too much."

Henrie pushed off Emma and dropped fully to her knees, Mina hurried to follow and keep the box aimed at her. They watched Henrie reach back and find the block under her shirt. Mina nearly dropped the brain box as Henrie grunted and tugged. The struggle reminded her of watching Capri overload the restraints on Outrider. Guaranteed harm, but no other option out. A faint shimmer of that smoky material billowed around Henrie, who must have also noticed because she pulled harder. The material flickered and retracted as the device ripped free from her back.

Henrie caught herself from falling over. "Tin-Man's cousins can suck it."

Neither Warden knew what that meant, but Henrie looked relieved. Mina checked their standing, the others were holding their ground but couldn't put either monster down. Comps were dispatched to downtown, because of course Capri sent Pawns too. More ways to split their attention. She suspected Capri would soon be on the ground, expecting them to surrender her Guardian any second. Mina wanted this device, and Henrie, far from where Capri could get her hands on them.

She crouched down in front of Henrie. "Wanna see a spaceship?"

"More space," Henrie groaned.

"We have a movie room," Emma offered. "And lots of snacks."

The shouts from the other three were getting louder, even with her comm volume turned nearly to mute.

"I promise we'll bring you back down as soon as this is over." Mina saw Nek swirling on her display. "How long until you can move her?"

"Five seconds," Nek answered.

Emma squeezed Henrie's hand before they backed off. "My room is the fourth door down. Nek can show you. Crash there if you need to."

Henrie sucked in a breath as the air around her blurred and she was gone. Mina's visor fuzzed over and she felt herself reappear inside her Thunderbird. The control panel lit up as she was secured in the chair. Across the crater, Emma's Drake shook to life. A spark of blue energy rolled over her wings as Mina took to the air.

29

We Did Get Better, Right?

"This monster took one of my tails!" Sean yelled across their channel. "Give that back, you ass."

"We'll reattach it, I promise." Mina flew across the city to join him and the overly appendaged lion-monster. Why did Lenians like adding so many arms?

"Which fight do you want me on?" Emma called out.

"Stay with those two and put that lizard down."

Zane locked his Jackalope's antlers in some of the spikes coming off the back of the lizard-monster. He tried tipping the creature, but as soon as he snagged any leverage the spikes retracted into the monster. Only to then shoot back out and shove him off. Steph was keeping the creation inside the crater, knocking it back with either a wind gust from the Pegasus's wings or a stomp from a hoof. The squirming pincushion would bounce back toward Zane and they'd do the whole routine again. With Emma there in the Drake, she helped on both fronts. Biting the lizard's tail to pull the monster further inside the crater while also denting a spike or two with each swing of her own tail. Mina didn't like the amount of scrapes and punctures on the Jackalope, but at least in the crater they weren't doing any worse damage to the city.

Sean wasn't having as much luck across town. The Lenians used a cluster of car dealerships for their second landing zone. The drop alone sent a shockwave through the cars underfoot and the monster had immediately begun scooping up crushed hunks of metal to chuck in every direction. The Kitsune created its own amount of damage while crossing the city, but she could tell Sean tried being careful about where he put his feet down. Mina made a mental note to see if something could 'accidentally' happen to that Hephaestus building downtown while the Comps were flying around. The upside of their location, there wasn't a large amount of people and there was plenty of space for those onsite to run once the monster arrived. As Mina got closer, the area looked mostly clear. The Kitsune kept the Lenian creation in place by wrapping its legs and most of the arms up with its tails. Sean initially sounded confident that he could keep that up until the others were free, until two arms broke one of his tails and the fight turned on him.

Mina worked up an electric blast on her way over, releasing the charge as she sank talons in one of the free arms. The Lenian metal buckled as the Thunderbird squeezed and pulled. A roar, very close to her head, filled the air. The creation shook its massive mane and strands of twisted metal slapped across her screens. Her Thunderbird lifted, not by her doing, and then was quickly pulled toward the ground; she let go to avoid doing more damage to the lot. The previously wrecked cars below shook from the force of the Thunderbird pushing itself back into the air.

"These moving spikes are not fair," Zane said.

"Try thumping it down," Emma said, "I'll whack-a-mole a few more."

Mina couldn't take her eyes off the spider-lion to see how the other fight was going, but she liked hearing them come up with attack plans.

The lion-monster grabbed two of the Kitsune's tails and yanked the Guardian toward one of the dealership buildings. Mina sunk her talons in the lion's shoulders and tried pulling the pair back, but Sean was forced to release two of his tails in order to stop himself from destroying the building.

"I'm not usually for audience participation," Steph said, "But you'd think some of this crowd would lend a hand."

Mina checked her dash, pings from helicopters were scattered along the edges of both fights. They didn't want Mina to fry their systems with her push this time around. Speaking of, she went straight up in the air and charged her next shot. If the robotic beast wouldn't let her take it up, she'd put this thing in the ground.

"Good news is the ground crews aren't shooting at Comps," Steph continued, ending in a grunt as her Pegasus likely took another kick at their lizard-monster.

Mina swiped over to Comp2876's feed, feeling like she was in a constant loop of playing catch-up as she remembered there were Pawns downtown too. There were military vehicles scattered through the streets, soldiers posted on corners and took shots at MegaPawns attempting to close in. During the two seconds she dared to watch, soldiers picked up the 'take out the middle' tactic from watching the Comps work. She saw 2876 giving a *Great job!* to a group as it flew by. "Everybody loves our robots."

"Such a proud mom," Zane said. "They'll all get-ahh!"

"What was that?" Mina turned as her burst went off. She'd been aiming down, but the blast wasn't as dead on as she'd intended. The near miss didn't bother her as much as the sight of the Jackalope on its back at the edge of the crater, the lizard crawling over him into The Park proper. Emma's Drake had the tail in its jaws, attempting to pull the creature back. A move that was working until Mina heard a snap over their comms and saw the tail break off at the base. The newly freed lizard-monster bolted for The Park and city beyond. "Zane, talk to me."

"Spike. Broke one of my screens a little. All good." He sounded shaky.

Mina hoped that was a 'threw up' shaky and not 'secretly punctured' shaky, a quick check of his vitals confirmed he was physically okay. She threw herself back at the lion. "Fall down already."

A flash on the dash grabbed her attention. *Capri located!*

Good ole Comp2876 at work. In the small feed that popped up, Mina saw Capri strolling through downtown with her Pawns. Mina wanted to ask what she liked down there so much. Capri appeared to be having a heyday with no Wardens around to stop her. The feed showed her take a swipe with her blast saber at a military vehicle. The slice cut the jeep nearly in two, leaving a red hot scorch mark across the concrete and building behind the vehicle as well. What caught Mina's attention was the hand holding the saber. Specifically the fact that she could see Capri's actual hand. The suit retracted from the weapon during her attack, Mina watched the material reform as the smoky version they'd seen on Henrie.

"Mina!" Sean yelled.

"Sorry! Yep." She sent another blast at the Lenian lion, finally knocking it down to one knee.

Sean yanked an arm out, sparks of electricity from severed cables surrounded the Kitsune as he tossed the piece on a pile of destroyed cars. "Now we're even."

"Technically, it's ahead in the arms-to-tails ratio."

"Not the time."

"No yeah, you're right." Mina scooped up the discarded arm in her talons and bashed the claws against the monster's head as her energy blast recharged. She opened a channel directly to Nek. "I think Capri's Pak is acting up."

Their waves filled the edge of her dash. "I noticed that too. My estimation is excessive stress on the system. The Lenian device is still connected to the Pak."

"Even being off Henrie?"

"Yes. The signal is weak, but there."

"Bring me back up. Please." Mina switched over to the team comm. "I have a bad plan and no time to explain it."

"I think we could use any type of plan right now," Emma said.

"Good. Zane, I'm pulling you off the lizard. Come pin some of these arms down for Sean."

The Jackalope hopped to the order, leaving the Drake rolling with the monster across the highway as the Pegasus tried stomping down more of the spikes. Zane spoke only to her, "And where are you going?"

"Thunderbird will stay here, keep the monster where it can shoot." She locked her systems on the lion, setting the energy blast on repeat. "I'm going up to Outrider."

"Mina, what are-"

"Remember when I said no time to explain?" Mina felt bad for cutting him off, but their time was very short. "Be right back, I swear."

She went weightless as Nek triggered the teleport, braced herself during the short trip, and hit the floor running once inside Outrider. "Where's the device now?"

Nek rolled across the panels next to her. "Medbay with Henrie. We moved her there immediately upon arrival."

Mina bolted through the halls, bursting in the room as Henrie pulled a gray shirt on to cover the large bandage taped across her back. The Comps had found her a training outfit to change into. She looked initially frightened to see Mina there, but seemed to register the coloring and relaxed. The Lenian block sat on one of the beds nearby, a small floral hair clip laying next to it. Mina snatched up the device and dropped her helmet. "In the alley, you kept apologizing. Saying you didn't want it. Why?"

Henrie nodded at the block. "There's a glitch in her program. When I fought you guys, this pulled the suit from her. She hated it."

They knew from Nek that traditional Warden training was years of hard work. Something sought after by many, but gained only by a worthy few. Add in Capri's twisted commitment to the Collective and it was no surprise that losing the suit would incite panic. "Her suit keeps glitching. If we can force it to break further, we might get the Pak off."

"How will you get close enough?" Nek asked. "She's utilizing a full guard of MegaPawns this time around."

That was the bad part of her plan. "We give her what she wants. We drop her Guardian. She'll come running."

Nek became a bright ball of white. "That is not advised."

More notes of damage to her team pinged away on her armband. She needed to move. "You said this has the same altered signal as her Pak, so shouldn't it open the Guardian? I can hide inside and ambush her."

Nek relaxed slightly, tinges of color around the edges of the white ball. "This is not advised."

"I said I had a bad plan."

"I'll go," Henrie said. "She won't be alone in there."

"Absolutely not," came from Mina.

"Extremely unadvised," from Nek.

Henrie's eyes darkened as she stared Mina down. "Capri has damaged my life in ways I have no idea how I'm going to fix. She threatened every single person I care about. She's beaten me and mentally tortured me for days. You have a way to get up close and kick her around. I am going."

Mina could only nod. Nek sighed. The two were weightless within seconds, dropped at the feet of Capri's dark Guardian in the bottom level of Outrider.

"Oh, that can go straight to hell," Henrie said, taking in the multiple eyes and drooping tendrils.

"Whatever this is might have come from there." Mina directed her around to the right leg. Cut in the side, matching the other Guardians, was a square the size of a Pak. She pressed the block in and waited. Nothing.

"I think it's a little crooked." Henrie reached out to adjust the position. As soon as her fingers touched the device, the Guardian's tendrils rustled.

"Guardian unlocked." Nek rang through the otherwise empty room. "I'll move you in."

The control room was tight with the two of them. Mina loaded the device in her Pak and pointed for Henrie to take the seat as she crouched beside it. She noticed a rosy glimmer cross the dash as Henrie sat.

"So the plan is to jump her?" Henrie asked.

"Let me jump her. You go for the Pak." The window of the Guardian became streaks of light. The teleport was just long enough for Mina to feel she needed to say something. "Sorry about shooting you, by the way."

Henrie dropped a hand to her side. "You didn't know, but thanks."

The Guardian appeared in the now empty crater, one edge newly crushed from the Jackalope's fall. They'd have to wait for Capri to reach them. Comp2876, who'd been keeping visuals on Capri, informed them the second she disappeared from downtown.

"What are you doing?" Steph asked.

Mina cringed. "The bad plan is in action. We got this."

"We?" Emma asked.

"That was the, um, royal we."

"Is Hen-"

Mina shut her comms down, electing to avoid a lecture mid-battle. A ping appeared on her heads-up display, the heat signature of a Lenian teleport dropping not far away. As the air cleared, Capri was running for the Guardian. They lost sight of her as she disappeared off to the right. The dark dash before them pulsed, she'd connected her Pak.

"Nek put us here. How is she getting in?" Henrie whispered.

Mina realized she didn't know how someone got in without a teleport. Their answer came when the Guardian bent closer to the ground. Capri must have jumped and pulled herself up one of the tendrils while her beast bent forward. She reappeared at the end of the nose, one hand remained covered by the broken material. A patch on her left thigh flaked away as she stood on the snout. The suit was leaving her piece by piece, Mina noticed particles floating their direction. Capri couldn't see them through the tinted screens; an advantage they wouldn't have for long as a seal popped and the center screen began to rise outward. Mina made a note to ask about the emergency exits on the other Guardians later.

Mina activated the sticky boots and angled herself on the side of the control room to get a small running start once the panel was fully open. A useless endeavor, as Henrie pounced from the seat once there was enough room to dive for Capri's legs. The pair rolled over the short snout and off the edge of the Guardian's face before Mina cleared the dash.

"Emma's gonna kill me." Mina scrambled to the end of the nose, finding both hanging from tendrils below. Henrie looped a length of a strand around her arm for extra grip.

Capri kicked at Henrie. "You insolent little-"

"I don't know what you're saying, but bite me, space hag." Henrie kicked off a tendril to swing herself backward, on the return she aimed both feet at Capri's hands. Mina watched Capri slip another foot down.

"Everyone is better at comebacks than me." Mina pulled one of her blasters. With the adhesive active on her boots she could stand on the end of the nose and take shots at Capri.

The ex-Warden dropped further on the tendril in her haste to leave the line of fire. "This is mine, Blue!"

"Agree to disagree."

Capri attempted climbing her tendril, but the other hand of her suit turned to smoke and she lost more of her grip. Henrie jumped to Capri's tendril and let herself drop straight at Capri's head, who backed further off. Mina needed to get down there. If Henrie was doing this bare-handed, Mina could figure it out. She put her blaster away, flipped herself around with a tendril in hand, and deactivated her sticky boots. Nothing more complicated than getting off the climbing wall at the gym.

With one small jump Mina was out in the air. Zipping down the front of the Guardian. Ready to intervene on Henrie's behalf and keep her from more direct harm. Capri shook their tendril, attempting to throw Henrie off, but the other girl wrapped a section around her arm again and kept herself in place. All Capri did was knock Henrie against Mina's strand. The jostle pulled the tendril out of Mina's loose grip, leaving her fully falling through the air for a brief second. She regained her hold, but came to a jarring halt far below the fighting pair.

"Totally what I wanted." She dropped the short remaining distance to the ground and unloaded both blasters, deciding this was her best way to help. Mina took shots at any smoky bits of suit she could see as Henrie kicked at Capri from above.

Their joint efforts paid off as Capri lost her hold and slipped to the ground, landing right next to Mina. Henrie wasn't too far behind on coming down, Mina expected she'd have some kind of burn on her arm after that stunt. The alien huffed as the left shoulder of her suit broke apart.

"Looks like your suit also disagrees with you," Mina said.

Capri tackled her, the reaction Mina wanted. That gave Henrie a spot to land without being in immediate danger. Mina let go of her blasters, opting to block the pummeling Capri was giving her with one arm and reach for her own Pak with the other. She unloaded the block, pieces of the misty material immediately began moving towards it. With a small boost, Mina bashed the smooth side of the block into a deteriorating section of Capri's helmet, connecting directly with her head underneath. As Capri rolled away, Mina watched a batch of material remain around the device. Henrie came up behind and kicked the back of Capri's now exposed head, putting her flat on the ground.

Henrie scooped up one of Mina's blasters and clicked. "I forgot that stupid part."

Capri pulled one of Henrie's legs out from under her, sending the girl to the ground. In a flash, Capri was on top of Henrie, who used the blaster to block hits meant for her face. A trail of material hung in the air between the Lenian block and Capri, Mina watched a wisp break off her back and join the cord. Mina flipped the device over, now barbed side out. With as much boost as she could put in the swing, Mina slammed the device in Capri's ribs, pulling back with another boost to rip the barbs from her side. Capri, distracted by the pain, paused her attack on Henrie. Mina watched another length of material along Capri's back turn to smoke. Unsure how much longer they could keep up this fight, Mina made a grab for Capri's Pak.

The pad flashed several colors beneath her hand as the Pak resisted. Capri, again lost in her assault on Henrie, paid her no mind. Mina used a boost and the Pak lifted from the ex-Warden. Large strings of suit material followed, the pad flashed white rapidly as she backed away from the pair. Mina dropped the Lenian block and crushed it beneath her foot, causing every floating piece of suit to redirect toward the Pak. As the rest of her helmet melted away, Capri finally realized what was going on. She whipped around as the last pieces flaked off her arms, leaving her in a green activewear set she must have made Henrie steal. Emma was right, that store did have cute stuff. If Mina survived this next bit, she'd hit them up tomorrow.

Capri launched off Henrie, sprinting directly for Mina. "Give that back!"

"You're unfit for duty." Mina waited until Capri was almost on her, when it'd be too late for Capri to turn back, and tossed the Pak over her head towards Henrie. "But I think she stands a chance."

30

Three Good Bois

While the sentiment was nice, Henrie could tell the throw would fall severally short of where she currently sat. She kicked up from the ground, stumbling a few steps because her equilibrium had taken a beating over the last few days, and got herself under the Pak right as it came down.

The pad glowed a rosy pink in her hands, Henrie liked that. Instead of smoke, solid material rolled out over her arms. She didn't like that as much. The Pak drifted along her right arm and down to her hip, that was weird to watch but okay. She'd never worn the full helmet before, making for a bizarre feeling as her head became fully encased, but the view was good. Capri, who'd gotten herself stopped and turned, wore a look of horror as the suit completed itself with a rosy pink band rolling down Henrie's side.

Henrie noticed the rather high degree of pain throughout her body decrease immediately. She'd refused anything more than a light pain reliever up on Outrider, having spent so much time not feeling her own body lately, and didn't appreciate the suit negating that decision. Nevermind that she did feel a hell of a lot better. This didn't feel as dangerous as the blooms Capri sent her, but was something she'd bring up later.

Capri bolted back toward her. "Take that off!"

Henrie was surprised to find she understood Capri. She didn't know how the suit was doing it, but assumed that was the source. The syncing was far better than what Henrie had been dealing with over the last few days.

Cutting out the delay let Capri yell at her in real time. "Take it off!"

"I don't have to listen to you anymore." Henrie planted her feet, dipping right as Capri got close. Easier than expected, something extra pushed around her knees and along her back, she lifted Capri off the ground and tossed the alien over her head. She turned to the sputtering Capri. "I can see why you like this thing."

Capri's head tipped, her blue brow furrowing, and she appeared confused. Henrie realized what was going on, Capri was now the one who couldn't understand her. Which took the fun out of insulting her. As the alien's confusion shifted back to anger, Capri gave another scream and lunged. Henrie caught Capri across the face with a punch before the alien got all the way back up. The hit sent her back to the hardened ground of the crater.

Notifications filled the edges of Henrie's vision, updates about fighting elsewhere in the city. The scrolling text was distracting from the fight directly in front of her. She kicked Capri again, sending the alien rolling several feet. Henrie turned to Mina and gestured at her helmet. "How do you stop the stuff popping up?"

"Think 'clear' and it'll go away." Mina jogged over, grabbing her weapons on the way.

Capri was back to her feet, trying not to tip to one side as a knee almost gave out. Henrie thought *clear* and her field of vision expanded. "Handy."

Mina aimed at Capri. "Lots of tricks we can show you."

Capri screamed, "I will rip that Pak off your dead body!"

"Did you tell your team that too?" Mina asked.

"She can't underst—wait, what?" Henrie asked. There was a metallic groan behind them, she turned enough to see the Guardian folding in on itself. The other two weren't paying the disappearing monster any mind, so she let it go.

"Leave that out, did she?" Mina shot at the ground in front of Capri, keeping her at bay. "She killed her team on the way here. That's why Outrider crashed."

When Capri screamed this time, there was an accompanying foot stomp. Her face conveyed that she did not appreciate being the odd-man out in this conversation.

"Really need you to stop screaming," Henrie said anyway as she closed in on the alien, kicking a foot out from under Capri. As she fell, Henrie caught one of Capri's arms and twisted it behind her back to force her further down. "My head has been through the wringer these last few days."

A set of opened cuffs appeared from Mina's Pak, she handed them over to Henrie. "I thought you might like the honors."

"Oh, yes please." She pulled Capri's arm harder than necessary as she snapped on a cuff, there was a distinct pop from the shoulder.

Bursts of pain broke out over her back, her tender spine wasn't thrilled with the new additions. She turned to see Pawns closing in from the other side of the crater.

"Don't let them get together." Mina tossed one of the gun-things over to Henrie.

She caught the weapon but wasn't falling for this a third time. "I can't use these."

"Think 'attune' and it'll give you an option." Mina took shots at the nearing Pawns, running to the left to split the group.

Henrie did as she was told and saw *Attune blaster to system?* appear before her eyes. She thought *yes, duh* and the coloring along the bottom of the weapon changed from teal to her pink. Before taking a shot, she kicked back at Capri. Connecting with enough of the alien's chest to send her back to the ground. She moved away from the alien, running in the opposite direction of Mina. Her shots didn't land as often as the other girl's, it'd been awhile since she'd been at a shooting range, but she kept them off herself or from getting too close together. The Pawns returned shots, two got around them and hovered over Capri.

"They're going to take her!" Mina shouted.

Henrie made a run for Capri, but hit a wall of air that bounced her back. Capri wasn't happy about the change either. She yelled up at the Pawns, "Leave me here!"

The space around Capri turned wavy and blurred. They glared at each other until Capri disappeared. Henrie chucked the blaster at where Capri had stood out of frustration.

"We're not done yet." Mina ran over to her. She held out a hand toward the blaster, which snapped back to her palm. The bottom reset to her blue before both weapons returned to her Pak. "The others need help putting those monsters down. I have to get back to the Thunderbird."

Henrie turned to the Guardian they'd brought down, now a ball of material floating several feet over the crater. A faint sheen of pink around the edges. "How am I supposed to use that?"

"Same as the other stuff, you think of a form and it'll do it. I would love for you to have the proper time and space to decide what fits you best, but we gotta move." Mina was tapping on her armband. "See you out there."

"You're leav-" Henrie didn't bother finishing because Mina was already gone. "Okay, yeah. I got this. I guess."

"Best to not put too much pressure on it," Nek spoke directly in her helmet. Henrie jumped, they must have noticed. "My apologies."

"Yeah, not big on voices in my head right now."

A small circle of colors appeared in the corner of her visor. A message scrolled out next to it. *I can communicate like this, if that works better?*

"For now. How much in my head are you?"

Myself? None at all. The Pak only provides me vitals.

Capri did plenty with only access to her vitals. "But it also knows what I'm thinking."

That is a connection between you and the Pak directly. And only from you to the Pak. It can't make you do anything.

She gave the pad on her hip a little tap. "Good to know."

There was a crash from beyond the crater. Henrie caught a flash on her wrist, discovering she wore an armband like Mina's. There was a scrolling transcript showing that the others were talking on a channel together, her own name flew by several times, but she needed a minute alone in her head.

"No pressure." The others were all creatures of fantasy and myth. Zane was in a straight up cryptid. All Henrie needed to do was pick some funky little beast. A simple task, except she'd forgotten every single mythical creature she'd ever heard of.

Henrie shook her arms and focused on her breathing. The first image that popped in her head was the dumb little robot dog her parents bought when she was six because she'd been begging for a pet, but her mom was deathly allergic to dogs. The metal beside her shifted, she watched sheets pull away from the mass and form a set of paws as they touched the ground.

She'd begged for so long, always insisting she'd keep the dog far away from her mom. Pillars stretched down from the mass and took shape as the legs. The remaining mass elongated and formed the body, a short snub of a tail popped out the backend. Fine bits of metal split to replicate fur. Patches tinted with her rosy preference.

Once Henrie learned what hypoallergenic meant, she'd obsessively researched every single option but was always shut down. More of the mass formed sheets, building three columns that rounded into necks. Henrie liked where that was going. She watched each sprout a head. Short ears, all pointed and alert, popped out the top of each. Long snouts stretched out as the Guardian shook each head in turn. The one on the left sported a pink spot on the side of its nose.

"You're going to get all the skritches." She ran around to the right leg like Mina did before, finding the same smooth square patch waiting for her. Henrie lifted the pad off the Pak, a thin line of that smoky material keeping them connected, and placed it on the Guardian. Above her, each head let out a growl.

Nek spun on her visor. *Moving you in.*

For the first time, Henrie was excited about being teleported somewhere. She was dropped in a seat as the dash came online before her. A pulsing spot told her that was where her team chat was happening. Henrie took a deep breath and added herself. "Hey, gang."

A lot of hollering–good, bad, and stressed–came back to her.

"Cerberus, huh?" Emma asked.

"Always wanted a dog. Now I have three." She grabbed the controls in front of her and pushed her Guardian to run. As they leaped over the crater's edge, a pulse of energy rippled through the air around her. Henrie was about to ask if anyone else saw that when she heard Sean come across the channel.

"Did that happen to everyone else too?"

Nek spread across the top of the dash. "Full Warden team is now online! Maximum power now available."

"We were running at low power before?" Steph asked.

A whoop came in from Mina. Henrie spied a bright blue energy ball aiming for the lion across town. She eyed a new glowing red icon on her dash, somehow knowing what the button would do. Emma's Drake was on its back and trying to push the lizard off, but several spikes were stabbed in the Guardian's stomach, locking the two together. Steph's Pegasus rammed the monster the best she could but wasn't having luck knocking the thing over. The Cerberus bolted down the highway, Henrie hoped people were off the roads by now. Her Guardian locked in a bite on the salamander's neck with its right head. The middle, where Henrie sat, caught the arm swinging for her. The left head, where the pulsing icon hovered over on her dash, gave another growl from deep in its throat. Her control room vibrated slightly. When the Lenian creation retracted its spikes from the Drake and shot them toward the Cerberus, Henrie hit her shiny button.

Fire rolled out through the teeth of the Cerberus's left head. Heating the spikes until they melted against the lizard. The monster roared and tried pulling away from her, tearing more of its own metal in the process. The Drake clawed at the lizard as it got out from underneath, the Guardian's tail whipped around and smashed the lizard's head, caving in one full side.

Henrie was hit with a flash of memory about the Mooneater and felt queasy. Her Cerberus released the monster and backed off. Steph took her place to stomp the Lenian creation into the rubble that was once an offramp. The creature stilled and stayed down.

"You good?" Emma asked.

"First-time jitters," Henrie said, hoping that'd be a good enough cover.

"Zane is head of the Nervous Stomach Committee," Sean said.

"I have pamphlets," Zane added.

"You three need a hand over there?" Emma asked.

Henrie turned her Guardian toward the other fight. They were a decent ways away in the city, but given the size of the Guardians she could see them clearly. The Lenian lion-monster was missing several arms now, frayed bits of metal hung from spots that were once joints. A stump of an arm flailed at one of the Kitsune's tails and missed the Jackalope's antler coming in from the side. The monster tipped and the Thunderbird sent an energy blast to fully knock the creature over. Henrie remembered standing at the feet of these robotic nightmares. None of the fear was there anymore. She sat back in her seat, feeling proud that she'd shaken some part of the trauma from these last few days. Though she couldn't be sure if that fear was her own to start with or something Capri put in her head.

"We're clear," Mina called out. "Which means these are going to disappear any second."

Sure enough, her dash alerted her to something pushing on the Guardian, like she'd been bounced when going after Capri. She tried to dig in her paws but lost that fight. The monster between them disappeared.

Nek's waves rolled along the dash. "Comps have confirmed Pawns were removed from downtown. Recalling everyone to Outrider."

She thought to compliment the glorious Guardian more but felt sure the Cerberus knew her deep appreciation. The idea of going back to space wasn't exciting, but Outrider treated her far better than the Lenian base had. Not to mention, space felt better than facing her mother. The idea alone put a familiar tightness in her chest. Henrie muted her outgoing chat, letting the banter from the others fill the space around her. With a thought she dropped her helmet and laid her head down on the control panel.

On the edge of her vision she could see Nek's waves pulsing. "Warden Henrie, are you-"

"I need a minute. Please. Sorry."

"I understand. Of course. I'll have you up soon."

Henrie tipped her head to look out the screens as they fuzzed over from the teleport.

She took a deep breath in as the Guardian landed in the lower level of Outrider. The others were being teleported out to the center of the room.

Emma immediately jogged over toward the Cerberus and waved up at her control room.

Henrie pushed the breath out, shakier than she expected. Weirdly enough, she found herself picturing that mental cage Capri constructed for her. Tried locking her worry away in there instead. The sniffling little version of herself there wasn't time for right now. She didn't expect the cage would hold, but it would do for now.

31

We Should Get Matching T-shirts

Mina got eyes on everyone - specifically Zane - before telling them to head home and check in with their families. She took it as a sign of growth that she'd remembered the others did have concerned parents to consider. They were all a fair bit more damaged than their last go around, but everyone was in one piece. Henrie looked reluctant to go home, Mina expected there was a difficult conversation waiting for her there. The team agreed to meet back up the following night if nothing else happened.

Her and Zane were dropped off near Restoration to retrieve his car, opting to take the drive back home as part of their cover. The trip took longer than usual due to blocked off streets and added traffic of others getting through the city. They were met by his parents rushing out the door as they parked on the street. Their story was that they'd been at Restoration originally, tried to get out of the area, and met a little trouble downtown - to cover their hits. His parents bought the story and insisted Mina stay until they saw her parents come back.

She ended up spending the night. All good by her, their guest room was plenty familiar. His mom wanted to call her mom, but Mina insisted they were bunkered down at the lab and unable to be reached. Mina rambled something about a panic room that Zane's mom didn't seem to buy, but she also didn't push.

The next morning, she asked Nek to send a fake text as her father saying they were heading back to the house in order to get herself out of there. Mina could tell Zane needed the space. With her there his parents always wanted to entertain and fill up the time, she assumed the behavior might be an attempt to offset her neglect with smothering. They watched her cross the yard, Mina waved from her door like always. She stayed planet-side long enough to shower and change before sending herself up to Outrider and getting to work. Mina was unaware hours had gone by until there was tapping at her workshop door.

Steph stood in the doorway. "We thought we'd chill in the movie room. Unless you have a lot to do?"

"No. No, just filler stuff." She snatched the new watch cover for Henrie. "Everyone here?"

"Yep. Emma gave up some of her loveseat."

"Nooooo."

"They're too cute." Steph led her through the halls back to the movie room.

Sure enough, Henrie sat at the edge of a cushion on one side of Emma's loveseat. Mina expected her back didn't like too much pressure on it right now. Their newest edition looked rough—a frizzed out ponytail of drooping curls, face red and raw, and fresh bandages across several parts of her body. At least she wasn't forced to cover up anymore, the loose shorts and tee appeared more comfortable. Emma sat perched on the arm of the other side, one leg tucked in the cushion. Like she wanted to give Henrie as much space as possible without fully giving up her ownership of the seat. Sean was lying across his chair like normal. Steph took the same spot on the opposite side of the couch from Zane, who scowled as she came in.

"Your parents never came home, did they?" he asked.

Mina gave a weak smile. "Their bags are at the house. Which is close enough."

"No, it's not."

"Them being home is not a good thing, remember?"

"This is more about you having Nek lie to my parents."

"Were you up for another ten rounds of board games or did you enjoy the twelve hours of sleep?" She waited for him to say something else but he only sunk down in his seat, choosing not to fight anymore. Which made her feel horrible all the same. "I'm sorry. I was wrong to ask Nek to do that. I should have told you I wanted to go home. If it helps anything, I got some odds and ends done up here. First off, Henrie, this is for you." She handed the watchband over. "You can load the armband of the suit separately and put that over it. This way Nek and all of us can communicate without anyone being the wiser."

Henrie looked at the band and pulled the Pak out of her pocket. "I've, um, I have been thinking. I'm not sure about this."

Emma stiffened on her perch. "What?"

"How can you not be sure?" Sean sat up in his chair. "We're awesome!"

Zane tossed a pillow at him. "Henrie's intro to this was a lot harder than ours, cut her some slack."

While she knew Zane was right, Mina had almost responded the same as Sean. She was confused at how this was a hard decision. The Pak chose Henrie, even while on Capri. And she didn't want to keep it? Didn't want the suit, the Guardian, the robots, or the spaceship? Who turned down a spaceship?

Steph leaned forward from her spot. "Is there something we can do to change that?"

Henrie placed the Pak and band in the space between her and Emma. "I have a lot of questions."

Mina's mental buffer wheel cleared away. "Oh! Is that it? Join the club!"

"Mina," Zane said in a way that sounded like he'd otherwise would have jabbed her in the side. He was out of pillows to throw.

"Sorry. What I mean is, of course you do. We all do. We have a list even. Emma, can you add her to the doc?" She caught a nod from Emma, who appeared happy to have a small task to distract herself with. "We probably hit some of your concerns on there."

Henrie glanced at the notification on her phone, but made no move to look at their curated list. She instead looked behind Mina to Nek's panel on the wall. "Why do the suits numb you?"

"We know that one!" Mina happily answered before Nek could respond. "That's a protective agent. The suits can heal some minor injuries. Bumps and bruises type stuff. The numbing is a side effect of the suit trying to do that on bigger wounds."

Henrie kept looking at Nek. "It's not something to keep a soldier on the field and fighting, all the while ignoring their damage?"

"Woah," Steph whispered.

Mina never considered that possibility. She turned to Nek, their waves remained relaxed as they said, "That is not the intended use of the feature."

"But has it been used that way?" Henrie asked.

"I can't speak to the intentions of every Warden, so I must concede that some may have done so. All parameters can be changed or deactivated."

Henrie looked to be considering that information.

That was a lot harder hitting of a question out the gate than Mina expected. The specifics of how the suits affected them was on her list; she'd been unsure of how to approach the topic. Mina moved herself a little more between Henrie and Nek. "See? We can talk anything out. Trust me, I have a million questions too. I'm positive you won't ask something we haven't thought of."

Henrie paled before her next question. "What's the plan if Mooneaters come around next?"

"Oh, well, look at that. You did it." Mina didn't even know what a Mooneater was.

"I think I read that name in the database," Steph said. "But I was only giving things a glance and didn't read too much."

Mina, at a loss, looked to Nek. They balled up tighter in their panel. "Their territory is a great distance from here. They're not a nomadic species, they would be no threat to us."

"What about The Hemlock Empire? Or Celestians? Or, um, what were those hollow looking things? Oh! The Sunderfolk."

Mina caught eyes with Steph, who gave her a shrug and mouthed, "Sorry."

Nek bunched tighter. "I've not run scenarios regarding other enemies arriving as of yet. Capri and the Lenians are our focus."

Mina stepped closer to Henrie. "To their credit, Nek did predict Lenians being the first to follow the Collective here."

"And what is that exactly?" Henrie stood, taking a second to steady herself, but remained staring at Nek. "Capri talked like she was a hero to them, but you work for them too?"

"Not anymore." Nek paced on the panel. "We believe that Capri was turned by an agent within the Collective ranks. They convinced her that we should rule and not simply protect as the Collective always has."

"But she never mentioned one person. Always the Collective. She's certain there's a reward waiting for her. I think her manic conviction is why that thing," Henrie threw a hand back to the Pak, "worked for her. She's insistent that the Collective is on her side."

"We're investigating that as well," Mina said. "To be honest, she monologued more the last time around. We didn't get much out of her this time."

"She lived here, right? Didn't she have stuff? Places she could have hidden, I don't know, some copy of their evil plan."

Nek, a loose ball of colors now, rolled along the panel. "Her room was searched, we didn't find anything. Either she destroyed all correspondences before we left for our expedition, or she kept them on her person."

Everyone looked at the glowing pink Pak sitting on the loveseat. That would be a smart move. Her own personal dimensional pocket to keep all her secrets in. Better than one of those electronic password journals by far.

Henrie scooped the Pak up. "And what if what she has in here says you're the bad guy?"

Mina didn't like how this was going. "Nek isn't-"

"Capri is far from the worst thing out there." Henrie looked around at all of them. "You have to know that. Your ship isn't telling you everything."

"Hey!" Mina shoved Henrie, both of them were stunned by the action. Steph and Emma were statues. Zane got to his feet, but didn't get closer. Sean pushed forward on his recliner. Mina stood her ground. "Nek is not the ship or some program in it. They are a living being and you will act as such. I get that Capri did a number on your head, but you need to calm down and see we're trying to help here."

"You can't just blindly follow-"

"We're not! I told you, we have our questions. Maybe we haven't pushed hard enough for your liking. Nek is dealing with their own trauma here. I told you Capri killed her team," Mina pointed back to the panel where Nek was slowly returning to waves, "That was their team too. Stopping Capri from conquering our planet nearly killed them the first time around. So back off."

Henrie looked around at the others. "You need to know what's out there."

"Okay, you got us, we haven't made a battle plan for every single bad guy in the books yet. You want that as your job?" Mina tapped Henrie's shoulders with the side of her hand like she was being knighted. "I declare you Battle Master. You can toil away and make sure we're ready for every odd foe that may fall out of the sky."

Henrie flinched at the contact, but didn't push her away. "I'm just-"

"Also, mind you, we've been at this for all of two weeks. I think we've done pretty well for beginners. Capri certainly underestimates us. I'm sure whoever comes next will do the same." She was not about to have someone walk in here and minimize all they'd accomplished while insulting a member of her team. Not on her ship.

Zane grabbed Mina's arm and pulled her back a step. "I think we got off on the wrong foot here."

Sean slid back in his seat. "Hey, Henrie, I would listen. I've never seen Mina get this worked up about anything."

"Same," Steph said.

Mina found she was breathing a little harder than expected. She loved her ship, she loved her team; alien lifeform and robots included. She'd protect them with everything she had in her. Henrie could easily kick Mina around, but she'd go down swinging. This boost of assertiveness was surprising. She'd always been fine disappearing into the scenery. Let Zane take the spotlight and be left to her projects. Not here. Not on Outrider. This was her home and she wasn't about to let anyone badmouth it.

Henrie started another protest, but deflated and dropped back on the loveseat. "I'm sorry. I just...Capri did..."

Watching the other girl crumble, Mina went from enraged to feeling like an ass. She'd been looking at Henrie like she was the bully here, but all Henrie was doing was reacting to the literal days of abuse she'd taken from every direction because of Capri. Yelling at her wasn't going to make recovering from that any easier, or make her trust them any more.

"Crap." Mina dropped to the floor, sitting at Henrie's feet. "I'm sorry. I shouldn't have reacted that way. You can ask Zane, I get a little overly defensive when robots are involved."

Henrie glanced his way, getting a response Mina couldn't see. "It's fine. I was-"

"Having every right to be suspicious." Mina caught the edge of a look from Emma. "Sorry, I keep cutting you off. I told Emma the other day I need her to be more suspicious for me. Because I suck at it." She took a risk and put a hand on Henrie's knee. "But we won't get anywhere being hurtful toward each other. That's not the way to get the answers we need."

"I'll help you build plans for whatever enemy you want." Emma sat on the loveseat next to Henrie. "We stopped monsters together once. Let us prove we can do it again."

Henrie rolled the Pak between her hands. "What if I can't do this?"

"All of us are sporting injuries that prove you can," Sean said.

"Not me!" Steph added. "Got lucky somehow."

Mina stopped herself from laughing, wanting to stay focused on Henrie. "When I first held a Pak, I assumed I'd only use one long enough to distract Capri and save the ship. These weirdos followed after me for some reason." A pillow from Sean hit her back. "We got very lucky that the Paks chose all of us. This one picked you too! I don't," she spoke slowly, unsure how Henrie would take her next statement, "I don't think there was a glitch in Capri's programming."

Henrie rubbed the touchpad, a rosy glow followed her finger. "She said so."

"I hate to compliment her, but Capri is phenomenal at programming. She reverse-engineered a way to block herself from Outrider within hours of waking up from centuries of stasis. The programs she built in those Pawns?

Hurt my brain. I couldn't make sense of it and the Comps barely broke enough to allow us to start tracking them. And while I did smash that block to be dramatic," she gave a quick 'sorry' look to Nek, "I bet if we looked at it, that code would be just as airtight."

"But the suit-"

"Was trying to protect the person that was worthy of it." Mina caught the sound of Zane clearing his throat. "Sorry, I cut you off again. My point is, this was all you."

"This is a lot to take in," Steph said. "But we're all here to figure it out alongside you."

Henrie looked to Emma. "How do I get the armband out?"

"Real easy." Emma reached over and showed her the combo. When the armband wrapped around her wrist, she held out the fake smartwatch to Henrie. "You can talk with us anytime on this."

"That's good because my phone is locked up for the next few years." Henri put the cover over her armband.

"How bad did that go?" Zane asked as he sat back on the sofa. "If you don't mind saying."

Henrie gave a weak laugh. "Unfortunately, it wasn't too hard to convince my mom I'd been having a sort of emotional breakdown. Told her I'd gotten in random fights and that's why I'd stolen the–oh," she looked at Nek, "I stole a Comp deck for Capri. I don't think it ended up being useful, but I will be sort of federally grounded if I can't return something to them."

Nek rippled across their panel in steady waves. "Easily arranged. We can fabricate a blank deck for you to return."

"You stole from the military?" Sean asked.

"Don't be impressed. I got out on luck alone. The only reason I wasn't caught for the food and clothes was because of the Pawn with me. And giving that security guard a bad concussion he couldn't ID me." Henrie looked embarrassed at that bit. "Oh! Can you make doorknobs? My mom also took that."

"As someone who's spoken to your mom," Emma said. "I'd advise against a suicide mission like that."

When Henrie gave a small laugh, Mina backed up to give them more space. "So, can I take this as you joining for sure?"

"I wouldn't mind kicking Capri around some more." Henrie poked at the pad. "What combo do I use to empty this thing out?"

Emma showed her on the armband how to pull up the inventory. "I'd say dump everything and we can start you off fresh."

Mina was glad she'd backed up as the Pak's contents spilled on the floor. Capri's stored belongings included a recon drone, the saber blaster, a standard blaster, a compressed pouch that contained loose Comp parts, and what looked like a slender hard drive. She grabbed the drive off the floor. "How tightly sealed do you think she has this?"

"We'll find out," Nek said as Comps appeared from one of the tunnels.

Comp2876 took the drive from Mina. *We'll crack it!*

"I know you will, buddy." Mina got out of the way as Comps grabbed the rest of Capri's items and disappeared down the hall.

"Can we go over the fight you two had with her now?" Emma asked. "I need to see the footage."

"You can see footage?" Henrie asked back.

Emma grabbed her hand and pulled her from the loveseat. The pair ran out of the room with Emma cheering, "Hard Light Fight Night!"

"Do we follow?" Steph asked, laughing. "Or hang back here?"

"Even with the risk of her stomping me," Sean stood up, "I want to see that footage too." Him and Steph jogged out of the room after the first pair.

Zane came over and pulled Mina off the floor. "Nice going there, Boss."

"I was too mean."

"You're passionate. You pulled back when you needed to. And you didn't try getting someone else to say it for you. Proud of you for that."

"Thank you. You are released from best friend duties and may join the viewing party." Zane was gone before she finished the sentence.

"Will you not be joining?" Nek asked.

"I will, but I was lucky enough to be there." She knew the initial footage they'd be watching was her own. There was a collective whoop from the direction of the training room. Must be Henrie's first dive at Capri.

"Thank you for what you said on my behalf."

"You're part of the team. You get a say and you get respect. Beginning, middle, and end of it."

"All the same, thank you." Their waves pulsed a brighter shade. "I should tell you, they've seen you dropping from the Guardian."

"Yeah. I figured." Mina slowly headed out of the room toward her hollering team. "Better go take my lumps."

32

Not in my Job Description

"**S**he needs time to settle," Gregory insisted.

"She needs put down!" Maxwell replied as Capri banged against the door of her room.

The fallen Warden had thrown an exceptional tantrum since returning. They'd experienced quite the battle throughout the base. She'd arrived raving and screaming to send her back. Gregory sent every remaining Pawn to hold her down, she'd destroyed a fair number with no suit and only rage fueling her. A well timed twitch of a discarded lion arm knocked her out long enough to move her upstairs. The Pawns deposited Capri within her chambers. The engineers then promptly welded the door shut for their own safety. As soon as she'd woken, the protest started anew. Listening to the constant pounding, the welds felt like only a temporary measure.

At first, they filled their time ignoring her by also ignoring each other. Maxwell was bitter over Gregory secretly changing the drop point of his creation. He felt that his salamander was not given the same chance of destruction being dropped in the crater alone and immediately surrounded by Guardians. His argument was that damage done to Guardians should also be considered, thinking to score major points for hits landed on the Jackalope alone, but Gregory refused to budge from their original agreement of damage done to the city itself. Not his fault Maxwell hadn't thought to

215

reprogram his landing spot too, though the idea had only come to him after seeing the fight scenario Capri had altered.

As the day wore on Capri chucked everything possible at the door. Maxwell's resilience broke first. He'd crossed over and started a casual conversation about nothing as her mad drumming went on. In a short lull from her fit of rage, he quickly conceded the loss and promised to tuck the pettiness away for a future day, as long as Gregory helped do something about the mad ex-Warden. Gregory agreed, a gracious winner as always, but needed time to put a solution together. Their dinner was overly noisy. The pair clanged silverware into dishes. Loudly repeated stories both knew by heart, but laughed uproariously as if they were new. Gregory at one point called all of his birds in to tweet out a song and Maxwell, for once, didn't complain. Anything to make enough sound to distract from her.

Once done eating they found themselves standing before Capri's door. Maxwell eyed the welds, making sure they would hold.

"Is this really how we solve this issue?" Maxwell asked. "Let her beat herself to death in there? Or starve?"

"No, of course not," Gregory scoffed. "That would leave us a body to dispose of and a workroom to clean. I have the Maintenance Crew in the vents right now."

There was a bang from somewhere on the other side, followed by a long hiss. A small cloud billowed out the top edge of the door. Capri's raspy insults and demands grew faint and then fell away completely.

"You killed her," Maxwell said.

"She's asleep. And now we can keep her that way until we decide what to do next."

"What's to decide? Dump her outside. Her kind can't last long in this planet's atmosphere."

"And then how do we explain the gross misuse of materials when the next check-in occurs?"

"Pictures of said body. Video from our workrooms."

Likely the right solution. The easiest, for them, for sure. This crazed, ex-Warden did little to win any real favor with them in her long weeks here.

Outside of providing a small amount of entertainment, when not issuing threats or abuse their way.

Yet.

Gregory sat on the floor, back pressed to the railing, looking at the hasty job they'd done on the door. Part of him itched to fix the seams, as useless as that was now. "Don't you feel bad for her?"

"Your first encounter started with her breaking your nose."

"Yes, yes. But think about it. She's been ranting about the Collective all this time. She doesn't even know!"

Maxwell got a mean glint in his eye. "You want to tell her that her precious Collective is gone before we kill her?"

"I don't want to kill her!" Gregory looked out through the railing at their base. "Look where our own loyalty landed us, stuck here wasting away. They tried doing the same to her, hundreds of years before us. I think she has a right to know what happened."

Maxwell sat next to Gregory. "I can't imagine she'll take that very well."

"That's why we're going to keep her sedated until we figure out how to slowly break the news to her."

Maxwell looked at a flashing notification on his tablet. "What if we don't have to be the ones to do it?"

"The Maintenance Crew are annoying, but that does seem overly cruel."

"No, not the baboons." Maxwell showed Gregory the screen. A high-priority message from the Council's Office sat waiting. Their check-in had arrived.

Any security footage would show the ex-Warden pressuring them to work for her these past weeks. Observe, observe some more, and then report–that was the Lenian way. They were gathering information on the crazed Warden and the new team. Any Councilor would accept that as an explanation of why they failed to inform them of anything until now, right? Gregory hoped so anyway, as he was out of ideas otherwise. "Yes, let's do it. Whoever they send can deal with her now. This has officially gone above our pay grade."

33

Freeze Frame

"So we count as therapy?" Mina asked Henrie as they sat at the front counter of Restoration. She'd been surprised to see her stroll in with Emma when the group decided to hang out while Steph and Sean closed up shop two days after their Lenian fight.

"My therapist pointed out to my mother that isolation was something I'd sought during my breakdown, so using that as a punishment might not be the best plan forward." She tipped back the last of her peach tea. "But Emma has to get me back by nine sharp or she chips away at the curfew."

"Good thing my cousin is obsessively punctual," Sean said as he wiped down a table.

"Is it bad to be on time?" Emma asked.

"How do you feel," Zane asked before the other two could start going at each other, "about having to do real, full-on therapy?"

"Honestly, it's not too bad." She rolled the cup between her hands. "I did have some stuff going on before all this, so it was probably overdue."

"Thanks, Capri-care," Steph said as she passed by with a broom.

Mina snorted part of her drink from her nose. "That was horrible."

Zane patted her on the back. "Humor is the best medicine."

Mina was glad they were alone, no one needed to hear her cackle like this. Henrie wasn't the only one feeling cooped up. Her parents slipping in and out of the house put her on edge, she never knew when they'd hang around long enough to force a conversation out of her. With The Expo so close, there was no chance of them leaving before then. She'd have to suffer their company for now, more reason to find any excuse to get out of the house.

Hurst on a whole bounced back quicker this time, even though the direct property damage to the city was significantly higher. They'd gotten lucky that with so much going on, no one caught their fight with Capri inside the crater. Anyone looking their way focused on the Guardian, especially after it started to change. Mina had been nervous to wake up and discover Henrie's face plastered all over the news, but the main chatter around town, while mostly on their side, was criticizing them for leaving downtown to defend itself against Capri and her Pawns. Mina felt annoyed, since the Comps were there and provided tremendous help, until Henrie gave her a small silver lining. She'd learned from some family friend that the military was boasting about their standoff with the Pawns. The fight allowed them to prove you didn't need a super suit to take the alien robots on. While Mina feared that would lead some more rambunctious civilians taking their chances with Pawns in the future, she would take the small win.

Henrie also gave them a major breakthrough on finding the Lenian base. While she kept most of what happened to herself, only walking Nek through the limited layout they'd allowed her to see. One fact she shared with them all was the planet being red. Mars was their target. The Lenian cloaking remained an issue, but Nek was working on a means of getting eyes on the planet. With luck, they'd figure something out and avoid the Hail Mary plan of sending Comps on a physical search of the planet. They wouldn't see it, but with enough time one would eventually smack into the base.

She didn't want to bother the Comps at all for now. They were dedicating a fair portion of their framework toward Capri's hard drive. Slowly picking away at her encryption to avoid any sort of trigger that might wipe all the data. Others were working on the extensive repairs the Guardians required. Along with the odds and ends of final repairs around Outrider. While training, the team was simply part of the buzz of activity on the ship. When not training, Mina worried they were getting in the way.

Which was why she'd suggested the group hang out here and revisit their list of questions. Prioritize what needed researched and delegate certain topics to people. Maybe determine if there was anything they could sort out on their own.

Essentially, she'd again given herself an excuse to sit with a tablet in hand and work as the others went off on tangents.

Mina tapped the tab labeled Earth Issues. "Okay, reel it back in for a second, I need a vote. I'm biased, and Zane will be too, but I need to know what you all think. Is the switch that leads to a secret lair in my parent's work office something that waits until after Capri? Or do we tackle that in some downtime?"

No one answered. She looked up, expecting they'd been too distracted to hear her. Instead she found everyone staring. "What?"

"What?" Zane asked back.

"The anatomy statue that's a switch. You were there."

"We were scanning papers and putting them back in the exact same place like madmen," Emma said. "Did not catch anything about a switch."

"Did I forget to mention it?" The continued stares told her yes, she very much had forgotten. "My bad. Hey, surprise, my parents are confirmed evil."

"Every teenager's dream," Steph said.

The office door snapped shut from the back. Steph and Sean jumped to their cleaning duties. Mina moved the tablet over as if she were showing Henrie and Emma something. Zane moved behind them. Their blockade effectively kept Henrie from being seen at most angles. Which didn't matter much, as Sam strolled behind the counter and toward the register. The four of them kept eyes locked on the tablet. Mina could feel Henrie's leg bouncing from nerves under the counter.

Sam tapped at the screen to pop the drawer. "Register is closed for the evening, folks."

"We were done," Mina said.

They didn't look up at anyone, only pulled the drawer and headed back for the office. Sam stopped by Sean long enough to say, "Quick reminder that the store needs to be clear of customers before final closing happens."

Sean nodded. "Yep. They were about to head out."

Zane sat back on his stool as Sam disappeared up the ramp. Mina pulled the tablet back and reopened her questions. Emma and Henrie remained shoulder to shoulder. Henrie gave them all a weak smile. "Thanks for attempting to human shield me."

"The least we can do until they calm down," Emma said.

Mitch contacted Henrie's mom about the incident downtown, but not until after the attack was over and she'd reappeared to give her own breakdown story. So Mitch, being the guy he is, immediately offered any support he could. He also offered her a job again, but Henrie decided to simplify things for the time being. Simple as they could be with superhero training now on the schedule. She'd been assured he'd love to see her at the cafe, so here she was. Sam offered a very blunt "sorry for your troubles" when Henrie first arrived and then proceeded to ignore their entire group for the rest of the night. Maybe they weren't as ready to forgive and forget. Or, per Steph's snooping, there was another explanation for Sam's continued fuming.

Mina eyed the two girls tucked in close together. Neither said anything outright to the rest of them, but also they didn't need to. Certainly not as Henrie's fidgeting fingers twirled around one of Emma's braids. She didn't see any issue with the two becoming a thing, certainly didn't think she could physically stop them from being together. Plus, she needed them to work. If only as proof that perhaps her and Steph could…maybe, be something… someday. She was well aware Zane's deadline was fast approaching.

Henrie sighed, "They're not wrong to be mad at me. I did some awful things."

"Under duress," Zane amended. "Sam is a good person, they'll come around."

"Maybe one day you can explain everything that happened," Steph offered.

"Oh!" Sean let the display case fall shut as he rushed over to the group. "New question, who plays you in the biopic they make of us one day?"

The team immediately spun off naming actors, Mina only recognized some of them. She found herself searching their names to check for accuracy. Zane tried telling them that, depending on when this fictional film was made, actors they named now would age out of the roles. Everyone ignored him for being no fun and went on picking their favorites.

When Steph and Sean started arguing about whether their suits should be done practically or with CGI, Mina knew she'd lost them for good. She closed the tablet and watched her team go back and forth with their debate. There'd be plenty of time for her list later. They'd get back to saving the world tomorrow.

About the Author

Tara Brazee is lost in a cornfield somewhere in Nebraska, but it's okay. There's wifi and D&D actual play shows to catch up on. When not writing about a group of quippy teens in her superhero series, she's tapping away on one of the many other tales trapped in her WIP pile–knights learning magic, newly sentient robots, and demonic bartenders trying to make rent coming soon. If she's not writing a book, she's reading one. Odds are that one day she'll be discovered crushed by the weight of her TBR pile.

Insta/Threads: @brazeetara

Tiktok: @tarabrazee